Pas de Death

3-2-94

For Susan

Find all the
orifices in this book
and solve the mystery!

Best wishes,

Jerry

Pas de Death

L.M. Vincent

A THOMAS DUNNE BOOK

St. Martin's Press New York

Design by Basha Zapatka

Library of Congress Cataloging-in-Publication Data

Vincent, Lawrence M.
    Pas de Death / L.M. Vincent.
      p. cm.
      "A Thomas Dunne Book."
      ISBN 0-312-10521-5
      1. Physicians—Missouri—Kansas City—Fiction.
    2. Murder—Missouri—Kansas City—Fiction.   3. Kansas City
(Mo.)—Fiction.
    I. Title.
    PS3573.I486P37   1994   93-40499
813′.54—dc20   CIP

First Edition: March 1994

10 9 8 7 6 5 4 3 2 1

For Sharon, who keeps me on the music.

The author gratefully acknowledges the help and technical advice provided by Dr. Lars Crabo, Dr. James I. Kustin, Dr. Corinne L. Fligner, Dr. Barry Logan, Dr. Gary K. Stimac, Dr. Greg Schmunk, Dr. Robert M. Varnell, and Denise Truzinski, M.T.

Pas de Death

1

"ARE YOU SURE THIS IS OKAY . . . I mean, they can't see us, right?"
he asked in a hoarse whisper.

"Not a chance. Don't worry, I said it would be fine. Now
there's a real nifty lift coming up soon. . . ."

Placated but still stiff, Dr. Townsend Reeves squirmed self-
consciously, the considerate arts patron who settles for a restrained throat clearing when he feels compelled to hack his
lungs out. At six foot four, Townsend was not designed for sitting
in standard theater seats, and a college basketball knee injury
didn't help any. He slumped down and stretched his legs into the
aisle.

Like truants, they had sneaked up to the balcony of the new
Performing Arts Center of Missouri State University and concealed themselves in the darkness on the left side aisle of the fifth
row back. Townsend's sometimes wife, Leslie Rosenthal, who
had hatched the scheme, seemed comfortable enough, curled up
in the velvet seat to his right in a contorted Martha Grahamesque
pretzel position. Leslie, of course, was a dancer.

"What are you worried about, anyway?" Leslie added distractedly, not taking her eyes from the stage. "Nobody knows you
from Adam. But if Paul were to get wind of *me* being up here, it
could really be taken as a disloyalty."

The rear of the main floor below them was out of view, but as
far as Townsend could make out, the only other spectators were
the raggedly attired and bored members of the Moreau Com-

pany—some of the girls actually knitting—lining the perimeter of the empty, harshly lit stage. Quite possibly he and Leslie were the sole privileged gate-crashers at the closed rehearsal of *Desdemona*. Presuming, of course, that no other outsiders were similarly concealed in the shadows of the mezzanine.

"Here it comes." Leslie nudged him to pay attention as if he needed the cue.

He didn't. Townsend's eyes were glued to the body of Felicia Bradley like those of a hungry dog following a hunk of hamburger in a trainer's hand. From afar, she promised a striking beauty, and Townsend knew from photographs that he wouldn't be let down if he were fortunate enough to get closer. She was sleek but not angular or sinewy. Her line was lusciously padded and perfectly proportioned.

The lady could dance—even an unseasoned eye could appreciate that Felicia Bradley had it and knew how to sell it. Later, Townsend would try to articulate (to himself, of course) what set her apart, his mind settling on modifiers with overtones of sexuality. At the moment, however, he was wordless, even breathless, just knowing that she had pushed his button.

"This is it," Leslie's whisper reminded him.

Felicia and Gerard—the other, less interesting half of the duo in Townsend's estimation—had separated, and the dissonant chords of Aaron Dijulio's score were increasing in intensity. Felicia, crouching low to the ground with arms outstretched, sprang forward into a split leap. In midair she convulsed her upper body opposite to her forward momentum, comparable to any virtuoso NBA pro move to the basket. Gerard caught her high under each thigh and let her falling weight carry him to the floor into his own 180-degree split.

"Ouch," Townsend muttered under his breath, utterly taken by the move but preoccupied by matters of physics and flesh. Common sense and medical training told him that Gerard should have ripped his groin apart, but he was proceeding with the rest of the dance, an unfazed Superhero Rubberman. Sliding into a split was one thing, but with a 120-plus pound cargo load? Something special. But then again, mused Townsend, maybe he himself could defy bodily harm at the prospect of a spread-eagled Felicia Bradley plopping into his arms.

"Pretty amazing, huh?" Leslie said expectantly, enjoying Townsend's response.

"She's incredible."

"I meant *him.*"

"He must be wearing a steel-plated jock strap."

"They don't wear jocks, asshole—they wear dance belts."

Townsend snapped from his reverie at the anatomic term of endearment. Wasn't that an affectionate sphincter reference, just like old, happily married times? High school chums grinning and flipping each other off? Or was her word choice painfully literal, like Freud's cigar being just a cigar?

Their reconciliation was not going well. They still loved each other, but the anxiety and doubts pervaded, like two nations on the brink of war. Both yearned for any resolution. After the split-up almost a year earlier—legal separation with actual divorce proceedings on hold—Townsend had relinquished his medical staff position and followed Leslie to New York. A gesture of good faith and effort if there ever was one, but he had lasted only six months in Leslie's cramped Upper West Side apartment. All plans of self-discovery and expanding his horizons quickly dissipated into restlessness and depression. He retreated to hometown Kansas City, feeling equally unsettled and aimless, living the cliché of "going through a rough time."

Townsend, even in his glory days as a college All-American basketball player, had never been particularly known for his transition game. Maybe he would have had more insight into Leslie's career had his own professional limbo not been in the way. Heaven forbid he was "sexist"—that obscenity spat with finger-pointing intensity and revulsion by a generation blessed with feminist consciousness raising. More likely, he was just self-centered and competitive and consequently threatened by his wife lapping him on life's track. After all, didn't Leslie's newly acquired stature as soloist with the New York–based Paul Gruenfeld Dance Company make his own adult accomplishments as radiologist at St. Michael's Hospital pale by comparison?

Purely good luck had brought Leslie back to Kansas City and provided the opportunity to remortar their crumbling marriage. The Gruenfeld Company, along with other major troupes from New York and elsewhere, were in a monthlong summer residence under the auspices of the National Dance Festival. To Townsend's continual irritation, though, Leslie had refused to move into their jointly owned house in Westwood, instead opting to share a dormitory room on campus with two other company members. Townsend understood her argument intellectually, but remained totally learning-disabled at fathoming it emotionally.

Townsend peeled his eyes from Felicia. The two performers had again split to opposite sides of the space, and Leslie was clearly tracking Gerard. Townsend cast a penetrating glance at Leslie's dark, dramatic profile and wondered if she were equally captivated by the male half of the team.

Gerard Moreau was no wimp, well over six feet tall with the muscular definition of a professional athlete. He was in his midthirties, face rugged and leathery like a sportsman (or peasant, by Townsend's way of thinking). His dark hair was close and evenly cropped, and though beardless, he was too hirsute to ever look clean-shaven. Perhaps women were taken by the grace and strength with which he moved, but Townsend found him unctuous and could easily picture him on the streets of Naples selling knockoff Rolex watches.

"Fool! You try to kill me?" An enraged Othello shattered the trance of what had been a romantic dancerly embrace. "Other leg! And Christ, you're not on beat!" shrieked the heavily accented Gerard, wringing his hands through his head bristles and then shaking them, convulsively, heavenward. "What takes it for your little brain to comprehend?"

The abruptness of the outburst sent Townsend's heart racing. Then, from some misplaced sense of propriety, he felt embarrassed, like an accidental interloper wanting to gracefully excuse himself from a domestic spat. Leslie revealed no discomfiture.

She was smiling, seeming to enjoy the commotion. The female members of the troupe, leaning carelessly against the walls, displayed an even more muted reaction. Hardly any took notice, and those knitting kept at it without pause.

"Face it, Gerard. You haven't the slightest idea what you want!" countered Desdemona, hands defiantly on hips and chest heaving.

"*I* don't know what I want? You kid me?" cried Gerard in disbelief, exhibiting the arrogance perfected by generations of his French countrymen. "You dare question *me?*" His eyes, at first rounded in astonishment, narrowed into slits. "I want someone taking direction, bitch!"

"Take direction? I have some directions for you! *Eat shit!*"

Last echoing word. Felicia flung her head back and made for the door, detouring only to grab her dance bag from the floor against the back wall.

The tape of the musical score, which had not stopped playing, could be heard again, a soft, lyrical refrain that contrasted jarringly with the real-life spectacle. Felicia stopped short of the door and began rearranging items in the bag, a casual, premeditated exit.

Townsend inferred that such displays of artistic temperament were commonplace, and smart money knew who would blink first. The pressure to finish setting the piece was intense. With the premiere of *Desdemona* just over a week away, the heat was squarely on Gerard. Expectations were high; the hype had been carried to a fever pitch by Gerard's brashness and boasting. The piece could be no less than brilliant, the dancing flawless. And Felicia Bradley was the centerpiece, the exquisite glue holding it all together.

Felicia was fishing inside her bag, as if the most important thing in the world at that moment was somewhere to be found there. Gerard was facially contorting, gesticulating, and muttering in his native tongue. With forced composure he walked to the far end of the stage and turned off the tape recorder. For a few seconds he stood in silence, smothering his internal flame, the weight of the world first settling on his eyelids, then pressing down upon his head. Eventually he opened his eyes, lifted his chin off his chest and took a cleansing breath.

"All right, why don't we try again from 'ta-da-da-ta-da-da,' " he said contritely, rewinding the tape. "You keep in extra step, Felicia dear, if you wish. I work around it."

"It can wait," announced Felicia Bradley. "I'm having a smoke first." She pulled a pack of cigarettes from her bag.

"*C'est bon,*" Gerard responded as if he had thought of it. "We break for five, then." Gerard Moreau had not simply swallowed his pride, he had been tube-fed.

Townsend had just read a lengthy article about the Gerard Moreau Dance Theatre in Leslie's latest issue of *Dance Magazine*— the glamorous pair of Gerard and Felicia had, in fact, graced the cover. The article was the standard whitewash, but Leslie had supplemented it with the nitty-gritty. While the new company had only recently burst upon the scene, both dancers were well seasoned.

Gerard Moreau had trained in classical ballet with the Béjart Company in Paris before moving to the U.S. in his early twenties. On an impulse he switched to modern dance, ultimately performing supporting roles in the Graham and Taylor companies. While *Dance Magazine* attributed his mobility to "a conscious effort to absorb a variety of dance styles as preparation for his ultimate goal of breaking new ground in modern choreography," his rampant ego and general inability to get along with people had been the real motivation. By the time Moreau had settled in with Paul Gruenfeld's troupe three years earlier, Felicia Bradley was the leading female in the company and the well-established partner of a pushing-fifty Paul Gruenfeld. Gerard Moreau became the successor to Paul's signature roles, and the partnership with Felicia took off. Few in the dance world were surprised— Paul Gruenfeld not among them—when Gerard announced that he and Felicia, whom he had secretly wed, were leaving to seek greener pastures.

The defection generated considerable bad blood. The Moreau Company consisted of twelve other dancers, each lured from the ranks of other New York companies by promises, and in some instances outright deception. Hardest hit, of course, was Paul Gruenfeld, who took it in the pocketbook besides being personally devastated. The loss of his two stars had sent the company scrambling and thrown their repertory into chaos. Questions about the drawing power of a "starless" company had resulted in enough performance-hall back-outs to force cancellation of their annual spring tour, the major source of company revenue. A large grant from the National Endowment for the Arts, which had been in the bag, fell through.

The financial hurdles could be overcome, but Gerard's betrayal of Paul Gruenfeld was another matter. Gruenfeld had discovered Felicia Bradley as a seventeen-year-old corps de ballet member in the Chicago Opera Ballet, trained her in his style of modern dance, and nurtured her into the consummate Gruenfeld dancer. Their relationship, while a platonic one (Gruenfeld himself gay), had been ongoing for over fifteen years. Gruenfeld had lashed out publicly, and a verbal war between Moreau and himself had been ongoing in the press for months. The festival was the first opportunity since the rift for both mentor and ingrate protégé to share billing, and the potential for confrontation had aroused considerable speculation. That both companies had been invited to the festival in the first place appeared an inexcusable *faux pas,* but knowledgeable sources suspected that the National Dance Festival director, William Davidson, had done it intentionally to generate publicity.

The upheaval in the modern dance community had rippled into the nondancing life of Townsend Reeves. When Leslie had traipsed off to New York a year earlier to take a shot at professional dance, even her supportive family had counted her out. Talent and determination were irrelevant. Leslie Rosenthal was a twenty-eight-year-old midwesterner with no contacts and only regional performing credentials. Townsend had the scenario figured. She'd chase her lark for three months or so, come to grips with the real world (personally enriched for having tried), and be content with her lot as hospital social worker and doctor's wife in Kansas City. Maybe she had the grit to hold out for six months. However long it took, the wanderlust would expend itself, and Leslie would settle down and get pregnant. Townsend's expectations made their separation a little easier to take.

Something went awry. Leslie, always a fan of Gruenfeld and his style of modern dance, enrolled in his Upper West Side school. Her technical proficiency and the forceful dramatic quality of her dancing did not escape notice, but the fluke of circumstance made the difference. Within a month of her arrival, the shake-up and Felicia Bradley's departure opened up a rare company slot, and Leslie Rosenthal became a card-carrying member of the American Guild of Musical Artists and a Paul Gruenfeld dancer. The irony of the situation was not lost on Townsend, who directly related Leslie's nongravid state to a greasy French egomaniac.

"So what do you think of the piece so far?" said an enthused Leslie. "Isn't it fantastic?"

Townsend nodded noncommittally. The dancing was superior and the choreography interesting and innovative, but without the luxury of an uninterrupted run-through, he couldn't tell how the work held together. For certain, the adaptation was only loosely tied to the original Shakespeare—thematically, the plot boiled down to "boy meets girl, boy kills girl, boy kills himself." Townsend thought that costumes might help.

"What about the costumes?" he asked.

"I haven't seen them. Very basic, I would imagine," Leslie replied. "You know . . . more abstract."

Townsend nodded again.

"What do you think of Felicia? Ready for a cold shower yet?"

Was Leslie goading him? Hadn't he already said that he thought Felicia incredible? Was this a test? And did the correct answer mean she'd start sleeping with him again?

Since Leslie's arrival, Townsend had found himself crippled

by common conversation. Her merest utterance provoked cerebration over nuances and innuendos. Defensively he misdirected conversation or resorted to quips with her, choosing words with the care he'd use to pick scraps from a fish carcass.

"I took a shower this morning," he replied.

"Boy, are you ever hard to talk to these days." She shook her head, her thick black bush of hair bobbing from side to side. Before New York she had never been permed, and Townsend still couldn't get used to it. The hair was an obvious change that belied more subtle underlying ones. He liked neither the hair nor the changes.

"Okay. I already told you she's incredible. But I don't need a cold shower. Just pack me in dry ice and come back for me in a week."

"Can't you even take a joke?"

Townsend was formulating his reply when Leslie went on.

"Anyway, not that it matters, but she's best admired from a distance. She dances like an angel—I take that back, she's much too sexual and powerful."

"An angel on anabolic steroids."

Leslie smiled. "In person she's an absolute bitch . . . real poison."

"Frogman isn't exactly Mr. Chips."

"Not by a long shot."

"So I suppose they were meant for each other. A marriage made in heaven . . . like ours."

"More like a marriage made by Immigration," replied Leslie, ignoring the personal allusion.

"I don't follow."

She shushed him.

Gerard was fiddling with the tape recorder controls, and music spurted in unconnected bursts. He continued the process of playing and rewinding, searching for the right measure and eventually getting close enough. Felicia, meanwhile, had sauntered back to the center of the space. Gerard scurried to her side and assumed a noble posture. Two measures later, Othello took Desdemona in his arms and they were carried by the music.

Townsend sensed movement from the corner of his eye, a brief alteration of dimness. Paranoia, he rationalized, redoubling his efforts to focus on Felicia. Always the obedient, well-behaved child, Townsend wasn't a natural rule-breaker—such was the humiliation associated with his only significant juvenile misdeed in memory, lifting a Butterfinger at age seven. Could a thirty-four-year-old physician be anxious over the prospect of being discovered and chastised by a pimply freshman volunteer usher?

The sense of another presence in the balcony, real or imagined, continued to unnerve him. He heard a soft creak, unmistakable despite the ongoing musical score. At first he resisted the urge to look, then finally indulged himself, indiscreetly twisting around in his seat to scan the near void behind and across from him. Leslie was haloed in blackness, and if she had heard anything, she wasn't paying any mind.

A chill passed across the back of his neck, as if the skin there had suddenly become oversensitive to the weight from his collar and was retracting from it. The chill penetrated, transmuting into a vague sense of queasiness. A formed shadow was slowly making its way down the far right side aisle. Its progress was marked by the sequential flickering of a faint amber glow from floor-level low-voltage aisle lights transiently eclipsed by the mass.

The figure stopped nearly even with Townsend's row and stood still, strangely composed. A tubular shadow levitated forward, stopping when parallel to the ground. A similar but foreshortened appendage then rose, and shadows linked. Abstractly, the form had coalesced into a shadow puppet, perhaps the head of a dragon or dinosaur, or an enormous pointing hand. The left side of Townsend's brain, however, perceived a man aiming a handgun, the forearm of the firing arm steadied by its leveled counterpart, the supporting arm crooked at the elbow. The arms were smoothly sweeping in unison, tracking like a spotlight in time with the music. Panicky, Townsend squinted back to the stage, searching out the point of focus. Felicia Bradley stage left, recumbent, a murdered Desdemona. Gerard stage right, anguished and remorseful, moving across stage within the sight of a gun.

In a balcony where he didn't even belong, Townsend Reeves responded like a startled junkyard dog. Not a thought for potential dangers, best- and worst-case scenarios, let alone the more mundane and immediate physical obstacles. Leslie, for one, sitting directly in his path, unaware and enraptured, legs crossed and bouncing innocently in time with the music. There were also his own legs—his 38-inch inseam—and the standard dimensions of theater seat rows, complicated by the randomness of the seats left in their upright position and, of course, the darkness.

Townsend's ankles caught on the base of the end seat with the initial lunge. Leslie was the first to go, partly because of his haphazard attempt to shield her with his arm as he stormed past, but more the result of 220 pounds of forward momentum smacking her blindside. She toppled into the aisle with a grunt— fortunately no feminine scream to give herself away—and Townsend, gaining traction by grinding her flesh into the floor, scrambled onward like a tenacious defensive lineman in dogged pursuit of the man with the ball. He tumbled clumsily, pathetically forward, the clatter of seats echoing in the theater.

Townsend was prone, no more than halfway toward the form no longer evident, when the full balcony lights came up. He froze in place. He had not heard any previous words over the din, but in the relative quiet, a dominant voice, an angry *"What is this?"* from the stage was quite clear. A pissed-off Moor, in whose voice the last word stretched to nearly two syllables and was likely accompanied by considerable spray.

The music continued, but obviously the dancing had stopped. Townsend stayed low, panting and taking inventory of multiple points of pain: both shins, his left knee (that old injury site), ribs, cheek, wrist on the right, both forearms. The wounds of a hero, but Townsend had serious doubts they would be recognized as such. He'd be hard-pressed to explain a phantom assassin without sounding like a basket case. Who would believe that someone may have been trying to kill Gerard Moreau? At the moment, seeing the emptiness where the form had been, Townsend wasn't quite sure about matters himself.

Postponing the inevitable, Townsend looked back at Leslie. She was slumped on the floor twenty paces away in a half-sit, rubbing the small of her back, leaning her head against the seat back of the next row. He thought he saw a trickle of blood from her nose—suspicion confirmed when she placed the back of her free hand against her upper lip, pulled it away, and scrutinized the warm smear at the point of contact. She met his eyes with hers and, facial expression transformed from flaccid bewilderment to tension, mouthed her own animated *"What is this?"* Spasmodically she began shaking both arms in a body language suggesting, in a different context, the universal reference to a woman with really big breasts.

Townsend placated her in mime, an economical downward patting motion with both outstretched hands. The compressed message falsely implied that there was a reasonable explanation, that all was under control.

Leslie's stinging rebuttal was an eyeroll of such expanse and sweep that Townsend could imagine both her eyeballs getting stuck off to the side, deep within their sockets. Every bit of the fallout from the swiped candy bar incident couldn't hold a candle to the humiliation conveyed by that single ocular motion. And things weren't getting any better.

Again, Gerard's voice.

"Who is up there? Who in God's name makes such a racket?" Then, directed to someone on stage, "Go there and see what goes on, for Chrissake. . . ."

Townsend motioned for Leslie to keep down, then sheepishly stood up. The balcony had become center stage; all eyes from down below were upon him. Gerard stood near the front of the proscenium, suppressed rage in his eyes. Felicia was still recumbent, now lounging, casually curious. Two nondancers, probably the stage manager or assistants of some type, were now also onstage, peering up intently. And without exception, all the girls scattered around the perimeter had set down their knitting. Townsend, in the spotlight, had their undivided attention.

"Sorry," he began anticlimactically.

No response. All expected more from the oracle, had not yet accepted that their mahatma could very well be a horse's ass.

Townsend cleared his throat and spoke more loudly, "Sorry to disturb you. I . . . uh . . . tripped."

A disbelieving silence from below. Continued anticipation, universal expressions of intensity, except for Felicia, whose face now seemed to convey vague amusement.

Gerard, totally nonplussed, turned to the nondancers. "Who is this imbecile? Do you know? Is this some joke? Does anybody know this imbecile?"

The nondancers shook their heads, prompting Gerard to glance furtively across the stage, nonverbally querying all the other stage inhabitants. They all shrugged and shook their heads. No one admitted to knowing the imbecile. The scene was taking on a surreal quality.

"I'm Townsend," he volunteered in a friendly offhanded manner, tacitly accepting the conferred role and pointedly not offering his last name. "I'm really very sorry about all this, but . . . uh . . . I was in the theater the other night and I . . . lost my keys. Fell out of my pocket. I was just up here looking for them. I didn't intend to disturb anybody . . . really very sorry."

Townsend considered the whole explanation quite plausible, and was rather proud of it, considering the stress and mortification he was working under. He had not even sounded breathless, and the beads of sweat on his face were probably not visible from the distance. Best of all, he had shielded Leslie, who really had something to lose. As she had said earlier, no one knew him from Adam; but how would they construe a member of the rival dance company spying on their rehearsal? Or worse, how would her own director, Paul Gruenfeld, react to such a revelation? Top priority was to distance himself from Leslie, make as graceful an exit as possible under the circumstances. Leslie could sneak out on her own.

Townsend nervously lowered his head to scratch his temple, and glanced over at Leslie. Expecting some show of gratitude, some acknowledgment of his fleetness of thought, he caught instead the tail end of another major eyeroll.

"Get out of here!" screamed Gerard, fuse finally igniting the explosion of what was now mock anger. He grinned broadly for all to see, his desire for showmanship and male dominance coming to the fore. The outburst was cathartic, the tension of the moment dissolving into sputters of laughter across the stage.

"I'm on my way," Townsend replied with forced calmness. But he didn't move, instead staring down his adversary from the fifth row of the balcony. The laughter in the theater faded.

Townsend Reeves had eaten enough crow. He had apologized, he had demured. But this leader-of-the-pack bravura from Gerard was too much to take. Gerard was a bully, albeit veneered by Continental machismo and artistic temperament. Townsend had been willing to keep himself in check for Leslie's sake (not that she had reciprocated with her own show of support), but he had limits. Given Gerard's nongraciousness, Townsend wasn't about to walk out a buffoon.

"Have a good rehearsal," he calmly added after several long seconds had passed. "I'll be back for my keys later." If anyone wanted, they could interpret his closing remarks as a threat. As it happened, some did.

Maybe I should have let that prick get shot in the head, Townsend thought, as he deliberately wove his way along the remaining seats in the row toward his original aisle destination. Or had he imagined the whole thing? Had there been a man with a gun after all? Regardless, Leslie's reaction really irked him. He couldn't have expected much from some unstable French dancer, but Leslie? Who had humiliated him more? Townsend was trying to mentally reconstruct what had set him off, what shape the shadowy form had really taken, but his thoughts were a muddle.

Startled, Townsend nonetheless hesitated for only an instant when he saw the body. Under other circumstances he might have audibly gasped, even jumped backward, snapped so from his reverie. Perhaps he had blown his quota of adrenaline; hormone depleted, his flight-fight response had mellowed into detached self-containment. Gerard and the rest of the dancers, watching him from the stage, observed only a pause, natural enough, just as the imposing stranger completed threading his way along the narrow row and stepped into the aisle.

Townsend took in much during that instant, in the same way he might pattern read an X ray, absorbing the image in its entirety rather than consciously analyzing the individual components in a systematic way. The body was lying in the row directly across the aisle, knees slightly bent, submissively belly-up. The feet, closest to the aisle and to Townsend, were sporting well-worn beige Hush Puppies; exposed ankles revealing thin cream-colored ribbed socks. The slacks were also beige and quite wrinkled; the polo shirt was red, the vertical orientation of the insignia suggested the Polo player of Ralph Lauren rather than the horizontal Lacoste alligator. Slender, tanned body, no appreciable flab. Mostly salt but some pepper hair, crew cut, hairline receding.

Nowhere in the visual tableau was there a gun; not on the ground, not in either visible hand. He had apparently hit the deck at the onset of Townsend's ruckus, and was lying-in-wait, cowering. He brought his index finger to his lips, imploring Townsend to remain silent.

Townsend walked past, sauntering up the aisle. Leslie wasn't the only one he was shielding, and ironically Townsend had blown her cover. He heard directives being issued from stage, and the houselights went off. Someone, presumably Gerard, was again searching for the right measure of music. He pushed open the double doors and entered the glaring brightness of the upper mezzanine.

Outside the theater, Townsend didn't bother to wait for Leslie. He was in no mood to explain himself, and the situation was laden with fight potential. Best to let things cool off. She would undoubtedly crawl out to safety in the dark balcony and escape via the back stairwell. The dormitory room was an easy walk, and that, after all, was where she had chosen to stay. Townsend had done his share, it was up to Leslie to fend for herself.

And so, for that matter, could the curiously supine Paul Gruenfeld.

2

HE SHOULD HAVE CRACKED A WINDOW— the inside of the car was suffocating. The vinyl upholstery of Townsend's twenty-year-old banana yellow Chevy Nova was black, and the June afternoon was typical—blue skies and scattered cumulus clouds for looks, oppressive muggy heat for real. He eased his bottom onto the hot seat and hastily opened the driver's side window, then leaned across the seat to open the passenger side. The maneuver was automatic, nearly a ritual. He needed an air-conditioned car in the worst way. He was probably the only person above the poverty level in Kansas City who didn't have an air-conditioned automobile, and certainly the only doctor in Kansas City without one.

The car was an affectation, enduring the heat his penance. Townsend was the progeny of a wealthy and well-known physician, a pillar of the medical community, eight years deceased. His mother, now remarried and living in Santa Fe, had been the stereotypical 1950s doctor's wife—Donna Stone or Margaret Anderson in a bigger house—well meaning, subservient, and hopelessly oversocial. From his teens onward, Townsend had rebelled against the career and the life-style, not that he harbored deep resentment toward either. Simply a matter of the road not taken.

Townsend had wanted to be a professional basketball player; at least he had wanted his shot. He had been good, very good. Two-time All-American for the Missouri State Wildcats by his junior year, point guard for the 1971 Division Championship team. From the limited perspective of his nonjock premed friends at the time, even good enough to date Cindy Mitchell, the best looking and most sexually liberated of the cheerleading squad. His glory days had been spent in Woolcott Gymnasium, just on the other side of campus, where he had been a celebrity, cheered on by thousands of adoring fans. A far cry from the bumbler who had just made a scene in the Performing Arts Center.

Townsend twisted the key in the ignition; the engine turned over immediately. Maybe his father had been right, though. Considering the five starters for that team, outcomes were unimpressive. Paul Molina was a banker at Great American Savings, Steve Price owned and operated a body shop catering to the university crowd (cleverly named "Crash Course"), Lamar Oates had his own rib place. Not to put down his former comrades-in-arms— they were all decent, upright, moderately successful individuals, and Lamar was raking it in loin over rump. But as for fulfilling the B-ball dream, only Roger Nelson had been drafted, and he had washed up after a year of handing out towels for his Washington Bullets teammates. Still with his hands in the game, to his credit, he was an assistant coach at Iowa.

And what about Cindy Mitchell? The perky blond dish who, out of some perverse nurturing hang-up would go all the way with him only after games they had *lost*. In victory, Townsend couldn't even unbuckle her bra, which put a damper on the season the Wildcats went 21 and 2 in the conference. Townsend recalled his own private hell on three occasions at the free throw line, clutch attempts at the buzzer determining the outcome of the game. To his credit, he never threw a brick, providing the game winners twice, and taking his single failure in stride.

"Dammit, anyway, Town, you did your best. You can't make them all . . . we can't win them all."

"I know, coach."

"Good effort, anyway, huh? That's all that counts. Effort. Don't feel like you let the team down, okay?"

"I'll try not to, coach."

"Chin up. Keep the whole thing in perspective."
"I'll try, coach. Can I go now?"

When last heard from, Cindy was in Omaha, the mother of five kids. Against odds, her marriage was intact, maybe because her husband was a moderate failure. After all, he was an insurance man for the Prudential, not an NBA celebrity.

For that multitalented championship team—viewed by many sports observers as one of the best collegiate teams Kansas City had ever mustered—hoops had not prevailed in real life. One assistant basketball coach for a mediocre Midwest team. And the only persistent celebrity was Lamar Oates, barbecue baron, who had his picture on a sauce label. Could Townsend have proved the exception, a slow white guy with brains and grit anchoring an NBA franchise?

Townsend and his father had discussed the road not taken in one of their less volatile career discussions.

"There's a damn good reason why that road is less traveled, boy . . . because nobody who takes it ends up making a decent living. Maybe Frost should write some poetry about making a decent living."

"Robert Frost is dead, Dad."

"I know that, boy. Just because I'm a rich successful doctor doesn't mean I'm illiterate."

The father-son conflict had reached a head after his junior season. After much shouting and screaming, final resignation. To the adult Townsend, the extent to which his twenty-one-year-old version would go to please his father was unfathomable. Getting the grades up, getting into medical school would have highest priority. Good-boy Townsend (then also known as D.T., short for Down Town, a reference to his outside shooting proficiency), to the astonishment and dismay of fans and boosters, opted not to play basketball for the Missouri State Wildcats his senior year.

Franklin Reeves had always been confident and dogmatic, his arguments rational and persuasive. To a healer, basketball was trivial. He attended a handful of his son's home basketball games, but never on call nights. Pointedly, he never arranged or switched call duties to watch Townsend play, despite a regular season schedule available months in advance. Townsend's basketball life was an incidental to which he gave notice in passing. He congratulated his son on his performances absently, almost by rote, in praise of the Protestant work ethic for a job well done. Three years after his father's death Townsend learned the complexity of the truth.

His mother had put their stately Mission Hills house on the market, and Townsend was in the basement clearing out his father's old office desk. He had leafed through the file folders of clipped journal articles and handwritten notes—an intimate reference file, lovingly sorted, organized, periodically purged and updated—giving a final look before tossing each one into the trash. The folder following the one labeled THYROID DISORDERS was totally unexpected: TOWNSEND, ALIAS 'DOWN TOWN.' Contained within was virtually every press clipping from his high school and college playing days. More surprisingly, Franklin Reeves had kept a detailed tally of every game, handwritten in his pinched scrawl, a compulsive record of his son's statistics on index cards. Franklin Reeves, who had convinced him to give it all up for his own good, had been Townsend's biggest fan.

I did what you wanted, I did it for you, and now you're dead, and where the hell does that leave me?

Townsend was daydreaming, automatically having taken the circuitous, scenic route to his home in Westwood—heading west on Fifty-fifth Street, Loose Park with its ducks and joggers on his right. All looked overheated, but at least the fowl could cool off in the pond. He turned on the car radio, caught three words of the local newscast—

". . . Little Jesús Sanchez . . ."

20

—and promptly switched it off. Enough about little Jesús Sanchez. The press was giving enormous play to the nine-year-old Raytown boy with end-stage liver failure. They had been milking the story for days, badgering the dying kid and his widowed mother to death, pulling the collective heartstrings of a four-state area to sell more newspapers. Fund-raising efforts for a transplant were in full swing, but no suitable donor organ had been found and time was growing short, Jesús languishing in the pediatric wing of St. Michael's Hospital, Townsend's old stomping ground. Townsend hoped the kid got his liver, but the media play was offensive. The only decent copy to come out of the whole tragedy was the campaign slogan, a publicist's masterstroke: *"Save Jesús."*

The small Tudor on Westwood Drive was a pleasant walk to the Country Club Plaza and a stone's throw from the two-lane road that demarcated Missouri from Kansas. The location was ideal, the house a scaled-down replica of the palatial homes along Ward Parkway Boulevard and the posh Country Club District. The neighborhood was a mix of old-timers and realistic yuppies, all of whom took equal pride in their quaint, well-kept neighborhood. Townsend's domicile was among the most neatly manicured, with evenly trimmed laurels marking the property boundary and freshly mulched beds of juniper, boxwood, and silver queen euonymous. The centerpiece was an ornamental crab apple that was spectacular when covered with blossoms in the spring, but even now respectable, crammed with its petite red fruits of summer. Juxtaposed beside it was its protector, a mature red oak. A manageable amount of yard was weed-free and compulsively edged. With time on his hands, Townsend had sought the therapeutic effects of gardening to good advantage. But an experienced gardener would have noted the imbalance. The perennials were there—snapdragons, daylilies, hyacinths and tulips, and irises—but the lack of annuals was palpable. Annuals were Leslie's responsibility, but she hadn't been around that spring to sow them.

Not bothering to garage the car, Townsend went through the front door, confirmed that the day's mail was its customary disappointment, and headed straight for the answering machine. Three blinking red message lights, and hopefully one of the callers was Leslie. He didn't have time to check before the phone rang.

"Les?"

"Less? Less than what, man?" The voice was male, the accent British, the tone loud and overly cheerful.

"Howard?"

"More or less. Is that the right answer? Is this some kind of phone game, like letting Prince Albert out of the loo?"

"Out of the can, not out of the loo. The joke doesn't work with 'loo.' "

"Ah . . . well you know what they say about American humor."

"Sorry, Howard, I was expecting Leslie."

"Well, you certainly should be sorry, Townsend. I've rung you twice and got your blasted machine both times! Don't you believe in returning your calls, sport? It could be someone with good news or money, in this case, good news *and* money."

"I'm all ears, Howard," said Townsend, trying to conceal his disappointment. Not that Howard Gorell wasn't a charming and entertaining conversationalist, but Townsend already knew Gorell's reason for calling and was more concerned about keeping the line open. Rarely did Townsend regret not having Call Waiting, but this was one of those occasions. Two of the incoming calls were accounted for, but maybe Leslie's was the third.

"I just got in. Had I known you weren't calling to ask a favor, Howard, I might have even called you back."

"Well, that too," replied Howard.

"You need coverage, and you'll pay me handsomely for it."

"Precisely."

Dr. Howard Gorell was a British-born and -educated gynecologist who had done postdoctorate infertility training in Boston and decided to expatriate. Finding competition on the East Coast too intense, he had migrated to Kansas City and established himself as the best in the region. A prisoner of his success, Gorell operated out of four suburban clinics and had privileges at three hospitals in the metropolitan area. Breaking away for vacations or meetings was nearly impossible. Townsend knew him from St. Michael's, and was occasionally called upon by Gorell for fill-in office ultrasound.

"Where and when?"

"The Lenexa office. And how does tomorrow sound to you?"

"You believe in giving a man a little notice?"

"In your case, do I have to?"

"Point well taken."

"I'll be gone until Tuesday, but I've canceled just about everything. Most of my patients can afford to rest for a cycle. There might be a few stragglers next week, but Rita can call you if we need you. Tomorrow presented more of a problem, but I've lined up everything in the mornings. First one's at eight-thirty. The usual procedure. I'll be able to handle most anything by phone."

"From where?"

"Nassau. Some dreadful fertility society meeting. But I intend to redeem it on the beach. You'll have the satisfaction of knowing that you've postponed the inevitable bleeding of my ulcer."

"Money talks," responded Townsend. They both knew the money issue was irrelevant. The work would keep his mind occupied for a while, and at least get him out of the garden.

"Easy money, my friend. And my eternal gratitude, priceless beyond measure."

"Have a good time, Howard, don't worry about a thing. Gotta go now."

"Bless you, my son."

The first and third messages on the answering machine were Howard's, the second was from a national locum tenes firm. The recording informed him that fill-in radiology jobs were available in Fort Scott, Kansas, and Omaha, Nebraska, for the last two weeks in June, and was he interested? Several months earlier Townsend had notified the service of his availability, but neither Fort Scott nor Omaha particularly struck his fancy. Besides, he wouldn't consider leaving Kansas City for medical mercenary work as long as Leslie was in town. In fact, to date he had turned down all offers from the service, although they were calling him with job openings on almost a weekly basis. There was plenty of work locally if he really wanted it, and if he felt this unsettled at home, what would it be like on the road?

Townsend dialed Leslie's dormitory room, number already committed to memory, and let it ring twelve times before giving up. Where the hell was she, and what was taking her so long to get back? He tried to remember her schedule. It was just after 3 P.M., and if the Gruenfeld Company was rehearsing, she would have mentioned it prior to their undercover outing. He knew they were rehearsing later that evening, since she had declined his dinner invitation specifically because of the conflict. He tried her number again, thinking he might have misdialed the first time. No answer.

Townsend was restless, a bored child completely surrounded by toys. He wanted to stay near the phone, which ruled out going for a run, shooting some hoops at the park, or wandering around the Plaza. It was too early to eat. Nothing ever any good on afternoon TV. He was gardened out. He was three months behind in his radiology journals—they were grouped together in a magazine rack beside the sofa in the den—but he wasn't in the mood. Ennui had settled upon him like a bad case of indigestion.

When the phone finally did ring, Townsend was puttering around the house, straightening the odd picture on the wall, picking crumbs off the kitchen countertops, rearranging coffee- and side-table knickknacks like chess pieces on a board. He sprinted from the living room to the wall phone in the kitchen, and cut the second ring short.

"Les?" he blurted, out of breath.

There was a pause at the other end, followed by a female's drawn out, opened-ended "No . . ."

"I'm sorry, I mean 'hello.' "

"Is this Townsend?"

"Yes, it is. Who's this?"

"I'm glad you made it home all right. I wasn't sure if you could get in without, you know, without your keys. But I suppose you have a spare set." The voice was deep, the delivery self-assured and provocative. Townsend had never called one of those 900 number fantasy lines, but it occurred to him that this woman would be a shoo-in for the job.

"Who *is* this?" he asked again.

"You don't know me. My name is Felicia Bradley." She stopped there, letting it sink in, anticipating and rewarded by a lengthy silence on the other end. "Are you there?"

"I know who you are," said Townsend, recovered enough not only to reply, but to fake nonchalance. "How did you get my name?"

"I got it from *you*, of course. You gave it to the entire company this afternoon, didn't you?"

Townsend knew he was being toyed with, but there were worse things than being toyed with by a beautiful woman.

"Just Townsend. I said I was Townsend. But there must be quite a few 'Townsends' in the directory, and it must be tough tracking me down considering it isn't my last name."

"You're right. What if I told you that I found your key chain on the floor of the balcony, and there was this little I.D. tag with 'Townsend Reeves' written on it?"

"I'd say you'd be pulling my chain, and not my key chain, either. Mainly because..." and here he reassuringly squeezed the corrugated ellipsoid deep in his right pocket, "I don't have any I.D. with my keys. The only thing on my key ring besides my keys is a rubber prune."

"I mustn't torture you any more," she said, laughing. "Leslie gave me your name."

"She did? When?"

"Don't worry, Townsend. What do I care if you watch our rehearsal? And I'll have to admit, I loved it when you rattled dear Gerard like that. It was wonderful. Made my day."

"When did you see Leslie?"

"I stepped out for a quick smoke and saw her coming down from the balcony. I put two and two together. I had heard through the dance grapevine that she had a local significant other."

"Just Leslie?"

"Pardon?"

"Was she by herself?"

"Yes, of course she was. What? Were you having a party up there or something?"

"No. Never mind."

"Well, anyway, to get to the point, we had a brief but nice little chat, and of course the subject somehow turned to you, your being a doctor and all."

Townsend felt it coming. She wanted his signature on a prescription blank. Some innocuous pharmaceutical that could calm her down if she were a bit tense, or perk her up if she were a bit tired. Maybe something to relax those exhausted overworked muscles, or take the edge off that constant, nagging pain. Valium. Dexedrine. Percocet. Townsend had always been amazed at the gall of people who felt that a casual acquaintance with an M.D. with a valid DEA number entitled them to free prescription services. The practice was medically unwise and ethically dubious. And Townsend, used to pleasing people and always feeling guilty about refusing, had come up with a suitable reply. Being a radiologist, he didn't have need of a Drug Enforcement Agency number; thus, he wasn't authorized to write prescriptions for most of the desirable remedies. It was a lie, of course, but most of them bought it and didn't push matters further, aside from asking, "Well, then, do you know a good gynecologist?"

She went on.

"Do you know anything about ankles?"

The question seemed naive, almost comic.

"Ankles? Do I know anything about ankles? Well . . . I suppose. I know that I like them with a nice taper. . . ."

"Touché."

"Okay, I know a few things about ankles, more because I used to play basketball on weak ones than anything else. But I'm not an orthopedist, I'm a radiologist. What's your problem?"

"Well," she began, gathering her thoughts, "I've had chronic tendinitis on my right ankle, but it seems to be getting worse. And

I *know* you're a radiologist; Leslie told me. That's why I called. I went to the university health service yesterday and they X-rayed it. I wondered if you could take a look at them? The X rays."

"What did they tell you over there?"

"They didn't tell me much of anything. You know how those doctors are."

"Right. I'll be happy to take a look." The X rays, he knew, would show absolutely nothing. But he was intrigued with the prospect of getting up close and personal with Felicia Bradley. He knew enough about ankles to know that he didn't want to turn away from a finely turned one.

"You live close to the Plaza, right?" she asked.

"Very close. Five minutes."

"Perfect. I thought, that is if you wouldn't mind, and if you were free right now, I could hop in a cab—"

"No need for that," Townsend gallantly offered without hesitation, assuming her offer of taking a taxi was pure fabrication. Felicia Bradley had no intention of taking a taxi, but he didn't begrudge her the insincerity. She was too well mannered to just snap her fingers.

"I'll just drive on over and save you the trouble," he continued. "No problem at all. Are you in the same dorm that Leslie's in?"

"Dorm?" Felicia Bradley cut a laugh short into a snort. "My dear Townsend, I don't stay in dorms. My room is at the Fairmont."

The phone rang soon after Townsend had made his hurried exit. He had taken time only to brush his teeth and fluff up his curly brown hair with a controlled scalp massage maneuver in front of the mirror. In L.L. Bean denims and his KANSAS JAYHAWKS, 1988 NCAA CHAMPIONS T-shirt he was casual but presentable. After the obligatory four rings, per the program, the answering machine kicked on.

Leslie Rosenthal left a wordy, rather disorganized message. She wanted to know what the hell had happened, anyway; she hoped he had a reasonable explanation but couldn't possibly imagine one. She would be at rehearsal that evening until late, not to bother to try to reach her that night since she intended on crashing as soon as she got back to her room. She'd call him tomorrow. She'd forgotten to ask him if he was interested in going to the gala tomorrow night. He could think about it. No pressure. And, by the way, Felicia Bradley caught her sneaking down from the balcony and was pumping her for information about him. Ostensibly Felicia wanted medical advice, he might even get a call from her, so not to shit a brick. And if Felicia did call, Leslie admonished him, he had better hang on to the family jewels.

3

HE DECIDED TO LOCK HIS NOVA upon sighting the pickets. Not that he expected anything. The last time he had seen a picket line this far out in the suburbs, a troupe of matrons was protesting the sale of dirty magazines at a nearby 7-Eleven. They had shortly abandoned their vigil, probably because all the walking was playing hell on their varicose veins. Support hose could do only so much, and apparently the ladies weren't committed enough to subject themselves to vein stripping. Townsend had crossed the line, with no compunctions, to buy a large raspberry Slurpee.

This was no 7-Eleven, however. The Lenexa Women's Specialty Clinic was a boxlike single-story structure set apart from the more clustered office parks that had sprouted up in Overland Park and neighboring Lenexa, Kansas, over the past few years. It had formerly been a local real estate office, long since abandoned by the Realtors for high-gloss office space in one of the neighboring towers more appropriate for an upscale clientele. When Townsend was growing up, the whole area was farmland. Then, road names like Quivera and Pflumm had conjured up images of the sticks, sweeping wheatfields punctuated by the occasional farmhouse, sinewy country men with farmer's tans and prominent Adam's apples. But development to the west and south had since been cancerous, fed by greed, an inferiority complex endemic to the entire region, and the absence of geographic obstacles; specifically, any respectable elevation or, heaven forbid, a decent body of water. The Kansas landscape was undeniably bleak, but native midwesterners always defended the special beauty of the plains. In Townsend's estimation, scanning the vista during that morning's drive, man hadn't exactly improved on nature.

They marched in a casual loop around the front entrance of the clinic, no more than two dozen of them, carrying placards and wearing sandwich boards. They had gotten an early start; it was just past 7:30 A.M., another blue-sky day with the unexpected pleasure of a cool breeze. In three hours, though, it would be a scorcher, the asphalt underfoot exuding heat like smoldering coals. Not only was Kansas geographically deprived, it was meteorologically without merit. Townsend absently squeezed the prune on his chain; then pocketed his keys and walked across the parking lot toward the marchers. With dread he surmised the message even before he could make out the crudely lettered slogans and the full-color blowup of macerated fetuses. Crossing this picket line had not been in the job description; Howard hadn't mentioned this nasty business.

Close enough to pick out ABORTION IS MURDER and TWO PEOPLE ENTER, BUT ONLY ONE COMES OUT ALIVE, Townsend assumed the worst and felt the heat creeping into his face. What was the deal? Howard Gorell wasn't an abortionist, he was a fertility man, for Chrissake.

He took a calming breath and tried to appear inconspicuous as he crossed the near side of the marchers, timing his penetration in advance so as not to break stride or bump anyone. His chosen opening, between a severely myopic matron with short dark hair that wanted washing and a male geriatric with drooping paunch and freckled tonsure, proved relatively unimposing. Still, once engulfed by the ring of humanity, Townsend experienced a rush of paranoia that brought Custer and Jonah to mind. Then the cannibals from Tarzan movies, crazed primitives desperate for a respite from nuts and tubers. He was in hot water. The borders of the giant amoeba, restlessly shifting, undulated around him.

He maintained an even casual pace, and at the halfway point experienced a soothing detachment, as if he had stumbled into the eye of a hurricane. The chanting sounded more distant. The picketers took no notice.

And why should they? He was of the wrong biological persuasion to want an abortion, for one thing, he assured himself flippantly. Besides, in no way did he look like Howard Gorell; he didn't even look medical. In a lavender Lacoste shirt, khaki slacks, and saddle Oxfords, he looked downright collegiate. There was the small matter of the white coat, however; neatly folded and tucked under his arm, which he now hastily rolled into a compact tube that would be less obtrusive. As he assessed the situation, the docile protesters couldn't care less. He was an innocent bystander, surrounded at the moment only owing to a temporary fluke in some cosmic time-space continuum.

When Townsend spotted the sign printed with BRITISH ABORTIONIST GO HOME, he faltered and let his lower jaw succumb to gravity. If they weren't at the right place, they at least seemed to know where they were. The placard carrier, an immaculately dressed portly man in his fifties, stood firm between Townsend and the clinic entrance. The man smiled. His glance took in the balled up white coat in Townsend's armpit. In cautious rejoinder, Townsend pursed his lips ambiguously.

Gaze flung heavenward, the man began mumbling, lip-synching to an inaudible rhythm. His head initially outlined a circle in space, but subsequent orbits became smaller and smaller until movement compressed into a violent shaking, then an intense tremor. Fleshy jowls vibrated like the buttocks of a shimmying stripper.

"Gawd . . . I say *Gawd Awmighty,*" he supplicated.

"Praise the Lord . . . Praise the Lord. . . ." A chorus of subdued repetitions, a verbal chain reaction, percolated from the former marchers, now a stationary audience.

"Praise the Lord," the leader encanted, stretching his syllables like taffy until the words snapped to pieces. He resumed eye contact with Townsend and smiled demonically.

"Amen . . . praise the Lord. . . ."

"Uh . . . excuse me," Townsend piped unobtrusively, edging

around an invisible but palpable pulpit. In response, Elmer Gantry sidestepped into his path. Then he extended his free arm, as if to bestow a blessing.

Townsend noticed that the man had chunky, workman's hands, and that his tailor had overcut the suitcoat sleeves by a good two inches.

"Pardon me but—"

Images had blurred into a distorted, surreal montage. It was the second time in as many days that he had experienced such sensory overload; this time more tactile and auditory than visual. Rather than a cognizance of gradations of darkness, a form in the shadows, there were points of moistness against his cheek. The spittle peppering his face was spewed from the sloppily articulated *S* in "sinner." The full phrase, screamed with the conviction of sudden and orgasmic revelation, had been *"HERE'S your sinner!"* Loud, distinct, and to the point. References to his being a murderer, with full crowd participation, followed soon, and persistently, thereafter. By then, though, the hand of blessing had coalesced into a single pudgy finger of accusation, and the accuser's face had been transformed into the puffed, purple-faced countenance of someone choking, a cartoon character containing a fiery explosion inside his mouth.

The placard was swooping upon him like gigantic bird wings. Townsend deflected the force of the strikes with his left forearm and grabbed at the oversized swatter with his free hand. In the process, his white coat fell from armpit to asphalt. The cool breeze thrust upon his face by the fanning placard might have provided comfort against the heat if not for the stinging blows to his face, the shrill admonitions of a maniac, and anxiety over reinforcements attacking from behind.

Eventually the cardboard fell to the ground, and Townsend was dodging a flimsy T-shaped wooden frame of one-by-twos. Out of fear or impatience, or perhaps vexed by the symbolism of being on the vulnerable side of a swinging crucifix, Townsend switched to the offensive. He clutched the zealot's wrist and yanked it forward and groundward, at the same time shifting all of his body except for the firmly planted foot at tripping's distance. The man plummeted like a wounded bull. Only the balance of a running back or divine intervention could have detained nose from intimate conflation with asphalt. Townsend Reeves, confident of that inevitability, wasted no time to confirm and ran like hell to the shelter of the Lenexa Women's Specialty Clinic.

"What the hell's going on here?" Townsend demanded, bursting through the clinic door and forcing it shut behind him like a fugitive. He twisted the knob, preferring a more substantial barrier, like an iron bar. Fortunately the mechanism went unchallenged—no one came after him, no fists pounded on the glass.

The contrast from the heat, noise, and violence of the outside to the cool quiet haven was striking. The waiting room was tastefully and predictably decorated, the decor restful, professional, and totally impersonal. It was also empty. Townsend regretted he hadn't allowed the calm to overtake him before shooting off his mouth. The outburst had been indecorous, guffawing at a funeral. Maybe no one had heard him.

But Rita Babcock, out of view behind the partition separating the reception area from the business side, had most certainly heard him. Alarmed, she had spilled most of her first cup of decaf on the countertop as she lunged across to stick her head through the opening to check out the disturbance.

"Goodness gracious, Dr. Reeves." Taking appraisal of the situation, she pulled her head out of view, haphazardly blotted at the spilled liquid with some Kleenex, and rushed around the corner to join him.

"Why, your face is all scratched! Don't tell me those idiots—"

"Who are they? What's going on here?" he asked with feigned calmness.

She scrunched her lips together and shook her head in disgust. "Damn them to hell! Let me get some peroxide for you."

"It's all right. It can wait. I don't understand why those people are out there."

"Come on, now; let's have a seat." She had assumed her protective take-charge and nurturing-nurse persona, leading him backward to the sofa and sitting down beside him.

"I'm terribly sorry about all this. Did they get physical with you?"

"We got physical with each other," Townsend clarified.

"Good—not about you," she quickly corrected. "But now I'm justified in calling the police. Maybe they can shoo them off before the first patient arrives. This situation is absolutely ludicrous."

Rita Babcock was Howard Gorell's man Friday. She was a registered nurse, somewhere in her forties, with a pleasant and soft Virginia accent. She was attractive despite too square a jaw and strawberry blond hair that was pompadoured and starched in the anachronistic style of a southern beauty pageant contestant. Her fitted white lab coat and matching white slacks indicated an elevated professional status—health care delivery rather than bedpan transport.

"Exactly what situation is this?" Townsend asked. "Howard didn't mention—"

"Well, they're not worth mentioning." she interrupted. "You know as well as I that we don't do abortions here."

"Then what's it all about?"

"It's ludicrous, as I said already. Absolutely ludicrous." She took a deep breath, composed herself enough for an explanation. "Howard's had this patient for years. Big-time endometriosis, multiple laparoscopies for lysis of adhesions. Finally she conceived, but it was an ectopic. He couldn't salvage her ovary or tube on the one side, and most of the tube on the other side had already been removed. Her pelvis was a mess. Got the picture?"

Townsend nodded.

"She's thirty-nine by this time and she and her husband still desperately want a pregnancy. So Dr. Gorell decides to go in vitro with her." She noticed some coffee splatters on her jacket and patted them absently.

"Anyway," she continued, "after two more unsuccessful attempts, Doctor goes for broke and implants seven fertilized ova. Unfortunately, five of them took, and we're stuck with this high-risk mom with quints."

"I think I heard about this," interrupted Townsend.

"Well, you shouldn't have; that's the problem. After she delivers healthy triplets—precious babies, two girls and a boy—*Star Magazine* does a piece on her. Infertility success story, high tech enters the bedroom and all the rest, okay stuff, really. But then they have to mention, like an aside, that originally there were five embryos. They didn't specifically say what had happened, but the implication was enough for these crazies to pick up on."

"Selective termination?"

"Misnomer, it's hardly selective, it's all chance. The two embryos that happened to be most accessible to the needle, the sacs that technically were easiest to inject with ethanol were . . . injected with ethanol."

"Not much choice in that situation," said Townsend. "If he had let her go, she probably would have ended up with some surviving as preemie disasters, or maybe lost them all."

"Of course. But tell *them* that." She dismissed the goings-on outside with a wave of her hand. "But enough of that. You need to get cleaned up. We're going to be hopping this morning. Follicle-size checks on seven women on Clomid or Pergonal. And then I just got a call a few minutes ago from an AID patient who had a positive LH dipstick yesterday morning, so we'll have to work her in sometime for insemination. I'll be lucky if I get my coffee."

"An AIDS patient?" asked Townsend, perplexed.

"AID singular. A-I-D. Artificial insemination with donor sperm. We use frozen thawed."

Medical lingo was specialty specific. Not only did laypeople not understand medical terminology, but the widespread use of acronyms ensured that many physicians didn't even understand each other. The number of insider terms correlated directly with the rate of growth of a specialty. Predictably, the field of infertility evaluation and treatment had a burgeoning lexicon.

"Ah," said Townsend. "Let me get this straight. The AID patient is functional hormonally and otherwise, but she can't get pregnant because her husband—"

"Righto. Hubbie's sperm isn't up to snuff. So she charts her temperature or we can monitor her follicles with ultrasound, or simpler yet, we pick up her luteinizing hormone surge using a urine dipstick test. Twenty-four hours after the LH surge, we supply the sperm. The others coming today are being stimulated for ovulation induction. If the time is right, they'll get an HCG booster and hubby will have to take off work for some afternoon entertaining."

"Not as spontaneous as being in the backseat of a Fairlane 500," quipped Townsend.

"It can be a real chore, believe me," said Rita. "I don't know if Doctor told you," she went on, "but we're gearing up our lab for the trickier stuff. IVF-D, as opposed to AID, is in vitro fertilization with donor sperm. Or we can use hubby's in most cases. We retrieve the ova, fertilize it in a petri dish, then return it to the uterus. But now we've got GIFT and ZIFT. . . ." She smiled expectantly.

Townsend said, "I think I lost you after Harpo, Chico, and Zeppo."

"GIFT is gamete intrafallopian transfer, where we put the egg and sperm directly into the fallopian tube, usually with the laparoscope, but now with ultrasound we can do it through the uterus with a hysteroscope. With ZIFT, we put the fertilized egg directly into the fallopian tube, Z standing for zygote. Honestly, Dr. Reeves, you should come and work for us more often; you'd learn a thing or two."

"Fortunately for everyone concerned, I'm getting paid just to find those little eggs and measure them suckers."

"You're a practical man, Dr. Reeves. Well, let's get ready then. You know where the lab is—straight down the end of the hallway, past the examining rooms and Dr. Gorell's office. Lenny is back there; he's new since you were here last. He can get you some hydrogen peroxide for your face. Anything else I can do for you before we get going, Dr. Reeves?"

"Please call me Townsend, Rita."

"All right, Townsend, but not in front of the patients."

An old-fashioned prim and proper southern gal, thought Townsend.

"Oh, by the way," he said, looking out toward the window, but seeing nothing through the drapery. The spoil of battle was somewhere out there on the parking lot. "Is there an extra white coat around here?"

"You played basketball for the Wildcats, didn't you?" Lenny was a bookish-looking black of average height in his twenties, with dark-pigmented acne scars and tortoise-shell glasses. Not the basketball type, and he had to have been in grade school during Townsend's playing days. He handed Townsend the brown peroxide bottle and an individually wrapped four-by-four gauze pad.

"Thanks. How did you know that?"

"I think I've heard my uncle mention you. Lamar Oates, he's my uncle. My last name's Oates too. You know him, right?"

"Sure, I know Lamar. We were teammates. Haven't seen him in a while, though. You be sure and send him my best. Tell him I'll take him on one-on-one anytime. If he loses, he gives me a slab of pork ribs."

"And if he wins?"

"Unlikely. But I'll ultrasound his gallbladder for free. The King of Cholesterol probably has gallstones by now."

Lenny smiled. "They took out his gallbag last year. You'll whip him though, my money's on you. He's put on some weight being around all that barbecue. It's the best, that barbecue."

Townsend nodded in agreement, concealing his preference for Hayward's, the main ribhouse competition. He had removed the gauze wrapper, moistened it with the peroxide, and was dabbing his face.

"So . . . you play hoops?" A negative reply was obvious, but failure to ask could be taken as an affront to Lenny's masculinity, and Townsend was consistently well mannered.

"Naw," answered Lenny. "I haven't got the hands."

Or the speed, or the height, or the coordination, Townsend added to himself. He viewed the young man sympathetically. From his speech and affect, Lenny was the product of an upper-middle-class suburban neighborhood, a token black in a white school. Were he raised in the inner city, he would have been terrorized, a continual victim throughout his wonder years. Even in the suburbs, Lenny probably had a rough time of it. He had survived, though, painful adolescence behind him, bright and articulate, a nice kid. Still, he came across as a nerd.

"I'm going to be a senior at KU," Lenny offered, a shade defensively. "Then I want to get my master's in laboratory science. This is just part-time summer work for me—I fill in for Denise, the regular tech. I'm really sort of a trainee—"

Rita's voice from the intercom interrupted him:

"That fresh frozen should be thawing, Lenny. Mrs. Humphrey's coming in half an hour."

"Okay. As we speak," Lenny responded to the air. "Excuse me," he reluctantly said to Townsend, leaving him to minister to himself.

Lenny went to a workstation on the other side of the lab. The lab itself was a fairly small but functional work space, lined on all sides by countertop over steel floor cabinetry, and identical wall-mounted cabinets. There were three sinks, two large refrigerators, and a fume hood tucked away in one corner. One decent-sized window looked out onto the parking lot, shaded by simple white Levolors.

Four tall stools demarcated the four separate work spaces along the counter, each with a large and imposing microscope before it. A smaller worktable in the center of the room held the most imposing microscope of all, a tandem-teaching scope that would allow two people to simultaneously examine the same slide. The entire apparatus was hooked up to a monitor, so live-action images—aimless but frantic herds of sperm, perhaps—could be projected on a larger viewing screen. Of the two chairs facing off before the large scope, one was a standard gray steel chair, the other an Early American reproduction, painted black with gold accenting: a university alumni chair. Townsend spotted the crimson and gold central emblem on the chairback: Harvard, where Howard had done his postdoc. Howard's special lab chair, the only wood furnishing in the whole room, to be graced by no bottom besides Howard's.

Townsend watched Lenny pick up a metallic canister that resembled a thermos. He struggled with the cap, trying to untwist it. For an instant, Townsend thought about offering to help unscrew the lid for him. Then it was too late. Indeed, Lenny Oates had not been lying when he confessed that he didn't have the hands.

The technician trainee had managed to unscrew the cap, but in his effort lost his grip on the canister. He responded like someone at whom several balls are thrown at once. Attempting to regain the one, he lost control of the other, the lid falling to the ground and rolling on the linoleum like a dropped coin, while the main canister, frozen vapor pouring out from its open end, skidded across the countertop.

Lenny lunged after the canister, diving onto the counter in a headfirst slide. His grasp was ineffectual; in fact, he propelled the missile further toward the sink, a smoke-breathing fish flip-flopping its way to water's edge. The canister recoiled off the far side of the sink, and still on the fly, bounced against the opposite side. In the process, a small plastic vial, attached to a cane contained in the thermos, was thrust out of its housing. Both the contents and the housing rattled against the sides of the metal sink, eventually coming to rest at the bottom. Frozen vapor was now billowing from the sink, and through the mist Townsend watched Lenny, prone on the counter, making fumbling jabs into the pit, a Boy Scout attempting to salvage a hot dog that had fallen into the campfire.

"Aw, shit," whined Lenny.

He leaned more deeply into the abyss, straining to see through the vapor cloud, and in reaching further, accidentally bumped the faucet handle with his shoulder. Water cascaded full force into the fog, splattering off the sink bottom, hissing and dramatically enlarging the cloud.

"Aw shit!"

Lenny composed himself enough to regroup. He turned off the water and hopped down from the counter. Townsend, in the meantime, had come to his side to lend moral support. Both of them gazed into the sink as the fog gradually lifted. Lenny ignored the metal canister and carefully pulled out the plastic cane from the bottom of the sink. The cane was designed to fit in the center of the canister; it was fitted to hold several vials, miniature test tubes. Only one tube had been secured to the cane; it was now only partially secured. It was also uncapped and filled with liquid.

"It's ruined," lamented Lenny. "Water and the liquid nitrogen got in it. No way it's not ruined."

"That, I take it, is—" began Townsend.

"—Mrs. Humphrey's frozen sperm," Lenny finished, making it sound almost proprietary, like Mrs. Paul's Frozen Fishsticks.

"Well," said Townsend, "it was an accident, wasn't it? And accidents happen, don't they?"

"I'm dead meat. Babcock's gonna kill me, and then she's gonna fire me."

"Isn't there any more?"

Lenny, anticipating the question, shook his head vigorously, cutting Townsend off without uttering a syllable.

"Maybe you can order another batch . . . more frozen sperm?" Townsend suggested hopefully.

Lenny gave Townsend a "you're incredibly naive" look. "No way," he said. "The soonest we can get more in from the bank would be Monday. And sperm on Monday isn't going to do Mrs. Humphrey a helluva lot of good today. I'm dead meat."

"There's got to be a way—" Townsend stopped midsentence. He didn't like the way Lenny was looking at him.

"There *is* a way," Lenny said emphatically.

Townsend pretended not to pick up on it. "I'm sure Rita will understand. I'll vouch for you."

"Dr. Reeves . . . you gotta help me out . . . you just gotta!"

"Lenny, I don't think it's really wise—"

"You're not HIV positive, are you?"

"No, Lenny, I'm not HIV positive, but that really doesn't have anything to do with it. You see, it really isn't appropriate—"

"You gotta help me, Dr. Reeves! Please, man, you gotta save my ass!"

"Lenny, you seem like a really nice kid, and I honestly would like to help you out—"

"Man, I'd do it myself if I could. But this is Lenexa, man . . . Mrs. Humphrey don't want no colored baby—"

Townsend noticed that in his panic, Lenny Oates was reverting to street talk. Maybe he had escaped from the inner city after all.

"You're not hepatitis-B positive, are you?" Lenny was continuing with his medical history, and Townsend found himself complying.

"No, I'm not hep-B positive. But it doesn't matter."

"Sure it matters! This is cool . . . this is cool. There's no problem with this . . . there's nothing wrong with this. You're not HIV positive, you're not hepatitis-B positive. You're smart, you're an athlete, you're a tall, good-looking dude . . . why, man, your genes can run circles around anything coming from a sperm bank. I mean, any woman out there would be dying to have your kid."

Not Leslie Rosenthal, Townsend thought with remorse. Was he resisting because of her? It went deeper than that. He had turned down the opportunity to be a sperm donor back in medical school. The notion of his parenting some anonymous child somewhere had given him the creeps then, and disturbed him even more now. He wanted his own kids, he didn't want his seed scattered about to any caller.

"I'm flattered, Lenny, I really am, but—"

"And most important of all, man, you're white!"

"I *am* all of those things, Lenny, but—"

"Please, man," Lenny was begging now, "you just gotta help me out. I'll do anything. My Uncle Lamar will do anything—"

Townsend didn't respond. He was asking himself a number of questions. Why did he feel so bad about this? Why was he always such a nice guy, feeling compelled to please everyone? Where was the sanctity of his semen? Was this any way to treat his own precious genetic material, his link with the past, his legacy for the future? Was he really willing to sacrifice the uniqueness of his being for this? Not for love, not for money even, but as a swap for some mediocre barbecue?

Townsend felt sick to his stomach. He looked pained, as if he had something in his mouth that tasted really bad but he couldn't spit it out.

Lenny Oates had taken the opportunity to open one of the overhead storage cabinets. He held out a plastic specimen cup with a gray top.

Townsend Reeves took the cup. He swallowed the bad taste in his mouth. He sighed heavily.

"Where's the nearest bathroom?" he asked.

4

THE MATTER AT HAND WAS IN HAND, and not an easy task. Townsend squirmed on the toilet seat and gazed down at the rumpled trousers and boxer shorts encircling his ankles. The cubicle was small, with large maroon floor tiles extending halfway up the wall to oak wainscoting; from there up it was flocked floral wallpaper of a similar dark hue. Even the sink and head were color coordinated, the antithesis of antiseptic white decor. A brass tubular fixture over the mirror shielded most of the glow of an underpowered fluorescent bulb; adequate illumination to masturbate by, but not enough to check out a blackhead or see if a piece of spinach was stuck in your teeth.

Townsend didn't find the atmosphere soothing. He was definitely not in the mood, although if Felicia Bradley had had her way with him the night before, his job would be more challenging still. Technical considerations aside, the situation was ludicrous. Leslie wasn't sleeping with him for reasons not clear to him. He had declined Felicia's charitable offer, again for reasons not clear to him. Nothing was clear except for the plastic cup in his grip. He pried off the cap and placed both cap and cup within easy reach on the floor beside him. He closed his eyes, leaned back, and mentally began reconstructing the events of the evening before, frame by frame, his own blue movie.

Felicia's room was on the ninth floor of the Fairmont Plaza. He had arrived shortly after 4:30, less than fifteen minutes after receiving her call. Off the elevator he had turned left, cued by numbers and arrows on a wall placard. The teal carpet was soft underfoot, the hallway deserted. Townsend traversed the entire length of hallway, passing nothing but a housekeeping cart; another placard below an exit sign at the intersection directed him to turn down the shorter of the two feeding corridors. Straight ahead was the dead end at Room 920; next to it in the corner the emergency-exit stairwell, then 919, Felicia's suite. On the doorknob the DO NOT DISTURB sign was flipped to the MAID, MAKE UP THIS ROOM side.

Townsend became guarded the instant he saw her. A man couldn't look at Felicia Bradley without aching. The initial sight of her took his breath away, and when Townsend got his first wind back, the whiff was permeated with Opium. She had showered and changed into a light blue silk blouse and a short beige skirt. Her long legs were filmed with nylons. More than splashing on some scent as an afterthought, she had bothered to put on makeup and fix her blond hair in a French braid. Late afternoon after a long rehearsal—if she hadn't done it for his benefit, then for whose?

She greeted him cordially, invited him in, offered him a beverage. He politely refused the drink, and surveyed the room, as he couldn't just stand there gawking at her. It was a standard, reasonably appointed hotel room suite in good order except for the still unmade queen-size bed. He spotted a feminine-looking suitcase set on a luggage rack in the corner, caught sight of three or four dresses hanging in the open closet. No male presence in the room. So where was Gerard?

"You don't drink? I'd think you'd want a little one just to relax. It must have been a very stressful day for you, you know, looking all over for your keys."

Townsend ignored the dig. "A little early in the day for me."

"I have a minifridge full of Lindt chocolate and Häagen-Dazs."

"I'll pass, but thanks anyway."

"At least make yourself comfortable," she said, leading him to the sofa. Townsend had seen more blatant come-ons, but only in films.

Felicia Bradley might have been a high fashion model: azure eyes, prominent cheekbones, full lips, a Nordic queen. She lacked the slinking carriage of a model, though, holding herself centered, the stance of a trained dancer. They sat down, Townsend taking a safe middle ground off to one side. She sat kiddy-corner at the end nearest Townsend, tucking her long legs under her, draping a long arm across the couch back. The tips of her fingers lacked an inch in lighting upon Townsend's right shoulder.

"You're quite tall, what? Six-three?"

"Five feet, sixteen inches."

"My, my, my," Felicia said suggestively.

"So, where are the X rays?"

"We have time for that, don't we? Why such a rush?"

"No rush," said Townsend hurriedly.

Felicia was a temptress, and she was trouble. Townsend had promised himself that he wouldn't nibble at any bait. He had hoped to keep the encounter on a relatively safe, professional plane. Her reason for wanting to see him was plausible enough, but what was her real angle? And why had he been so anxious to get within touching distance of this prize? An innate male craving for self-torture? To prove that the force of willpower could overcome awesome biological urges? So far, the battle was a draw, but Townsend was beginning to perspire.

The situation with Leslie was too precarious to even contemplate an affair. Were he to have one (and did he really owe Leslie fidelity after all?), Felicia was a bad choice. The entire dance community based in Kansas City at that time would know about the tryst within hours. Felicia collected trophies, was vindictive enough to flaunt her conquest under Leslie's nose.

"So . . . uh . . . where's Gerard?" The safest way to set limits, he reasoned, was to bring up significant others.

"How should I know?" she answered, not hiding annoyance. "I'm not my brother's keeper."

"He doesn't stay here?"

"His room's across the hall. I would have preferred him on another floor or, better yet, on another planet, but this is how the festival people set things up. They have a block of rooms on this floor. In New York we share a brownstone, but thank God it's big enough that we don't get in each other's way."

"I don't understand. Are you two separated?"

She blurted out a harsh, unamused laugh. "If we're going to engage in depressing conversation, I'd rather have you look at the X rays." Abruptly, she got up and went to the bureau and retrieved a manila envelope. She handed it to him, unopened, and plopped back down into the sofa, assuming her previously relaxed position.

Townsend undid the string clasp and pulled out the two standard views of Felicia's right ankle, a front and side view. He scooted to the opposite end of the sofa, turned on the end table lamp, and alternately held up each image to the beige lampshade, the closest thing at hand to a view box. Nothing visible, as expected. Normal bones, no extraneous calcifications, not even any soft tissue swelling to speak of. He looked a lot longer than he needed, partly to give her concerns adequate attention rather than a cavalier brush-off, partly to stall. Looking at X rays, he was at least on familiar grounds, in control. He usually didn't perspire when interpreting X rays.

The knock on the door was timid. The door cautiously opened and a wizened Latino woman in a yellow housekeeper's uniform peered around the corner. Felicia waved her in impatiently. A change of bed linens under her arm, the woman stealthily headed for the bed, a mouselike creature in look and action, with a hairy upper lip.

"What do you think?" Felicia asked, watching Townsend intently.

"The films are normal, but that doesn't mean much of anything. Most problems with the soft tissues, like tendinitis, don't show up on X rays."

"It hurts right over here." Felicia immodestly untucked her right leg, stretching it out on the couch, and rubbed the outside of her ankle. In the process, her skirt hiked up and the gap between her thighs was large enough to accommodate a reasonably-sized Crenshaw melon.

Townsend disinterestedly looked toward the area of her concern. Lateral side of the ankle. Probably a peroneal strain or tendinitis. He halfheartedly made the effort to examine the ankle himself, the physician laying on hands.

"Here, let me get these off, then." Before Townsend could protest, she had arched her back and levitated her buttocks off the divan. Deftly, she maneuvered her hands under her skirt and pulled her pantyhose down to knee level. Bringing knees to stomach in another single coordinated movement, she removed the nylons completely, wadded them into a ball, and haphazardly tossed them across the room. Smugly she held out her ankle, and Townsend found himself cradling it with both hands, the Duke gently supporting Cinderella's glass slipper.

Felicia smiled at a nonplussed Townsend. "Well?"

Townsend was for the moment overloaded in the observation department. He had observed a number of things, the first being that Felicia Bradley did not wear underpants, or, at least, was not wearing any that afternoon. She had quite casually, unabashedly, flashed him her pudenda, luxuriously feathered by golden lockets. Thus, his second observation, that she was indeed a natural blonde. Third, he observed that in the current context, "pudenda" didn't seem an appropriate term when applied to Felicia Bradley. Townsend recalled the derivation of the term—learned in medical school—from the Latin meaning "something to be ashamed of." Finally, he observed that Felicia was quite pleased at his discomfiture, and there wasn't a damn thing he could do to hide it. He had been paralyzed by the Mother of All Beaver Shots, frozen with Felicia Bradley's right foot in his hand and not knowing where to look.

So he looked over at the housekeeper, who despite being bent over the foot of the bed, was at that instant looking back at him. She regarded him passively, as if she were lost in thought, then set her attention on the progress of her hands, which had automatically continued smoothing and tucking in the neat flaps of the cover sheet. She completed the tight military corner, passed no judgment other than one of satisfaction with her workmanship, and proceeded to the head of the bed.

Townsend kept his head down and ineffectually prodded the area in question. He hit a spot and Felicia winced. Townsend shrugged. He didn't want to play doctor anymore.

"I know several good orthopods in town. If it doesn't get any better I'll be happy to refer you to one." He gently put down her foot, setting it close against the other one and eliminating any further viewing temptations.

"Don't you have any ideas of your own?" she asked, demurely tucking her legs under herself.

"It depends on what the problem is." Townsend was growing impatient. "Maybe ice it after you dance, or use heat, or some anti-inflammatories, if they don't upset your stomach. Hell, I don't know. I'm not in a position to prescribe anything for you, Felicia. Let me give you somebody else's name."

"I may take you up on that." She said more formally, "I appreciate your coming."

"No problem. Anytime. My little bit for the arts." He pushed his weight forward on the sofa. Things were winding down. Even the housekeeper was wrapping things up. The blanket had been securely tucked in, the bedspread centered and smoothed, the pillows fluffed.

"Would you be interested in going someplace for dinner and making an evening of it?" A last ditch effort, asked without much conviction.

"I had a really late lunch, Felicia."

"Then we can skip the dinner part."

Townsend didn't respond. He gave her a wry look: *You know how much I want it and you know I still won't anyway, so why don't you give it up?*

"I have some cocaine," she offered.

"I'm not in the market," he said.

"I guess you're just not interested, Dr. Reeves." She didn't need reassurance, she was just making conversation, constructing a word bridge to cross the awkwardness.

"You're wrong there. I'm very interested, just not willing."

"Loyalty to sweet Leslie Rosenthal?"

"Partly, but not totally."

"You like to work more for it, then?"

"I don't particularly like to work for anything. But let's just say the timing isn't right."

"Maybe some other time then."

"Maybe." He stood up and walked to the door. The woman was a head case and real poison, but he might still consider enduring her presence for another session.

"You're not irresistible, Townsend; don't let it go to your head."

"Apparently I don't have to be irresistible, just in proximity."

"Screw off."

Townsend had closed the door behind him without further comment, leaving Felicia Bradley alone with the lady with the mustache.

The incident behind him, Townsend was proud of himself. He had looked the enemy in the lips and walked away unscathed. He had preserved his virtue, saved himself for Leslie. And, if not for Leslie, he had saved himself for this. For Lenny Oates. For some women named Humphrey, a stranger, whose husband was shooting blanks. Pump priming courtesy of Felicia Bradley, he would manage, in absentia, to impregnate this stranger, another man's woman. And she would have a child, his child, lost to him forever. Townsend wanted to sow his seed in a garden of his own choosing, not have it bandied about like an ugly orphan.

He forced himself, once again, to recall Felicia, the temptress, thrusting her hips forward, reaching up, the nylons effortlessly sliding down her thighs like a frictionless puck on ice. He had seen it, in the flesh, within his grasp, the crotch of Desdemona. Townsend held the image, grimaced, and reached for the cup in the darkness.

5

INFERTILITY PATIENTS WERE ALWAYS PUNCTUAL, unlike the infirm Townsend had encountered at St. Michael's, an urban medical center. They were generally pleasant, well off, and incredibly compliant—model patients. In the sense that their treatment protocol was the focus of their lives, they reminded him of cancer patients. The similarity ended there. Instead of attempting to impede the explosive growth of cells inside them, the mission was to promote it.

The couples could be desperate, occasionally pathetic in their absolute commitment. With success, the rewards were great for patient and practitioner, but it was a gut-wrenching way to make a living. The husbands, dressed for success and on their way to work, generally accompanied the wives for the daily ultrasound ritual—usually four or five consecutive days each month—only one component of the therapeutic gristmill. The regimen—ongoing for months, sometimes years—required dedication, emotional support, and money, a roller-coaster ride with many small tragedies endured for the sake of a possible success.

With each ultrasound examination taking ten to fifteen minutes, Townsend was halfway through the caseload in just over half an hour. He was polite but subdued, concealing his distractedness, trying not to think about what Lenny Oates was doing with his body fluid at each moment. He knew more than he cared to, since a relieved and inappropriately enthusiastic Lenny had volunteered the information and Townsend had listened with more than a clinical interest.

His specimen would sit for twenty minutes until it completely liquefied. Then it would be washed with a culture medium—a concoction called Hams F10, centrifuged, and resuspended in half a cubic centimeter of solution. The end product was a syringe full of Townsend's signature genetic material, awaiting the arrival of the mysterious Mrs. Humphrey. If the gods were with him, Townsend prayed, Mrs. Humphrey would get stuck in traffic. Any delay would do, as long as the spermatozoa could shrivel and die, like the miniature pet turtle he carelessly left on the dashboard of his mother's parked station wagon during a similarly scorching summer over two decades earlier.

The women that morning knew the program, had gone through the numbers before with Howard. They all wore dresses or skirts so they didn't need to gown, just slip off the underpants and pull their apparel up out of the way. Without instructions, they shimmied to the end of the exam table and slipped their heels into the sheepskin-lined stirrups. The husbands would take a standard position of their own, suit jacket unbuttoned, perched on the end of the chair in the corner, expectantly and helplessly hunched forward. Rita stood at the table side, making introductions and pleasant conversation, but mainly serving as chaperone.

It's liquefied by now, Townsend thought, glancing up at the clock. Bathtime, wash 'em and weep. . . .

"Mrs. Braverman has had four cycles of Clomid, and she's on day 14 of her cycle," Rita was explaining.

A pleasant, plumpish-looking woman in her mid-thirties, patient number four had assumed the position; husband, portly and balding, had assumed his. The woman was cheerful, her partner, brow furrowed, less adept at camouflaging the stress. When push came to shove, the women always were inherently stronger.

Townsend, already gloved, nodded absently. The endovaginal ultrasound probe was where he had left it, sticking straight down into a plastic jug of disinfectant by the sink on the counter, only the handle exposed. The soaking solution revealed its worth by its strong acrid stench. He lifted the probe from the solution by its handle, holding it over the bottle for a couple of seconds to let the excess fluid drip back into the container. The instrument was a high-tech dildo, not anatomically correct, that housed an ultrasound transducer in its tip. When hooked into the hundred-thousand-dollar-plus ultrasound machine by its connecting cord, the transducer emitted and received reflected sound waves, and the gathered information was digitally processed into a two-dimensional image displayed on a television monitor. Since continually updated images were flashed on the screen at a frame rate faster than the human eye could detect flickering, the images were in real time, a motion picture. An incredible live-action voyage, the world view as perceived from the inside of a vagina.

Townsend took the technology for granted. He had performed hundreds of these examinations, and simply went through the motions by habit. First he dried off the probe with a paper towel. While disposable latex covers were available through medical suppliers, most doctors used the cheaper commercially available condoms. Howard was a Trojan man. Several red-foiled packets were folded, accordionlike, on the counter. Townsend separated an individual packet from the rubber chain and tore it open. He determined which way the prophylactic rolled, squirted a dollop of conducting gel from a squeeze bottle on the inner side, and unrolled the condom over the plastic probe. Finally, pointing the probe end directly toward the ceiling, he squeezed another dollop of the ultrasound goop on the tip of the covered probe for lubrication. A final flourish gave the mound of gel the same dropping curl that crowned a soft cone from the Dairy Queen.

"A little cold," he said, parting the woman's labia with the thumb and index finger of his left hand and carefully inserting the probe into her vagina with his right. For the prices they were paying, Howard could at least buy a gel warmer.

"Yesterday the biggest one was nineteen millimeters, on the left side," the woman offered, unfazed by the instrumentation.

She leaned up onto her elbows, and taking the cue, Townsend tilted the television monitor so everybody could watch.

The left ovary was easily seen; hormonally stimulated, it contained several round cystic structures—follicles at varying stages of development. Normally, without fertility drugs, there would only be one follicle each month—the dominant, or Graafian, follicle—to reach greater than ten- or twelve-millimeter size, the also-rans in the pecking order dropping out of the ovulatory race earlier in the cycle. The most mature of the follicles was destined to burst midcycle, releasing a ripe ovum. With luck at least one sperm, a fortuitously positioned pellet in a cloud of buckshot peppering the airspace of ducks in flight, would meet its mark.

"Right," said Townsend, quickly spotting the largest follicle, the main contender. He pressed the freeze frame button on the console, then used electronic calipers to measure the dimensions, moving the markers with a track ball. "Twenty-one millimeters."

The woman beamed and glanced over at her husband. He nodded, guardedly enthusiastic.

"Let me measure the others," said Townsend dryly. Between both ovaries, the woman had nine follicles, two approaching the size of the largest, the others considerably smaller. Townsend nonetheless measured each of them in two dimensions with the electronic calipers and track ball, recording the data on paper film. Howard expected as much. It was tedious work and overkill, an intravaginal Nintendo game without the sound effects or adventure plot.

The woman left in high spirits, as elated as she had no doubt been at the comparable time of her past four cycles. Unlike those other eventual disappointments, this could be the month. She would yet again self-administer an injection of human chorionic gonadotropin to provoke ovulation, and husband and wife would have unspontaneous couplings over the next two days. She'd pass the coming days on needles and pins, praying for her period not to start with all the fervor of a single college coed praying for the opposite. Menstrual blood meant failure, back to the stirrups, back to another cycle of clomiphene citrate.

A viable pregnancy wasn't an easy achievement under normal circumstances. Even with a sperm-egg linkup, as many as a third of fertilizations were doomed to fail in nature's weeding out process. That thought at the moment was encouraging to Townsend. He wondered about the success rate with a single shot of donated sperm on any given cycle. Assuming his sperm were feisty, energetic, and potent (and how could they not be?), odds were excellent that Mrs. Humphrey would come up empty. Nobody's fault, really, just part of the process. Townsend looked up at the clock without registering the time.

Bathtime over, now in the centrifuge, blinding speeds forcing the gametes to the bottom of the tube like commuters jammed into a packed subway car at rush hour. . . .

She was already in position on the examining table when Townsend finally saw her. He had been pacing in the lab—pointedly ignoring Lenny—waiting for Rita's summons over the intercom. He naively assumed his involvement with the sordid mess had ended with his jerking off in the washroom of the Lenexa Women's Specialty Clinic. He was wrong, as Rita had the gall to ask him to perform the insemination. An imposition, she knew, but would he mind awfully much? Townsend had been medically reared on the "see one, do one, teach one" approach to medical procedures, but was reluctant for a reason besides his failure to meet even those unstringent qualifications. Since Rita hadn't a clue, though, she couldn't be judged too severely.

"I haven't seen one," he admitted.

"Nothing to it. Simpler than a Pap smear."

"I haven't done one of those in a long time either."

"You look tired, Dr. Reeves. Are you okay?"

"Maybe I'm too pooped to Pap—"

Rita laughed, ascribing his reluctance to false modesty.

"I'll set her up, even put the speculum in, so you won't have to worry about pinching her."

Townsend said nothing, felt an itch beginning under his collar.

"I could do it myself," she went on, "but it's better if an M.D. does it. If I'd known this was coming I'd have arranged for another O.B. doc to cover. You know, these women have a lot at stake; they've been through a lot, and having a doctor involved—even if it's just for show—gives them more confidence. Reassures them. And I'm sure Howard will appreciate it and give you a little bonus."

"It's not about money, Rita, you know that."

"All righty then, I'll make an extra big batch of my special chicken and dumplings for you."

First barbecue ribs, now chicken and dumplings. What was this food business, anyway? In nine months would they ask him to wet nurse the kid in exchange for a tuna noodle casserole? Townsend Reeves didn't want chicken or ribs—he wanted his damn semen back.

"You wouldn't turn down my chicken and dumplings now, would you? It's my great-grandma's old Virginia recipe."

Townsend started to say something, but no words came. Instead, a barely noticeable grunt emerged from high in his pharynx as the air escaped from his nostrils. He smiled wanly.

"I thought not," a gratified Rita said, negotiations completed, hurriedly turning away to go about her business, which first involved retrieving a small syringeful of his genetic material from Lenny.

Again her voice, an interminable five minutes of pacing later, coming over the intercom. "We're ready for you in Room 3, Doctor Reeves."

Entering the exam room, Townsend was shocked by the thighs that greeted him. Forced apart by the stirrups, they were taut and unveiny, the musculature of a much younger Mrs. Humphrey than he had imagined. Preoccupied, he was only vaguely aware that Rita was introducing him and that Mrs. Humphrey was shifting up onto her elbows. He was looking toward the ground, not wanting to see her face.

"Don't get up," he said inanely.

Both women laughed. The idiotic remark had passed for

humor with a deadpan delivery; his pratfall coming across as calming bedside manner.

He couldn't avoid seeing the woman's face, albeit briefly, and acknowledging her smile of appreciation. A lovely open face, girl-next-door attractiveness without flashiness or hautiness. A blue-eyed brunette with hair cut perfectly straight across at the jawline and brushed away from the forehead. He gauged her to be in her late twenties. Why had he expected someone older? He had assumed she would be pushing forty, but reminded himself that her problem involved sperm, not egg. In all likelihood, with decent timing and the proper raw materials, Mrs. Humphrey would have no difficulty getting pregnant. No hormonal imbalances, no previous tubal infections or tubal pregnancies, no endometriosis, no ovulatory failure, no killer mucus. Just a husband with impotence. Maybe an old codger or some young exec cut down by mumps or a varicocele, or a vasectomy from a previous marriage.

And where was her lesser half, anyway? All the other patients that morning had been accompanied by a spouse. Was Mr. Humphrey away on business, unavoidably detained? Maybe he couldn't deal with the situation, too embarrassed by his own reproductive failure to witness his wife's insemination by donated sperm. The ultimate in sand being kicked into the face of a ninety-pound weakling. No fault of his wife's and the jerk couldn't handle things well enough to be there to support her. Even before sitting down on the stool and adjusting the gooseneck lamp to center-stage mons pubis, Townsend had concluded that Mrs. Humphrey deserved better.

Unfortunately, she's getting it, that's the real problem here.

Something else clued Townsend to the fact that Mrs. Humphrey wasn't a regular with the program. She was wearing a disposable gown, while her outfit—a black top and slacks number—along with her panties, were draped over the corner chair that Mr. Humphrey should have occupied. No one else that morning had to change, other than slipping down underpants; not a single woman had worn slacks. Mrs. Humphrey, ignorance born from lack of experience, was clearly out of uniform.

"Okay, we'll just get going here," Townsend said authoritatively. He was sweating but too much of a professional to let his hands shake. Mrs. Humphrey seemed not much better off. After the cordial introduction, she had lain back down and was staring up at the ceiling. Townsend saw that her hands were clenching the sides of the table; tendons of the back of her hands, flexing rhythmically, belied her coolness. In a perverse sexual world order, they were both virgins. He felt awkward, not knowing where to look, so he glanced around furtively, noting the bruises on the outside of her right calf, the calluses on the bottoms of her feet. Now that he had seen her, he felt a compulsion to look at her face again.

He made himself as comfortable as possible on the hard metal stool, moving the seat to a proper working distance. He gloved up and readjusted the light, though it needed no readjusting. A metal tray stand was within easy reach to his right. On it rested a shiny speculum, an all-too-familiar syringe—now with a long skinny plastic tube attached to the end—and a larger syringe filled with clear liquid and hooked to more standard-sized plastic tubing. All in order, professional readiness for a simple procedure. Townsend impersonally took in Mrs. Humphrey's spotlit genitalia and paused before beginning, like a concert pianist pondering an empty music stand and waiting for some minion to set the music down. There the analogy ended, since not only did Townsend Reeves lack music, but he didn't even know how to play the fucking piano.

"Rita?" He cleared his throat. Always the professional, even when playing doctor, Townsend managed to convey irritation and condescension just in the rearranging of throat mucus.

"Oh, yes . . . I'm sorry, Dr. Reeves." Apparently, Rita had been so taken by Townsend's beside manner and demeanor that she herself had forgotten that he didn't know what the hell he was doing.

"I've more or less explained things to Doris already—"

Her name was Doris, Doris Humphrey. . . .

"—but we'll go over things again for her as we do them." Once cued, Rita didn't miss a beat. She slipped a pair of latex gloves from her jacket pocket and expertly, soundlessly, slipped them on. Medical training imparted a detached coolness under fire, and Rita was well trained. Even under the most trying and stressful of circumstances, health professionals maintained a humdrum façade for their patients (to ensure patient confidence) and also for the benefit of co-workers (to protect their own professional egos). Scenes of panic-stricken, out-of-control physicians attempting to resuscitate a patient were mainly the stuff of fiction and television shows. In truth, doctors and nurses—and especially doctors—were consummate bluffers.

. . . the slippery newborn slides through the hands of the delivering obstetrician and plunges, headfirst, into the stainless-steel waste pail at the physician's feet. The doctor casually retrieves the wailing infant from the trash bin and holds him up for the mother to see.

"What a great baby you have," he says. "Usually we have to drop them on their head twice before they cry. . . ."

Rita eased her way over to the work area, a casual stroll to the foot of the table, and surreptitiously lubricated the speculum on the tray. She picked it up, feigning a handoff to Townsend.

"We're just going to put the speculum in now, so it will feel a little cold," Rita said, now at Townsend's side. Townsend noted the undeceitful usage of the royal "we." Rita gently positioned the metal retracting device internally and separated the duckbill-shaped ends by squeezing the handgrip. Mrs. Humphrey's cervix, a swollen fleshy flower sans petals, came into view. With any luck, Mrs. Humphrey had no idea that Rita, not Townsend, was at the helm.

"Now," the nurse continued, "Dr. Reeves will place a very small cannula into your cervical os and inject the donor sperm, then he'll flush out the syringe with some normal saline to make sure everything gets delivered and nothing important gets left in the syringe or tubing." The description was purely for Townsend's sake. She was giving instructions, talking him through it. Rita indicated the small syringe with a nod of her head, then tilted her head in the direction of the exposed cervix. *That* in *there.* She raised her eyebrows expectantly, a "get on with it already" gesture.

Townsend did exactly as he was told, aiming the tip of the small cannula at the bull's-eye, the dimple in the center of the cervix that was the outer door to the inner reproductive world. With the tip securely in place, Townsend Reeves slowly pushed in the plunger and injected millions of his personalized gametes—rinsed, spun, and dressed for a road trip—into the endocervical canal of his newfound acquaintance, Mrs. Doris Humphrey. On autopilot, he deftly switched syringes and flushed in any remaining stragglers. Simple for the hands, but heavy on the heart.

Rita nodded her satisfaction.

"Now, then, that wasn't so bad, was it?" she asked.

"No," Townsend sheepishly answered, mistakenly thinking the query was directed to him. He quickly covered his break in character with a concurring "No, not so bad at all, was it?"

"Didn't feel a thing," said Mrs. Humphrey, who somewhere along the line had loosened her grip on the examining table.

"Good luck, pleasure meeting you," Townsend said brusquely, and hurried out of the exam room for some fresh air. He didn't wait to see if there were any late add-on cases, he didn't wait to thank Rita or even say good-bye. Without breaking stride, Townsend slipped off and dropped his borrowed white coat onto the closest chair he could find. He would stop for nothing on his way out the door of the Lenexa Women's Specialty Clinic. Once outside, he stepped up his pace to a jog. The parking lot, thankfully, was empty of zealots.

The inside of his Nova was an inferno. He opened his window, leaned over and opened the passenger's side. Townsend needed air.

6

TOWNSEND SPOTTED HER AS SOON AS he stepped into the lobby of the Fairmont Plaza. She was lounging in the Queen Ann armchair, an alluring glimpse of calf from the side slit in the formal white gown. With her olive skin contrasting against the white, and her lush, undulating hair draped over one shoulder, Leslie Rosenthal looked a ravishing gypsy.

Seeing him enter, she stood up and hastily slid her palms along her sides from breasts to hips, straightening the clingy dress. He bent forward as he approached her—the lifelong habit of a tall man—and she stood on tiptoes, despite her high heels, to offer her cheek for a kiss.

Townsend wanted her lips, but was as intimidated as she by the threat of a lipstick smear. He pressed his mouth to her gently and squeezed her bare upper arms with both hands. Holding her for a moment, he absorbed her fragrance, luxuriating in her scent and the warmth of her body. From the corner of his eye he glimpsed a uniformed bellboy watching him enviously.

"I'm glad you decided to come, even if it was such short notice," Leslie said as they broke away. "What's that scratch on your face?"

"Someone tried to make me a Right-to-Life poster child. Long story. I'll tell you about it later."

"That's what you keep saying. Now *is* later. Tell me what happened at the rehearsal. I can't believe you made such an ass out of yourself! At least you had the presence of mind not to drag me into it!"

"I'll take that as a compliment," he replied irritably. "That's me all right, an ass with stage presence of mind. Let's not get on with this just yet, okay? Is this why you invited me, for a bit of formal browbeating?"

Leslie demurred, nibbling on her lower lip. "Sorry, Town, but I've been curious about it all day. I couldn't reach you last night or this morning, and admit it, you weren't very talkative this afternoon. All you did was grunt a lot. Anyway, I invited you because I thought you might want to come."

Townsend tried to leave well enough alone, but failed. "Pretty short notice, though, wasn't it? You must have known about this shindig for weeks."

"Give me a break, please. You were never known to behave yourself at company functions in New York, were you? Or do you need to be reminded?"

She had scored on that one. Townsend was the castigated, quasi-remorseful ten-year-old, trying to lose himself in the geometric designs of the parquet floor.

"I'll remind you. You sulked. Sulked. I didn't think it would hurt your feelings if I deprived you a chance to sulk. So I wasn't going to ask you. This afternoon I changed my mind. I thought about getting all dressed up, wanting to look good for someone. I didn't want to come alone. I wanted you to be here with me." She took in a deep breath. "I want you to accept this aspect of my life, Town."

"I accept it."

"Then I want you to consider being a part of it."

"That's damn hard with you in New York and me here."

"Maybe we shouldn't get into all this again right now."

"Okay by me."

"We'll nip it in the bud."

"Consider it nipped," Townsend said, his eyes again straying, unfocused, to the parquet.

Leslie repositioned a loose mass of hair back behind one ear with a slow sweep of her fingertips.

"So where were you this morning? I tried forever to reach you."

"Covering for Howard at one of his offices."

"Oh. How did it go?"

"The routine stuff," Townsend said, feeling the heaviness bearing down on him. It was becoming a chronic feeling.

"You don't look well, Town. I mean—," Leslie corrected herself, "you look absolutely great all dressed up like this. You could be a male model. I mean it, you should dress up more often. That suit is great. But you look a little pale. Are you sick?"

"I'm fine. Rough day." He sighed and looked at his watch. "Anyway, it's five of seven. Let's check out this bash."

The bellboy, still distracted from his duties at his station, watched the tall guy gently press his hand against the soft firmness of the babe's waist, then lead her in the direction of the ballroom. He watched her flick her hair back over her shoulder, then kept his eyes glued on a great-looking behind and thighs and long legs rhythmically pressing against her dress until the couple disappeared from view. Something was going on in that ballroom that evening, and not the usual fare. For the past fifteen minutes, a procession of fine-looking babes had passed through his lobby. Night duty had never been such a treat. Where were all the fat ladies?

Rank-and-file dancers never ascribed to being fashionably late, at least not to galas, receptions, or any other entertainment functions where free food was provided. The motivation was primarily economic, the lesson rapidly learned on the first tour. Baseline salaries were paltry—even for dancers in the top union companies—but touring afforded them additional per diem money for on-road living expenses. Per diems, combined with frugality, amounted to a considerable percentage of income. Traveling dancers would "ghost" in hotels, registering for single or double occupancy, then sharing beds and squeezing in extra bodies.

They commandeered extra soap, shampoo, and towels from un-guarded maid's carts (hand towels were used as mats for makeup on dressing room tables, washcloths were essential for makeup removal), and to avoid the cost of meals, they "camped out" in their lodgings, carrying an extra bag with hot plates and all necessary cooking and eating paraphernalia.

Receptions at the very least meant hors d'oeuvres, and in enough quantity, the morsels served not only as dinner, but could be warehoused in a large purse for next day consumption. Money matters aside, physiologic needs had to be met. Parties were often held after opening- or closing-night performances, when the dancers were both exhausted and famished. Demanding rehearsal and performance schedules allowed little time to eat, so attend-ance at the functions was guaranteed. The price to pay for a little sustenance was the dreaded hobnobbing with a bunch of giddy, admiring socialites.

"The peons are already here," said Leslie, taking in the par-tygoers meandering in small clusters around the ballroom. As expected, they were mainly dancers, revealed by relative youth, a well below average percentage body fat, and a spectrum of attire ranging from conservative to tasteless. With time, middle-aged ladies with big hips and sequined dresses would populate the scene, accompanied by scrawny husbands with paunches and suspenders visible under their suit jackets. They were the civic do-gooders, socialites, and board members, for whom the dancers felt little more than contempt. Not wanting to be envied or lusted after, only wanting to be paid more, the dancers made little effort at mingling, and could be downright rude. Company manage-ment took a different tack, however, smiling magnanimously, rubbing shoulders with the deep pockets, in general brownnosing and ass kissing anyone fiscally capable of becoming a benefactor.

The room was set up for over three hundred guests, Townsend figured, estimating thirty white-clothed round tables with setups for ten. Toward the front of the room were two separate buffet tables, at the moment empty and unmanned; a dais for a dozen or so people was at the rear. Smaller tables along the room's perimeter were set up for hors d'oeuvres. Townsend was impressed by the lavishness of the affair—remarkable considering that the impoverished dancers would have been grateful for pizza and beer nuts. He counted four separate bar stations displaying the expensive hard stuff as well as wine, and stifled a whistle.

"No orchestra," he said dryly, feigning disparagement.

"Free booze, free food, this is incredible," said Leslie. "I intend to pig out like I haven't in weeks, real food for a change." She looked like a gleeful child on Christmas morning, Little Orphan Annie entering the Warbucks mansion.

Townsend scrutinized her, finding it incomprehensible that she had fallen into this street urchin mentality. The product of an affluent St. Louis Jewish upbringing, she had made a decent wage as a social worker, and as a doctor's wife hadn't had to work at all. But the separation agreement of her own design waived her rights to community property, didn't even force a sell or buyout of the house. All she had shown concern about were her personal belongings and a small savings account she had brought to the marriage. This despite Townsend's remonstrations to force more material goods her way, a behavior that had utterly astounded his attorney, Ray Ripley. For reasons incomprehensible to Townsend, Leslie Rosenthal had willfully assumed the mantle of a monastic order. What was she trying to prove?

"What are you looking at?" she asked, conscious of his staring.

"I can take you out for dinner, you know. Anytime. Plaza III, Top of the Crown, Jasper's . . . you name it. No need to depend on the kindness of strangers."

"Thanks for the offer." She smiled weakly. "And let's not discuss it, all right?"

"Nipped," he said contritely. "And speaking of nips—"

They headed for the closest watering station. A handful of patrons were queued ahead of them. Leslie stood with him in line at the bar, rather than placing her order with him and waiting behind.

The feminist wants to order herself, Townsend thought meanspiritedly.

"This may be a pretty heavy happening, you know," Leslie mentioned casually as they waited.

"Oh?"

"Rumor has it that Rose Van Buren, who's paying for this whole thing, by the way, is using this occasion to announce her sponsorship of a new piece by the Moreau Company. Apparently, she's really taken a fancy to Gerard's work, thinks he's a bona fide genius."

"I get it," said Townsend. "This show of partiality and dispensing of big bucks adds some salt to Paul Gruenfeld's festering wound." He became more thoughtful, the encounter on the balcony again surfacing. Coyly, he asked how long this had been public knowledge and how Paul Gruenfeld was "taking it."

"The rumors have been going around since the start of the festival. Paul hasn't mentioned a word about it to the company. It's all gossipmongering behind his back."

Townsend craned his neck and gave the enormous room as much of a once-over as he could. "I don't see him here yet, do you?"

Leslie shrugged and shook her head.

"It's not just Paul's problem. Nigel Devon is really the one who's getting the shaft."

Townsend knew the name, knew the man was an obnoxious Brit who headed up the ever-floundering Kansas City Dance Theatre. Leslie intuited that Townsend wasn't fully comprehending.

"The Van Burens haven't contributed diddly-squat to the KC Dance Theatre," she said. "Well, maybe a little bit here and there—a pittance—but no real money. So in rides this French hotshot from New York, absolutely sweeps this woman off her feet—artistically, I mean—and she showers him with money. At least that's what the word is—we'll find out soon enough."

"Even in the artsy world of dance, it all boils down to politics and money, doesn't it?" Townsend inched forward in line—they were next to order. "But I'm sure Rosie knows which horse to back."

"Rosie? You know her?"

"Sure I know her. Do I look like I just fell off the turnip truck? I'm a well-connected guy."

He was exaggerating, of course, since he barely knew Rose Van Buren. He had grown up in Kansas City, though, and everyone at or above a baseline social echelon at least barely knew everyone else. Money was confined to specific geographic boundaries during Townsend's salad days, the elegant suburb of Mission Hills on the Kansas side, where Townsend had been reared, and the broad strip of affluence along Ward Parkway, stretching northward from Meyer Boulevard and surrounding Loose Park on the Missouri side. Further insulating this special economic breed was the limited choice of private schools for the progeny of well-heeled Kansas Citians at the time: Pembroke Country Day for boys; Barstow or Sunset Hills for girls. Townsend, an exception to the rule, had been a public-school boy at his father's stubborn insistence, reflecting the elder's sense of being a "common man," an affectation of having grown up poor. Townsend hadn't much objected, as he had been indoctrinated as "son of common man," and didn't want to play basketball with a bunch of rich pansies anyway.

The Reeves family contact with the Van Burens had been medical more than social. Dr. Alexander Van Buren, long dead, had then been a well-known Emeritus Professor of Pathology, as Townsend's father Franklin was later to become in the field of internal medicine. Both had academic appointments in addition to successful private medical practices, but Van Buren's income was vast and inherited—looking at slides of dead tissue was little more than an economic sideline.

The Reeves family had visited the Van Buren home over twenty years earlier, when Townsend was still in junior high. He remembered Rosie as a vivacious redhead with a great body, one of the best-looking and energetic grown-ups he had ever met.

"Let's be friends, just call me Rosie" was the first thing she had said to him after a rather stilted and uncomfortable introduction by his parents. In retrospect, they couldn't have approved of Van

Buren's second wife. Her youth was in stark contrast to the advanced years of Dr. Alex, by then a white-haired and slightly stooped man who seemed ancient to Townsend. He had been widowed more than a dozen years earlier, with grown-up children in college from his first marriage and a second household of two boys with Rosie.

Townsend strained to remember details of that evening. Rosie had to have been in her early thirties then—just about his own age now—and the old man Van Buren was well into his sixties. The adults had eaten in a formal dining room that could easily have accommodated twenty, but he was assigned to the breakfast room with the two Van Buren boys, Philip, about ten, and an even younger Brian. A black maid had served filet mignon. The dessert must have been crème caramel, but Townsend took it for tapioca. The disgusting stuff made him gag, but fortunately, the boys had been rewarded with Fudgsicles as a substitute. Townsend moped through the dinner (was his tendency to sulk established back then?), irritated with having to sit with the children. He wanted to be in the room with Rosie, his newfound crush. What else from the memory banks? Playing with Philip's Duncan Yo Yo; the kid couldn't even "walk the dog," and was impossible to teach. And the butterflies—of course, the butterflies. . . .

"Why don't you show Townsend your father's butterfly collection? I'm sure he'd be interested in that!" Rosie had suggested after dinner. Butterflies, of all things. Townsend didn't want to see the butterflies, and twenty years later he could barely recollect anything about them. At the time, he had been more preoccupied with sneaking peeks down Rosie Van Buren's blouse.

"What'll it be?" The barman, who looked like a displaced surfer, snapped Townsend from his reverie. Leslie assertively piped in her request for Scotch rocks; Townsend self-consciously asked for a bourbon and 7-Up. If only Leslie had let him order, the bartender would have assumed that the Scotch was for him. The beach boy, with a sly smile and flirtatious glance at Leslie, had the temerity to drop a cherry in the college freshman's special.

Townsend mumbled his thanks and quickly slurped the surface of his bourbon and 7-Up to keep it from overflowing. The cherry stem nudged its way into one of his nostrils.

"Enough small talk. Tell me already," Leslie prompted as they made their way past the bar customers that had formed behind them.

"Not so fast. Did you see anybody else up in the balcony yesterday?" Townsend picked out the cherry and ate it, and considered alternatives for the stem.

"Besides us? No one. I didn't see anyone, but I assume you must have."

"You ran into Felicia Bradley," he said, ignoring her lead. He put the cherry stem in his pocket. "That's what your message on my machine said." Townsend had confirmation of that from Felicia, but he wasn't ready to reveal his independent source. Townsend wasn't sure why he was giving Leslie the third degree. Not that he didn't trust her; he just wanted spontaneous, unbiased responses.

"That was later, after I had gotten down to the mezzanine."

"And you didn't see anyone else."

"I told you that already, Town. What's the point here?"

"Hold on a sec. If you ran into Felicia, you couldn't have snuck out right after I left. You must have waited awhile."

"I waited awhile. That was the prudent thing to do. And besides, there was more commotion after you left, so I stuck around out of interest."

Townsend furrowed his brow. "What sort of commotion?"

"Nothing major, just another diversion. I already told you that Nigel Devon is incredibly jealous of Gerard Moreau, for good reason. Well, shortly after your little scene Nigel made an entrance with his company, demanding the rehearsal space. He claimed that they were on the schedule for the main stage, and Gerard had run overtime. You can imagine how Gerard responded to that one."

"I suppose I hadn't helped his frame of mind."

"Not by a long shot. Gerard was fit to be tied. Nigel put up a good front for about ten seconds, but it was no contest. Gerard humiliated him—you won't believe this—actually called him a fag and a no-talent. As little respect as I have for Nigel Devon, it was still painful to witness. I actually felt sorry for him."

"That was it?"

"Basically, Gerard repeatedly told him to perform a sexual act on himself, and if he still had any problems after that, to take them up with William Davidson, the festival director. That was *really* rubbing it in. Davidson knows which side his bread is buttered on and will do absolutely anything to placate Gerard. Gerard knows it, and Nigel knows it. Besides, Nigel's lucky to be involved in the festival at all, and he knows that too. Davidson included the Kansas City Dance Theatre in this business only as a courtesy to the locals. On their own merits, the company's much too mediocre to have been invited."

"Spoken like a true elitist New Yorker, putting down all the rubes."

"Well, it's the truth, Town! Now *please* tell me what's going on!"

"All right." A collegiate-looking waiter with a tray of stuffed mushrooms brushed past and headed for an hors d'oeuvres table. Townsend took a rushed second sip of bourbon and began a purposeful amble in the same direction. Leslie, unaware that it was other than an arbitrary stroll, took his lead without watching where she was going, eyes fixed on him expectantly.

"I *did* see someone." Townsend began. "In the shadows. Someone else in the balcony with us. He was pointing down toward the stage, and as far as I could tell, he was pointing at Gerard Moreau."

"Pointing?"

"Aiming, so I thought. There's some question as to whether or not he had a gun."

"Gun? So you went after the guy? That's why you made the commotion?"

"Right. So you see, a logical explanation. I wasn't hallucinating or having some kind of mental breakdown."

Leslie wasn't satisfied. "But there wasn't a gun, right? You scared some janitor, or some poor innocent dance lover sneaking into a rehearsal like we were, absolutely shitless."

"Partly true, a reasonable assumption."

"Because if someone really had a gun, you were throwing your body in the line of fire. Not well thought out, Town."

"Not well thought out. But give me my due. As you recall, on the way past I pushed you down out of the way, in what might be seen as a true heroic gesture."

"I'm grateful, Town, really grateful that the big man was protecting the little lady, and it makes all my bruises easier to take. It's a good thing this dress is slit up the left; my right side is black and blue. But I still can't believe you'd go after someone with a gun like that. Really stupid."

"Try 'impulsive.' At the time I was thinking of Gerard Moreau; you know, he really means so much to me." Townsend hummed the first few measures of "The Man I Love." Leslie jocularly elbowed him in what would have been the ribs in a man of average size, but in his case was too low to make actual contact with bone or cartilage.

He went on.

"Like in the movies. I thought the guy was going to take a shot, and at my angle, I thought I could knock his arm, take him off his mark. He wasn't aiming at me, after all, he was aiming at Gerard. I was going to ram him from the side. Nick of time. Bullet ricochets harmlessly off the wall. Just like the movies."

"Except, Rambo, he didn't really have a gun."

"Probably not."

"Probably." Leslie sounded doubtful.

"I never saw a gun, but it was a little weird at the time, in the darkness, someone pointing like that." Townsend had led her on and dragged things out long enough. They were almost to the hors d'oeuvres table and he was ready to spill.

"You didn't see anyone in the balcony?" he asked her again.

"For the last time—"

"Sorry."

"Was it maybe Nigel?"

"Nope, definitely not Nigel Devon. And the guy wasn't a janitor, and he wasn't exactly a poor innocent dance lover, either."

"Oh?" It was said naturally enough. Townsend dismissed the notion that Leslie actually knew what was coming and that she was playing dumb.

"It was Paul Gruenfeld."

"Paul?"

Leslie hadn't an inkling, she had been blindsided. She swiveled directly in front of him, grabbing both jacket sleeves.

"Paul?"

"Leslie, you asked, and I told you. Now please," Townsend gently pushed her aside, "have the courtesy not to stand between me and the stuffed mushrooms."

7

"There's got to be a logical explanation." Leslie distractedly slid the small spicy meatball off the toothpick with her teeth and set the pick delicately on the side of her plate.

"You keep saying that," said Townsend.

They were rounding the room for the third or fourth time and had sampled every hors d'oeuvre to be had. In their circling, they had only briefly acknowledged Leslie's fellow troupe members, but engaged none in conversation. Okay by Townsend, feeling fortunate that Leslie was too preoccupied to socialize. He never felt comfortable around her cohorts; Leslie had attributed his unease to being closed-minded. Townsend maintained that most of them were flaky.

He leaned his head back to get the last drops of the watery bourbon and seven. "I think I'll have another. How about you?"

Leslie declined with a head shake. Her current concoction, an orange juice with a splash of grenadine for color, was being nursed with the care given a dying mafioso. Townsend admonished her to stay put and headed for the closest bar to get his third refill.

Townsend rarely drank spirits—he was a beer man, preferably nonalcoholic—but he relished mental numbness that evening, knowing his liver was not up to the challenge, not in party shape. Like anything else, drinking took practice to become really good at it. The body habituated itself to alcohol intake by increasing production of an enzyme, alcohol dehydrogenase, responsible for metabolizing the noxious substance. A teetotaling Townsend didn't have much stock of alcohol dehydrogenase on board. He was the boozing equivalent of a middle-aged executive deciding one Sunday morning to compete in a marathon. As it was, with two drinks down, he already had a buzz on.

They were managing all right; after a rocky start, he and Leslie had avoided their conversational tarpits. He was enjoying their closeness, their bantering, not feeling tongue-tied for a change. And after forcing her preoccupation with the mysterious presence of Paul Gruenfeld in the balcony of the Missouri State Performing Arts Center, her social expectations of him were minimal. He even sometimes forgot—but never for long—that an army of his sperm was advancing up the treacherous battleground of Mrs. Humphrey's fallopian tubes, and it took only one, one little infantryman sperm, to create a new life in her womb.

"Bourbon and seven," he told the barman, sliding his tumbler along the countertop. "No cherry this time, prick," he added.

"There has to be a logical explanation, right?" Townsend had sneaked up behind Leslie, who gave a start, then flashed him a look of disdain.

"I hope you don't embarrass me with your drinking," she warned. "You're not exactly used to it."

"You'll have to find out, you know." Townsend parried.

"Find out what?"

"Find out what Paul was up to." Compared to the more recent events at the Women's Specialty Clinic, the matter of Paul Gruenfeld held relatively little interest for him. He had dwelled on it enough, his bafflement evolving into perplexity, then diluting into a mild curiosity. Now the curiosity was blending into a rather pleasant high.

Leslie pursed her lips.

"You're going to have to ask him, that's all," Townsend pressed.

"Are you kidding? I can't do that!"

"Come on, he can't be that upset with you. Put the onus on me.

Tell him I forced you to bring me to the Moreau rehearsal because I wanted to look at Felicia Bradley's chest. Besides, he's probably figured it out anyway. Surely he remembers me from hanging around your rehearsals in New York."

"Maybe he made the connection, maybe not. Either way, I don't want to broach the subject with him. Paul is a famous choreographer and I'm just one of many lowly dancers. I don't have that type of relationship with him. Nobody does. And the whole issue about Gerard and Felicia is much too sensitive. It's an open sore, and he's really on edge. Our rehearsals for the new piece, *Outlaw,* have been incredibly stressful." She glanced around to make sure she wasn't being overheard.

"You see him here?"

"Not yet."

"It's almost eight. Maybe he won't show."

"He *has* to show," said Leslie emphatically. "He'd never let people think that this business with Gerard affects him."

"I'm not sure you'd hold Paul Gruenfeld on such a pedestal had you seen him squirming on the floor tucked between those theater seats. Maybe he's still trying to get old bubblegum off the back of his shirt."

"You're more than irreverent, Town, you're cruel. Do these people threaten you so much or what?"

Townsend let it drop. He admitted his tendency to ridicule the dance world at every free opportunity. It hadn't matter much until Leslie became a part of it and their dynamics had changed. "Sorry. Paul Gruenfeld is a great man."

"He's a genius." Leslie corrected.

". . . and I'm sure Gerard Moreau has some redeeming social value as well. Speaking of which, I haven't spied the Frenchman yet either. Where's Pepe Le Pew?"

"I'm warning you, Town, you better stay out of his way."

"Don't worry, I'm more interested in bumping into Paul. He owes me one. I kept my mouth shut. I did the guy a favor, and he'll probably thank me. He might even give you a leading part in his next new piece, seeing as you're a friend of mine."

"Right," Leslie smirked and drained her drink. "Looks like they're starting to bring out the food. About time."

Several waiters had begun their procession, bringing large covered serving trays from the kitchen. A chef, a caricature in his pristine white kitchen garb and Pillsbury Doughboy chapeau, was sharpening a large carving knife in preparation for the prime rib. Young women in brown uniforms and white aprons were readying themselves behind the large tables, preparing their stations. Others were hastily filling the water glasses on the dining tables.

"Townsend," Leslie said seriously—and she was always serious when she didn't abbreviate his name—"I'm sure there's a reasonable explanation for all this. With Paul, I mean."

"Of course there is, Les," he said assuredly. Then he felt a little light-headed, and a sly smile came to his lips. "Why, I bet," he said, forming the words carefully, "Paul's gun wasn't even loaded."

Leslie called him a shithead, and the two of them positioned themselves closer to the buffet.

Rosie Van Buren had made her entrance sometime between Townsend's second and third drinks. He sought her out in the crowd at every opportunity, fascinated by her and the memories of his adolescent past that she provoked. A mini-whirlwind of activity followed her around the room. She was as vivacious and animated as he remembered, always the charming centerpiece of conversation, waving her arms about, flinging her head back when she laughed. Had he seen her in twenty years? Probably not, other than her photos in the *Kansas City Star,* always associated with some social event or benefit.

Rosie Van Buren's looks had a long shelf life. She easily passed for someone ten to fifteen years younger than mid- to late fifties. A plastic surgeon could do only so much, though. Through the medical grapevine Townsend had heard that Mort Feingold had worked on her eyes and chin, but Mort confined himself to the neck and above. Perhaps someone else tucked her tummy or reconditioned her mammaries, but cosmetic intervention aside, women her age didn't look that good without effort and commitment. Rosie Van Buren undoubtedly frequented a health club and worked the machines, a mature—postmenopausal even—but still hot Lycra bunny.

"Why don't you go over and say something to her? You've been gawking for almost half an hour," Leslie finally said, blowing Townsend's notion that his monitoring of Rosie had been inconspicuous. The wait for the food seemed interminable.

"You mean Rosie?" By his tone he tried to deny any interest. "We can't sacrifice our primo buffet position, can we? The chow line's going to open soon, and we're going to be at the head of it." Unconvincingly, he added, "I've been looking around for Paul. Still haven't seen him, have you?"

When Rosie's subsequent movement toward the dais happened to nearly intersect their own entrenchment, Townsend took a gamble, a bold step forward prompted by a mixture of pride, sentimentality, and curiosity.

"Rosie, do you remember me?" He wasted no time in adding, "I'm Franklin and Margaret Reeves's son, Townsend."

Rosie Van Buren's response was effusive, and Townsend breathed a sigh of relief.

"Why, the last time I saw you, you were this tall gawky kid with knobby knees."

"He still has knobby knees." Leslie wasted no time in getting into the conversation and forcing an introduction.

Introductions also involved Rosie's escort, a tuxedoed ferret-like man recognized by everyone in the room but Townsend. William Davidson, a mediocre ballet dancer from the fifties, had sought the haven of academic and administrative dance positions and politically made the most of it. A natural self-promoter who persevered by default, he was an institution in the dance world. For the past several years he had served as director of the prestigious National Dance Festival, an appointment he had massaged into a full-time career. His connection with Rosie was obviously sycophantic, as he clearly was not "main squeeze" material for the likes of Rosie Van Buren.

"Leslie, honey, just call me Rosie, for gosh sakes."

With Rosie adept at taking the lead, the conversation proceeded seamlessly, Rosie making the most of Leslie's dance connection. She made glowing remarks about modern dance in general and Paul Gruenfeld in particular, then made the transition to the Gerard Moreau Company, about which she absolutely raved. Rosie was ebullient about dance—a classic balletomane—and seemed to take an immediate liking to Leslie. Or was she like that with every stranger she met? Townsend wondered if an inherent quality of social grace was that people never knew if you were sincere or not.

While the two women chatted, Townsend smiled sheepishly at William Davidson, whose own grin seemed frozen on his gaunt face. Every few seconds, though, the man would sniff, temporarily transforming the smile into a sneer. Content to exchange silence, the two men intuitively knew they had little in common, were both disinclined to small talk, and would not like each other anyway.

A potential conversational derailment came when the subject led to how Townsend fit in vis-à-vis Leslie. Leslie faltered. Townsend, who had been closely monitoring, piped in matter-of-factly with "We were married for six years."

"Well," said Rosie, unfazed, "I'm certainly glad you didn't let marriage get in the way of a pleasant relationship." And without missing a beat, "So how's your mother, Townsend?"

Attention now focused on Townsend, the passage of twenty years summed up in a matter of verbally packed moments. The subject even turned to their family dinner of over two decades earlier.

"Why, Townsend, I remember how you were in such an absolute *snit* over not being allowed to sit in the dining room with the grown-ups."

"Oh?" Townsend raised his eyebrows innocently and emitted

a half laugh, half snort. He could feel Leslie's eyes weighing heavily upon him. "I don't remember that. I remember the butterfly collection, though."

Rosie laughed, throwing her head back flirtatiously and revealing a long, wrinkle-free neck. Townsend silently complimented Mort Feingold on a job well done. He realized, too, that under the right circumstances, he could qualify as playmate material for this matron, the dream of twenty years earlier not implausible. The prurience of the thought bothered him, and he cast it from his mind.

"Funny you should mention those butterflies, since they play a part in this evening's big announcement." Rosie brightened and glanced over to William Davidson for a reassuring frozen smile. "As soon as Gerard gets here—"

"I've heard that the piece is to be entitled *Metamorphoses,*" said Leslie.

"My, rumors do get around!" Rosie replied good-naturedly. She looked again at Davidson, as if he were to blame. He did a sniff-sneer, shrugged innocently, and lapsed back into his smile. Davidson's face didn't betray impatience, but Townsend noticed that the man was habitually checking his watch.

"Well, it doesn't matter at this point, really, and the new piece I'm commissioning from Gerard is only part of the surprise. And I want everyone to be surprised!" Rosie said, wagging her finger. "But as for the butterflies, Townsend, many of the rarer examples were donated to the university collection—the collection is in Alex's name, in fact. We still have an extraordinary collection at home, though, but my son Philip—you must remember Philip?— is more inclined to moths. He's collected specimens from all over the world."

"He's welcome to the ones in my closet," said Townsend, immediately regretting the quip.

Rosie laughed, erasing any concerns Townsend had about the rudeness of his remark. Moths could be serious business to some people, he supposed, people like Philip Van Buren. But seriously ... moths? He was as nonplussed as he had been upon first learning about old man Van Buren's butterflies. The notion conjured up the image of a skinny mustached man in Bermuda shorts and a pith helmet leaping in a meadow while making uncoordinated swaths through the air with a net.

"You'd be amazed, really. Most people have the same reaction. But they're fascinating creatures, actually. You're welcome anytime to come over and have a look . . . just give us a call."

"I'll do that," Townsend heard himself saying.

"You're invited, too, Leslie."

"I'd love to see them, Rosie."

William Davidson pointedly cleared his throat. "I think we had better proceed with the announcement, since the food's about to be served," he said, punctuating his statement with a sniff.

"But Gerard's not even here yet!" Rosie protested.

"Well—," Davidson backed down from his position, not one to cross Rosie Van Buren's objections. Then, in a compromising tone, "Perhaps just some welcoming remarks, later we can formally—"

"Wait! Here come Philip and Felicia now!"

Townsend felt his throat tighten. Felicia Bradley, in a revealing tight wraparound outfit, distressingly similar in style to Leslie's gown, was now beside him, arm in arm with a bookworm in tortoiseshell glasses. Philip Van Buren had not changed much in twenty years, except for thinning and receding brown hair.

Introductions were limited, as Felicia quickly pointed out that she already knew Leslie and had just recently made Townsend's acquaintance; in fact, "only last night he was in my hotel room giving me some free medical advice." Townsend stifled a cringe by contracting the muscles of his jaw. He felt Leslie's eyes and resisted the temptation to look her way. *Let her stew on it for a while,* he thought. *I'm a free man, aren't I?*

Fortunately, there was something more pressing to discuss; namely, the whereabouts of the guest of honor, Gerard Moreau.

"I thought he was with you!" Rosie said to her son.

"But Mother, I assumed he was already here!" whined Philip.

"He's probably off humping some *corps de ballet* girl," Felicia said in a voice just loud enough to hear, but soft enough that everyone pretended not to.

"Hell's bells," sniffed William Davidson, "we really must get on with this thing; the press is getting quite impatient."

"Did you call his room?" asked Rosie.

"No," answered Philip."

"Well, why didn't you?" Rosie appeared agitated, losing some of her social cool.

Philip stiffened defensively, befitting any thirty-year-old man being called on the carpet by his mother in public.

"But Mother," Philip protested, "I saw no reason to call him, I told you I thought he was already here! We were just with Gerard not an hour ago—Felicia and myself—right before we went to the lounge for coffee."

"Well, call him now—or better yet—get up to his suite and find out what's keeping him," Rosie ordered. "We'll stall as best we can."

Philip, clearly humiliated, did a quick about-face and scurried away.

Townsend took advantage of the lull to utter a "pleasure to see you," echoed by Leslie, and they made a gracious exit from the group. Townsend was glad they could bow out before having to engage Felicia Bradley in conversation. Walking away, he heard her voice, more volume this time.

"He's probably humping some corps girl, I tell you—"

Leslie wasted no time, yanking Townsend's arm as soon as they were out of earshot. "What's this business from Felicia about last night?"

"She asked me to see her at her hotel room," he began matter-of-factly, continuing to walk toward the head of the buffet line.

"Ohmygod! I can't believe it! She actually *called* you?" Not the distrustful type, Leslie seemed amused, her response one of hearing juicy gossip. "What absolute cheek! That woman will go after anything!"

"Now wait a minute," Townsend protested.

"My God, this is incredible! Okay, fess up, Town, you didn't sleep with her, did you?" She knew the answer, or else was expert at maintaining a jovial façade.

"Who wants to know?"

"*I* do, shithead!"

"All right," said Townsend after mock hesitation. "No, I didn't sleep with her. I could have, you know, since women find me irresistible. But don't tell anyone, because I want all the guys to think that I did. So they can point at me on the street and say, 'Hey, there's that stud that humped Desdemona.'"

"That bitch vamped you, didn't she. I can't believe it!"

"Well, gentlemen never tell, but"—he conspiratorially brought her closer and whispered in her ear—"I actually saw her private parts."

"Ha! You mean her *public* parts! I can't believe it . . . you gotta fill me in! All the gory details!"

"Not on an empty stomach." The buffet line was about to open. Townsend gazed inquiringly at the chef, poised at the prime rib, knives sharpened. The chef smiled and gave a go-ahead nod, a green light for gluttony. Townsend, first in line, picked up a hot plate from the top of the stack and sidestepped down to the meat station.

"Prime rib or ham?" asked the chef.

"Yes," answered Townsend, holding out his plate.

In less tumultuous times, Townsend's eating habits were spartan, verging on the health-conscious. Significant mental preoccupation of any sort, though, provoked primeval face stuffing. Townsend attacked the buffet. With years of experience at the St. Michael's Hospital cafeteria salad bar, where management had been foolish enough to charge according to plate size rather than weight, he had perfected strategic food piling. His plate was a structural masterpiece.

His first modification upon leaving the meat station was to stack the ham directly upon the roast beef, surreptitiously dragging it over with his fingers. He then constructed a dam along most of the plate edge with the scalloped potatoes—the vegetable most closely approximating the consistency of mortar—forming a central swale for the green beans with almonds, creamed broccoli, curried rice, and salad items. The only remaining unguarded border was barricaded by two corn sticks; French bread crowned the ham. The swale progressively transmuted into a mound, but Townsend kept the slope well below the critical angle beyond which loomed the threat of erosion or, worse, a catastrophic foodslide.

Leslie insisted on sitting at a table near the dais, although Townsend preferred a location closer to the buffet. Reluctantly he followed her across the ballroom to the table of choice, still uninhabited. He set down his plate; a crouton slid off a vinaigrette-soaked leaf of romaine and impaled itself in the scalloped potatoes, confirming the adequacy of his design. Leslie eyed his plate knowingly, gauging his level of stress. Townsend's cool was betrayed by the contents of his plate.

Cognizant of her assessment, he sent her an unspoken *don't say anything* command; she responded, also telepathically, with an *I don't need to*. He then took his own disparaging inventory of her plate. Portions and selection were so skimpy that he could actually see intervening china. Little Orphan Annie got her shot at a food free-for-all and managed to come away with *nouvelle cuisine*.

"I think I'll get my dessert now, rather than waiting," he said, pure stubbornness revealing itself. Thus excusing himself, he returned to the dessert portion of the buffet and heaped a second plate with an assortment of layer cake, cheesecake, and a variety of pastries.

"They're for both of us," he said pointedly to Leslie, returning to the table. He set the sweet selection within her reach, confident that she would not indulge. Then he spread his napkin on his lap and sawed off a hunk of prime rib, extricating it from under the ham. The piece was within inches of his awaiting open mouth—

"Townsend! There you are!"

Rosie Van Buren's voice was normal in volume, but her tone was panicked. She had placed a hand on his shoulder and was gripping him, her face was next to his. He smelled her closeness, a sweet smell of mouthwash as her breathing wafted around him. Her chest was heaving.

"We need you! Quick! Something's wrong with Gerard! He's sick!" she whispered hoarsely.

Townsend was slow to register; Leslie's eyes widened.

"Please come! We need a doctor!"

Crap, thought Townsend. He looked at Leslie imploringly, but realized there was no escape from the situation. Rosie was pulling at his arm, dragging him from his chair without waiting for his assent. People nearby had started to murmur; something was wrong. Whatever it was, it was serious enough to force Rosie Van Buren to reveal cracks in her socially correct façade.

A smattering of images flooded Townsend's vision as he spun around from the table: Rosie's heaving bosom, a bewildered William Davidson on the dais, Leslie's hand gesturing him to hurry up, the napoleon on the dessert plate receding from view, a cluster of dancers by the table abuzz with gossip, the prime rib still speared on the fork in his hand. Townsend managed to clumsily shove the meat into his mouth before leaving the table.

Decorum was recklessly abandoned. Rosie bolted to the ballroom entrance, pulling Townsend along by the hand, the two of them weaving past partygoers en route to and from the buffet. As they made their way to the exit, the murmurs around them exponentially increased in volume. Like two stones being skipped across a lake, concentric ripples of surprise and curiosity emanated from their moving center.

"Philip and the hotel manager found him unconscious in his room," Rosie gasped as they ran.

Townsend tucked the wad of meat into the side of his cheek; the last thing he needed was to aspirate and asphyxiate himself. Food safely cached, his musing became more universal, the inchoate thought of anyone with medical training finding himself in a similar position.

I hope I don't have to do mouth-to-mouth.

"Did somebody call nine-one-one?" he asked.

"I think so."

"I certainly hope so," Townsend said, praying that the medics would get to Gerard before he did.

8

THE HOTEL MANAGER, A MARSHMALLOW OF A MAN, was waiting by the ballroom entrance, red-faced and completely winded. From the looks of him, he hadn't worked up a sweat in years and was a heavy smoker, the type who prematurely drops dead one day from a heart attack. Townsend worried that this could be the day.

"Come on," pudge-face puffed as they approached, encouraging them on like a sheriff greeting a late-arriving posse. With a head start of a few paces, the man took the lead with an accelerated waddle, but Rosie and Townsend flew past him and reached the elevator first.

The door was open, the elevator empty and waiting. Townsend saw that automatic operation had been bypassed with a key. The hotel manager, lunging into the confined space like a distance runner collapsing over the finish line, had just enough reserve to flop himself against the operation panel, turn the key, and press the 9 button. Thanks to the foresight of the little man, who had introduced himself as Oscar Brewer, they had wasted no time; the car was a nonstop express run.

"Left out the door," Oscar managed between pants, "all the way down . . . straight . . . then a right . . . Room 921."

The remainder of the ride was suffered in silence, except for heavy breathing. The color had drained from Rosie's face; she leaned back against the wall of the elevator, fingers intertwined and hands clenched and held up to her face in the manner of prayer. Townsend, taking advantage of the respite to chew up the meat in his mouth and swallow, sidled up beside her and put a comforting arm around her shoulder. All were in oxygen debt, but Oscar was having major problems catching his breath. He coughed and sputtered, bent over forward like an asthmatic. Townsend, from three or four feet away, could make out the acrid scent of his body odor. Finally Oscar composed himself enough to straighten up and yank at his underwear, retrieving material that had migrated several inches into the crevice of his buttocks.

The elevator door opened and Townsend dashed out, familiar with the territory from his recent trip to Felicia's room. He had already made the connection that Gerard's room was near Felicia's—across the hall, in fact.

The door to Room 921 was open. Gerard was naked, his hirsute body lying prone on top of the queen-sized bed farthest from the door. Philip was sitting on the nearer of the two beds. He jumped up when Townsend entered.

"Is he breathing?" Townsend blurted, crossing over to Gerard's motionless body.

"I . . . I think so," said Philip uncertainly. He looked terrible, pale and pasty. "I didn't know what to do!"

"You called nine-one-one, right?"

Philip nodded, then sank back down onto the bed.

Townsend confirmed Gerard's rapid respirations by placing his index finger under the dancer's nostrils. Then he wrapped an open hand around Gerard's neck and palpated the carotid pulse, which was fast but regular. Townsend concluded that Gerard Moreau was a sick puppy in need of a real doctor, not a radiologist. Most comforting for Townsend at the moment, however, was that mouth-to-mouth resuscitation wasn't required.

Preliminary assessment complete, Townsend was not unlike Philip, in that he really didn't know what to do, either. There was no equipment, no crash cart, no nurses around to give orders to. He shook Gerard by the shoulders, then pinched the flesh over his ribcage as hard as he could, with no response. He shouted

Gerard's name repetitively. He lifted his eyelids—both pupils were dilated but still responsive to light. Finally, he picked up Gerard's foot and stroked the sole with his thumbnail, beginning at the outer part of the heel and ending near the great toe. In response to the stimuli, Gerard's toes flexed downward. Townsend tried the other foot, eliciting an identical, normal response. Whatever was going on, it didn't appear to be affecting one side more than the other. Gerard's coloring was good also, with fingertips and toes of a normal pinkish color, rather than the bluish tint of cyanosis.

Townsend shrugged and shook his head, then turned his eyes back to the other bed, where Rosie was now seated beside her son, gripping his knee with both white-knuckled hands. Oscar had stayed well back by the open door, looking not much better than he had earlier.

"What . . . what do you think?" Rosie hesitantly asked.

Townsend shrugged again.

"He's breathing and pumping blood," he finally said. "I suppose he could have bled into his head, like from a ruptured aneurysm. But he doesn't really have any focal findings that I can tell. He's a young and healthy guy, so I bet it's drug related. Is he a druggie?" Townsend turned his attention back to Gerard, surveying both arms for needle tracks. Finding none, Townsend shrugged yet again and looked at the others inquiringly.

Philip dropped his head. "He did cocaine, I know that."

Rosie startled at the revelation. "How do you know that? You never told me that!"

"Would it have made any difference, Mother? All these types do cocaine, what's the big deal? And I know because . . . look on that table over there." With a tilt of his head he indicated the small oval side table by the bathroom.

Townsend walked over to the table and saw the a small compact mirror, beside it a single-edged razor blade and a red-and-white-striped coffee stirrer. Residual white powder could be seen on the surface of the mirror. Townsend sighed, took in a deep breath. Then he smelled vomit. He backtracked around the table and saw the mess on the rug, about a foot or so from the bathroom door. Perplexed, he looked over at Philip.

"That's mine," Philip answered weakly. He was perspiring, and his glasses had slid down his nose. He pushed them back up with a shaking hand. "I'm sorry. I got sick and couldn't make it to the toilet." Oscar was nodding his head in agreement, substantiating Philip's claim.

"Why is he naked?" Townsend asked himself aloud.

"Maybe he was about to take a shower," offered Oscar, now able to complete an entire sentence without gasping. "He takes a little hit of some bad stuff, maybe, before he goes in—"

"What can we do?" Rosie interrupted.

"I don't think we can do anything other than wait for the ambulance," Townsend replied, relieved at the prospect that his involvement was over.

At that instant, as if a vibrating bed had run amuck, Gerard began convulsing. The force of his seizures caused the loose headboard of the bed to bang a tattoo against the wall.

Rosie wailed.

"Shit!" said Townsend. He rushed to the bed and placed both of his hands on Gerard's shoulder blades, pinning him down so he wouldn't roll off and bang his head. Townsend felt like a jackhammer operator not physically up to the job. He pressed down harder, straightening his elbows and leaning forward with the weight of his upper body. Still, he couldn't completely stop the shaking that was being transmitted to his own body. Then the paroxysms stopped as abruptly as they had begun.

Everyone in the room was still. It was an eerie stillness, like the unnatural calm in the air announcing an approaching tornado.

Townsend relaxed his shoulders and straightened up, his heart racing. He didn't like the situation. Many in medicine thrived on the deities of sickness and death throwing down the gauntlet, but Townsend had never warmed to the challenge. He abhorred bodily fluids and found the company of naked bodies loathsome, unless they were of his choosing. Forced intimacy was his own personal nightmare.

"Just a seizure," he said matter-of-factly to the group, hoping to reassure them with his nonchalance. They looked as if they expected to see Gerard's bit-off tongue falling onto the carpet and flopping like a beached fish. Oscar, although still standing, was now leaning back against the wall, on the verge of passing out. Rosie was quaking pathetically and Philip looked as if he would vomit again if only he had anything left in his stomach to puke. Without doubt, grand mal events were ultimate showstoppers.

Townsend was gathering his thoughts when he realized that Gerard wasn't breathing.

"Shit," he reiterated, shaking his head as if to scold himself for hammering his own thumb. He was torn between his responsibility as a physician and his overwhelming urge to run away.

"Quick," he commanded, "get him on the floor; he needs to be on something hard."

Townsend didn't wait for the others to respond, which was fortunate, as they didn't. Grabbing the bedspread with his left hand and wrapping his right arm around Gerard's torso, he slid both Gerard and the bedspread onto the floor, rolling the man onto his back in the process. With little floor space for maneuvering between the two beds, Townsend slid Gerard around to the foot of the bed, dragging him on the bedcover. Then he knelt beside Gerard's head and felt for a pulse—it was present, but Gerard's chest was not moving. Townsend again put his index and third fingers under Gerard's nostrils, this time feeling no passage of air. Gerard was in respiratory arrest after the seizure.

A last desperate look toward the door, hoping the medics would arrive to save the day, then Townsend bit the bullet. He tilted Gerard's head back, checked with his finger that there wasn't anything blocking the airway, pinched Gerard's nostrils closed with his left thumb and index finger, and pulled the jaw down with his right hand. He inhaled as deeply as he could, leaned forward, and pressed his lips against Gerard's partly opened mouth. The smell of Gerard's breath sickened him, but there was no turning back. Townsend blew a steady stream of air, looking sideways to confirm that Gerard's chest was rising as his own air filled the dancer's lungs. He sat upright and wiped his mouth off with the sleeve of his jacket. Then it was time to administer another breath.

Townsend took off his jacket, loosened his tie, and rolled up his shirtsleeves in between subsequent breaths. With time, the job became increasingly distasteful. Townsend was feeling light-headed and winded from the blowing, but the nausea was worse. The smell from Gerard's mouth was fetid and vile, and it became progressively harder for Townsend to subject himself to it. Still he continued. Where the hell were the medics?

When the medics finally arrived, Townsend stopped in mid-breath.

"Respiratory arrest," he shouted to the two uniformed medics. "What the hell took you so long?"

Townsend didn't hang around to watch, but ran immediately to the bathroom, hopping over Philip's vomit en route. Then he kneeled at the altar of the toilet and vomited himself. He was vigorously rinsing his mouth out with water from the sink when he spotted a bottle of Scope on the counter. Townsend swiped at the bottle, scattering Gerard's other toiletries over the counter and onto the floor, and guzzled the mouthwash from the bottle like a wino.

Townsend disposed of all the mouthwash that remained, splattered his face with water and patted it dry with the only standard-issue hotel washcloth he could find in the bathroom. He neatly folded the towel over once and replaced it on the rack beside the two hand towels. Then, feeling remorse, he cleaned up the mess he had made on the floor, replacing the deodorant stick, the Brut cologne, the talc, and the toothbrush into an orderly array with the other toiletries by the sink.

By the time Townsend had composed himself enough to re-enter the hotel room, an endotracheal tube had been placed down

Gerard's throat and a stocky Hispanic—identified as "Manny" by his I.D. tag—was oxygenating Gerard by an Ambu bag. One port of the black bellows-type contrivance fit onto the exposed end of the airway tube; the other was connected by green plastic tubing to a portable oxygen tank. Manually squeezing the reservoir forced oxygen into Gerard's lungs, a much more palatable way of resuscitation than blowing kisses. The other medic, an angular Anglo, had just finished securing an intravenous line into the crook of Gerard's elbow.

Townsend positioned himself unobstrusively in a corner, staying out of the way. Philip and Rosie still looked in shock, Oscar had garnered enough medical curiosity to watch the proceedings dispassionately. The routine was a familiar one to Townsend, so his mind and eyes began to wander. He gazed around the characterless hotel room. There were no shelves with books to gauge the man by, no hints at all to his character or interests. And Townsend was yearning to know about this man whose life he may have saved.

Strange how their paths had crossed in two days. Only yesterday Gerard Moreau had been a vibrant, if not abrasive, force; now he was a dehumanized limp form being manhandled onto a stretcher. As with any tragedy, the suddenness of it left one disoriented. Townsend, who had instinctively hated Gerard, was rooting for him to pull through. Perceptions depended upon circumstance, and illness never failed to shuffle the deck of priorities. But then again, perhaps Townsend's change of heart had more to do with protecting an investment. After all, he had given the man mouth-to-mouth . . . could he have subjected himself to that unpleasantness for nothing?

Whatever had befallen Gerard was a scandal of considerable proportions—*Dance Magazine* would have a hard time whitewashing this one, Townsend thought. Even if Gerard survived, he probably wouldn't be fit to dance, or even choreograph, for a considerable length of time. And what of Rosie Van Buren's grand plans—had they been foiled by a skinny line of white powder? What would happen to the megabuck endowment?

Without Gerard, would the Moreau Company be able to perform at the festival, or even stay together as a unit, and what would Felicia do? Considering Felicia, Townsend was led to a more egocentric line of questioning. If the Moreau Company dissolved, Felicia might return to Paul Gruenfeld, which could put Leslie's newly earned position in jeopardy. Was Gerard's tragedy a blessing in disguise?

A more mundane thought occurred to Townsend as he imagined the scene in the emergency room. A young, well-muscled man would roll in, absolutely naked. Naked bodies "found down" invariably had interesting, if not prurient, histories: "Man discovered in bed with another man's wife escapes by jumping out window," or "Coitus interruptus secondary to cardiac arrest." Initially there would be raised eyebrows and black humor among the E.R. staff, but Gerard's history would ring flat, a disappointing "Undressed to shower for a party, man takes final snort." Without sex and violence, it wasn't much of a story.

Townsend surveyed the room again. He noticed that some of Gerard's clothes were neatly draped over the back of an occasional chair by the table. Casual clothes, though, just a pair of slacks and a polo shirt. A pair of Reeboks was on the floor by the same chair. No fancy party attire in sight—neither in that room nor in the bathroom, so they had to still be in the closet. The closet door was closed, and he was not inclined to open it. Townsend always set his clothes out on the bed before taking a shower, but was it fair to compare the habits of an obsessive-compulsive with those of a wild-and-crazy, living-on-the-edge dancer?

Now stripped of its covering, the bed Gerard had been found upon appeared undisturbed. A thin mauve-colored blanket was completely tucked in on all three sides; at the head, the top sheet was folded back evenly over the blanket. Townsend was absently staring at the bed corners.

"Any more information about this guy?" Manny asked in between squeezes of the Ambu bag. The collapsible stretcher, now loaded with its human cargo, had been elevated to its extended, waist-high position. Coldly efficient, the medics had prepared their charge for transport.

Townsend motioned to the table and the drug paraphernalia. "Besides that," snapped Manny.

In turn, they all shrugged, except for Rosie, who had fallen apart and was sobbing into her hands.

Philip asked if he and his mother could come in the ambulance. There was no room was the answer, but they could use their own transportation to meet them at the St. Michael's E.R.

"Somebody . . . somebody," choked Rosie, "needs to tell Bill Davidson what's happened . . . and Felicia."

"I'll take care of that, Rosie," said Townsend. "Don't worry. Just go on ahead to the hospital."

Oscar held the door open as the medics rolled the stretcher out of the room. Philip had pulled Rosie to her feet and supported her as they trailed behind the medics down the hotel corridor.

"Helluva day, uh?" Oscar said to Townsend.

"I've had better," he answered. He had moved toward the door, but stopped midway to open up the closet. He was distractedly assessing Gerard Moreau's wardrobe.

From down the hallway they faintly heard Manny squeezing the Ambu bag, punctuating silence with the honking sound of someone, in a distant room, sitting on a Whoopee cushion.

9

He did his duty, returning to the banquet to discreetly inform William Davidson and Felicia of the tragedy. As discreetly as possible, that is, given that every pair of eyes followed him from his entrance right up to the dais. He feigned casualness, measured his steps purposefully, relaxed the muscles of his face. All for naught, he realized on the way, as he had left his suit jacket in Gerard's room. Worse, his shirtsleeves were rolled up, his collar button undone, and his tie loosened and dangling. The messenger was positively disheveled.

The room was hushed. Davidson and Felicia had known something was amiss and were anxious, though making a brave front at the table of honor. Neither had touched anything on their plates, Townsend saw. He smiled at them as he approached, placed his elbow on the table and slouched forward, as if about to exchange a pleasantry. His message was unadorned: Gerard had been stricken ill, the medics had arrived and were in transit to the St. Michael's emergency room. As if to intentionally undermine his calmness, they both bolted up from the table, Davidson jolting it hard enough with his thighs to upturn their wineglasses. They rushed from the room, providing Townsend temporary relief from exclusive scrutiny. Townsend righted the wineglasses, blotted some of the wine with Felicia's unused napkin, and retreated back to Leslie and his table. The hush had turned into a buzz.

"Let's get out of here," he told her quietly, sitting down and putting the napkin on his lap. He scanned the eight other faces at the table, all looking expectantly at him, and smiled to put them off.

"Talk to me," she said.

Townsend mumbled the message verbatim, then added. "Looks like drugs, and looks real bad."

"Ohmygod—"

"Be cool," he hissed.

"You smell like mouthwash." Leslie screwed up her face.

"Better than barf," said Townsend.

"Do you want anything to eat first?"

"Not hungry. You about done?"

"I guess now I am."

"Did Paul ever show up?"

"Two tables over on the left." She indicated with her head.

"Talk to him?"

"No."

"Nigel show up?"

"Yes. At the same table as Paul."

The rumors and the sudden departure of Felicia and William, as well as the continued absence of Rosie and Philip, had taken most of the fizzle from the gathering's punch. But everyone knew that Townsend was privy to some facts; Townsend was naive in thinking they could be denied.

"So what happened, already?" a male dancer sitting across from them at the table finally demanded, the spontaneous spokesperson for the seven others.

Relenting, Townsend repeated the message without adornment. Everyone at the table sat in stunned silence.

"That's all I know, honest," he added.

He turned because someone tapped him on the shoulder, a rather scrawny man with an ill-fitting suit.

"Steve Rayburn of the *Star*," the man introduced himself. Beside him was a plump blonde who was testing the limits of a strapless gown. "And this is Sheila Mills. She's the dance critic; I'm here covering the news angle, the grant and the commissioning of the piece. So what's the poop?" He had a small pad in hand and pencil poised.

Townsend caught Leslie and Sheila nodding at each other in mutual recognition. He paused, not sure of what to say, if anything. All he had wanted was to get through the evening without his relationship with Leslie deteriorating any further. He was peripheral, not a major player, an innocent standing in the wrong buffet line at the wrong time.

"Steve Rayburn," the man repeated, changing tacts. He had deftly passed the pencil to his pad hand and was extending his right hand for a shake. "And you're—"

"Townsend Reeves." He shook the man's hand. "There really isn't very much to tell you. All I know is that Gerard Moreau took sick in his room and an ambulance was called, and they're taking him to the hospital."

"Which hospital?"

"St. Michael's."

"What's wrong with him? What happened?" Rayburn fired.

"I'm not sure. All I know is that he took sick."

Sheila Mills quickly whispered something in Rayburn's ear.

"Took sick? You're a doctor, aren't you?"

Townsend shook his head in denial. He had overdone trying to sound the layman, the syntax of Uncle Remus didn't ring true. "I'm not a real doctor," he said. "I'm a radiologist."

"That's a real doctor. And all you know is that Gerard 'took sick'?"

"I'm sure he'll be fine," said Townsend, switching from Uncle Remus to Pollyanna.

Steve Rayburn persisted.

"Was he conscious?"

Townsend was tempted, but couldn't bring himself to lie. "Not exactly."

"Was he breathing?"

"Of course he was breathing!"

"So what happened?"

"How the hell should I know what happened?" blurted Townsend in frustration. "I'm sure the folks at the hospital will be able to give you all the information you need, all right?" He was lifting Leslie out of her chair by the elbow. She resisted only long enough to lean over and pick up her purse from beside her chair.

As they made their escape, Rayburn shouted out after them.

"What happened to your jacket, doctor?"

"What *did* happen to your jacket, Town?" Leslie parroted when they had reached the lobby.

"I forgot it. I left it in Gerard's room."

"Why did you take it off?"

"I got hot giving mouth-to-mouth."

"Ohmygod . . . it's really bad, isn't it?"

"It shouldn't be; I don't understand it. He should be all right. He had to have OD'd or else had some idiosyncratic reaction to the cocaine. A transient heart arrhythmia, respiratory arrest—"

"There was cocaine there? You saw it?"

Townsend nodded. "But he was breathing okay at first, and when he stopped it couldn't have been more than a few seconds before I started breathing for him. So he shouldn't have had any significant anoxia, and he should pull through." The logic didn't reassure him.

"What do you mean by 'anoxia'?"

"Without oxygen, not enough oxygen to the brain. You see, if he was breathing and his heart was beating, adequate perfusion to the brain shouldn't be a problem. But he had a seizure, that part I don't understand. The seizure could occur secondary to anoxia, unless there was some direct CNS effect from the coke—" He was rambling, trying to put the pieces together. He felt out of his depth, lacking expertise.

"I don't get what you're saying."

"I don't get it either. They'll figure it out." He was pensive, making possible connections that he kept to himself. Abruptly, he turned his attention back to Leslie. "Did you drive here or what?"

"I shared a cab with some dancers from the company. I assumed I'd go home with you."

The new information jarred him, her intent was registering.

"Home? You mean *our* home?"

"I thought that was a possibility, I mean, it was an option." She tilted her head, the look was unquestionably seductive.

"Like being together tonight, you and me, really together?"

"Just an option, Townsend. Maybe this evening could give us a chance to settle some scores."

Townsend stood silently, considering. Leslie was surprised by his hesitation, then assumed he was trying to take advantage of her opening, wanting to punish her. He didn't have the willpower to refuse her, she reasoned. She looked stunning and sexy and she knew he wanted her and she was finally giving him the chance. And, truth be known, it was a chance she wanted too.

If there was a mind game, Townsend was playing it with himself. His libido had abandoned him. He felt lost and bewildered, left on a doorstep without his glands. His sex juices had been wrung out of him, a sponge squeezed to the merest dampness and handed over earlier that day to Lenny Oates.

The dilemma involved more than drive. His thoughts were far afield, and he couldn't focus them on Leslie. He would be distracted, he was in no condition to discuss their future. And she would be irritated at his spaciness, and become angry, and they would argue. Besides that, Townsend had decided to go himself to St. Michael's, as well as make a certain phone call. Leslie, beautiful Leslie, would be in the way.

"I don't think this is the best timing, Les. I think maybe I should just drop you off at the dorm."

"You're kidding."

"No, don't get me wrong . . . please. . . ."

"Well, it's a first, at least. I've never known you to turn down . . . opportunity."

"Neither have I, but this whole business really has me shook. This isn't the time. But I want to take you up on your offer. I've been waiting a long time."

"More like begging."

Townsend didn't take issue with her word choice. They walked to the parking garage in total silence and had sporadic, pointless conversation in the car. Fortunately the drive was a short one. Townsend dropped Leslie off at the campus dorm with an affectionate but brief parting kiss on the lips.

A burden lifted when Leslie left the car; one less strain, one less complication to occupy his thoughts. Townsend proceeded to cruise north on Rockhill Road, the scenic route to St. Michael's. He had passed Volker Park and the string of vertical fountains that at this hour were stunted, only bubbling up a foot or so. He couldn't pass the fountains without thinking of the sixties, with longhairs in tie-dyed shirts and bellbottoms parading their rebelliousness in the waters. Basketball or Frisbee in hand, he had watched them enviously with his best friend, Steve Becker. In those days, the feminine ideal had been Peggy Lipton of the Mod Squad. While the battles raged in Southeast Asia, two affluent midwestern high school jocks scoured the grounds of Volker Park for braless Peggy Lipton look-alikes in wet T-shirts. The innocent quest had led to some of Townsend's most vivid and sweetest memories.

Once beyond the spacious Nelson Gallery south grounds, Townsend meandered through the tree-canopied, intimate neighborhood of the Art Institute. It was one of his favorite parts of Kansas City, provided he wasn't trying to find parking. The area was grounded and established, as substantial as the stone masonry of the houses and buildings. It was a calm and artsy pocket of contemplation removed from the worldliness of the city, and more, it defined the boundary of elegance before the seedier parts to the north. Townsend turned to the right on Main and entered St. Michael's territory. Unlike nearby St. Luke's, St. Michael's was a knife and gun club, the primary designated trauma center. The journey from the Art Institute to St. Michael's was the visual equivalent of exchanging paint dribbles for blood splatters.

Townsend's parking sticker was still valid, so he pulled his Nova into the physician's parking area and found vacant his spot from days of regular and more gainful employment. He entered the hospital through the emergency room entrance, nodded at familiar faces—many of whom were not even aware that he had been absent from the staff for several months—and breezed past Perkins, the Jamaican security guard. He learned at the nursing station that Gerard Moreau had been stabilized and sent for a CT scan of the head en route to the ICU. Townsend checked out the E.R. waiting area and found it empty except for a mumbling old woman and a drunk; Rosie and the others had probably already settled themselves in the ICU waiting room, a more appropriate oasis for private handwringing.

He took a back staircase up a flight to the level of the Radiology Department and followed a long corridor to the corner CT suite. A sizable reading room was adjacent to the scanning area; the room was darkened except for a lighted panel of automated view boxes. A bearded figure with a dark lion's mane in a green scrub outfit was precariously leaning back in a swivel chair, perusing some images.

"Peter?" Townsend asked from the door. Since a radiologist colleague, Barry Zingesser, had been murdered a year earlier in a similar, dark reading room, Townsend was reluctant to approach from behind without giving ample warning.

Peter Weinberg gave a noticeable start before turning around. Everyone was still skittish, Townsend thought, and who could help it? The hospital had been violated by the murder of a staff member, and the place would never be the same.

"Townsend! My God! What brings you here?" The short, stocky resident—pursuing an extra postgraduate year as a neuroradiology fellow—popped up from his seat and met Townsend midway across the room. He clasped the tall man's arm affectionately; had it been physically possible, he would have given Townsend a hug.

"Just look at you!" he said ebulliently. "You look great, you lazy fart! And with a tie no less! You just come from Friday night services or what?" Peter Weinberg was a well-known local rabbi's son, and could easily play the part of a junior version. Instead, he had chosen the medical route, and would have done most parents proud. Unfortunately, he was the family black sheep. Peter's failure, which far overshadowed his academic and personal accomplishments, was his resistance to dating Jewish women.

"I never converted, remember?" smiled Townsend. The irony of Townsend's attachment to Leslie had always been the source of amused discussion between them.

Peter shrugged. "You're too tall to be a Jew, anyway," he said, grinning widely. "What brings you here? Slumming?"

"Nosing around. A head CT on a guy named Moreau come through?"

"You bet." Weinberg exhaled a half-whistle, half-swishing sound. "Major bad news. He's a famous guy, you know that? A citizen, not your typical St. Michael's clientele."

"The scans handy? I'd like to see them."

"They're on the board. You know him or something?"

Townsend nodded. "Or something." He followed Weinberg over to the view boxes, where Weinberg consulted a list of names on a lined sheet attached to a clipboard. Over his shoulder, Townsend skimmed the names on his own. "Moreau" was listed near the bottom, corresponding to panels number 47 and 48. The current case in view was on panels 14 and 15.

He waited while Weinberg entered the first two digits on a keypad, then punched the Find button. Case after case whirred by them in a blur on the revolving panel, until the mechanism automatically stopped at the programmed location. State-of-the-art viewing boxes were a far cry from the old stationary boards, which necessitated putting up, interpreting, and pulling down films before going on to the next case. The two-tiered monster box in front of them was capable of holding over two hundred separate films, immediately accessible with fingertip controls. The only disadvantage of the technology, and sometimes a major if not a damned inconvenient one, was when an individual X ray, improperly secured by a restraining wire, fell down into the apparatus, lost in the mechanical bowels until a serviceman retrieved it.

Weinberg stood silently in front of Gerard Moreau's films. No commentary was necessary, as student didn't need to educate teacher, and the films spoke for themselves. There were four sheets in all, each composed of twelve smaller image squares in a geometric matrix. Each separate image represented a cross-sectional view of a slice of brain, starting at the base and proceeding in sequential increments to the top. The exam was present in duplicate, the second two sheets covering the same anatomy as the first two, but obtained after the administration of intravenous contrast material for image enhancement. They told the same story.

Townsend scanned the sheets, visually absorbing their content in total rather than proceeding methodically from one small image to the next. A glance was all that was necessary. There were no tumor masses and no extravascular collections of blood within the brain tissue itself or in the spaces around the brain. The abnormality did not involve something present, but what was absent. The sulci of the brain, the convoluted channels normally coursing circuitously along the brain surfaces, were effaced, as were the normally seen fluid-filled cisterns. The brain was diffusely swollen, bulging from within the ungiving constraints of the calvarium.

"Well, piss—" said Townsend.

"A real shame. Thirty-five and an incredible specimen. You know, he was even on the cover of *Dance Magazine* this month."

"I know," said Townsend, thinking that they could be the only two physicians in the entire city who knew anything about *Dance Magazine*. Peter Weinberg was a Broadway musical enthusiast who held Fred Astaire in as high esteem as Harvey Cushing. He had taken up tap dancing himself early on in his residency, and loyally attended evening classes at least twice a week.

"So what's your association with Gerard Moreau? Friend of Les?" Weinberg asked.

"I happened to be on the scene," Townsend answered, choosing not to elaborate.

Weinberg whistled. "The medics said there was coke nearby. Bad shit. Looks like he arrested and got anoxic. The edema's pretty impressive."

"Don't you think a little *too* impressive?" asked Townsend.

"Meaning?"

"Granted, you see this degree of brain edema after respiratory arrest, but usually not until four or six hours later, right?

"I suppose so," Weinberg hesitantly agreed. "What do you make of it?"

"Nothing, necessarily, except it strikes me odd. I'm just not used to seeing diffuse edema this early on in the game. He coded less than an hour ago, and when I first saw him, he was breathing."

"Maybe he got anoxic before you got there, the damage was done, and he started up breathing again. That might figure."

"Possible." Townsend looked troubled.

"In any case," Weinberg continued, "I really don't think Gerard Moreau is going to be much use for anything now, regrettably. Except maybe for spare parts."

Lieutenant Tony Mauro of homicide had an unlisted number, but Townsend still knew it by heart, even though he hadn't spoken with the detective in months. It was nearing 11 P.M. when Townsend placed the call from the radiology office at St. Michael's. He tried to make the call sound as casual as possible.

"Hey, Tony," he said upon hearing a cranky hello. "A voice from your past. A hint. Tall, good-looking doctor with an outstanding baseline jumper."

"Son-of-a-bitch," replied Tony Mauro. "This is the amazing thing about telephones, you know? The thing rings and absolutely any shithead can be on the other end."

"I'm not interrupting anything, am I? I realize it's Friday and kinda late—"

"Right. Molly Fivefingers over here is really upset. My love life ain't much better than it's ever been, Dr. Townsend, in case you want to send me a sympathy card. What's on your mind—wait a minute—tell me you ain't calling on behalf of some stiff."

Townsend hesitated.

"Crap," said Mauro.

"It's not what you think. No dead body. I was just going to ask you a small favor, thought maybe you'd be up for a beer."

"Okay, I'll bite. I'm always up for a little brewski, seeing as it's my evening off and I don't pull shift this weekend. I'm dressed and ready for action."

"That would be great. I can meet you. Ten minutes too soon?"

"Fine, if it's someplace close. What say somewhere in Westport, or we could go to Milton's Taproom."

"Uh," Townsend paused, "I had someplace else in mind."

"Sure, I'm a sport. Your choice, doc, as long as there're some women around. You name it."

"Coffee shop at the Fairmont Plaza," blurted Townsend. He hung up the receiver without waiting for a response.

Upon his return to the hotel lobby, Townsend noticed some familiar faces exiting the ballroom; apparently the dance function was winding down but still had its stragglers. The bellboy in the lobby recognized him and gave him a peculiar stare, no doubt wondering for what conceivable reason the tall guy had ditched the babe.

Townsend arrived at the coffee shop ahead of Mauro and waited in the most private booth he could find. He fiddled with the plastic-coated menu, wondering if he could ever overcome his disgust at the thought of putting anything in his mouth. For the present, his diet would be liquid.

Within five minutes Tony Mauro showed, wearing jeans and a rugby shirt.

"Sorry I'm underdressed for a pickup hotbed like this. I don't know what got into me. I left my clean tux in the limo." He slid into the booth across from Townsend. Whatever clothes he wore, Tony Mauro bore the look of someone you didn't want to tangle with. He wasn't tall, but he was a wide body, the product of serious weight lifting. The sturdiness of his frame was complemented by rugged and intense good looks. His brown eyebrows were heavy and nearly met in the midline. When he wrinkled his brow, Mauro looked as if he had an elongated fuzzy caterpillar marauding horizontally across his forehead. "And do they even *sell* beer in this joint, or are we having cappuccino and little cucumber sandwiches with the crusts cut off?"

"Tough guys like you eat your petite cucumber sandwiches with the crusts still on," said Townsend.

"Anything so long as the rich doctor buys."

Townsend flagged down a senior citizen waitress and ordered two imported beers.

He had known the cop from the early days in his residency, when Mauro, then in uniform, was often responsible for delivering drunk and disorderlies to the St. Michael's E.R. Tony Mauro was real people, a street kid who had worked his way up, a gruff with ethics. While Townsend had been the basketball star at Missouri State, Mauro was being shot at, one of the tail-end troopers in Vietnam. Still worlds apart in background and sensibility, the two had a grudging respect for one another, cemented when they had been drawn together by the murder of Townsend's colleague Barry Zingesser a year earlier. Had Mauro attempted to deny the class resentment he felt toward Townsend, his flip antagonism would have carried a real bite. He had enough insight to realize that had he been the one born with a silver spoon in mouth, he wouldn't have spit it out, either.

"You never write, you never call. . . ." said Mauro.

Townsend smiled guiltlessly. Neither one had expected their relationship to be one of drinking buddies. Such was the joy of male friendship: no obligation, and despite the passage of time, things picked up exactly where they left off.

"Anything new?"

"Naw. Quit smoking . . . again," said Mauro.

"That's good. It's good every time you quit."

"So look," Mauro said impatiently. "You don't have to make conversation like I'm some broad you have to show interest in before you hose her. Just hose me, already, okay?"

Townsend began chronologically, starting with background

information on the Moreau and Gruenfeld companies. Mauro had only the vaguest notion of contemporary dance, but politics and conflict he could relate to, so it mattered little. Mauro made no comments except for "I'd finally like to see this Leslie of yours," to which Townsend offered getting him tickets to one of the festival performances. Mauro was receptive to the offer.

Townsend was surprised that Mauro didn't question his haziness about the encounter with Paul Gruenfeld in the balcony of the theater. The cop listened passively, not seeming to pick up on, or care about, the ambiguity. Townsend almost had the sense he was being humored.

The waitress delivered the beers at that juncture, smiling sweetly at both of them. A sixty-year-old in the uniform of a twenty-year-old, she had probably been a looker in the forties. Her wrinkles betrayed a tough life, but she was chipper, not defeated by time's ravages.

"Any questions, clarifications so far?" asked Townsend. Mauro didn't have his notepad out yet.

"Naw," answered Mauro, taking a large slurp of the froth and wiping off his mouth with the back of his hand.

"So I'm not really sure if Paul had a gun or not, or even if it was Paul that I saw. Because when I saw him on the floor, he didn't have a gun, although maybe it could have been under the seat."

"You've said this part already," said Mauro.

Townsend plodded on with his narrative. He mentioned what Leslie had told him about the confrontation between Nigel Devon and Gerard, then gave as detailed an explanation as he could about his efforts at resuscitating Gerard in the hotel room.

"I don't think he's going to make it," said Townsend.

"That's too bad," said Mauro, without sarcasm, but without real interest, either.

"I thought maybe you could look into this thing. On the Q.T."

"Let me tell you how this works, buddy." Mauro finished off the beer. He held the bottle up; an observant Helen by the register picked up the cue. "People kill themselves on drugs every day. I mean, that's why they have those public service TV commercials on all the time. You know, 'This is your mind on drugs'; 'Your mind is a terrible thing to waste . . .' "

Not wanting to come off sounding pedantic, Townsend didn't interrupt to inform him that the latter was a slogan for the United Negro College Fund.

"It's not a very practical use of taxpayer's money to chase around after every stinking OD. I mean, who gives a shit? Now, if the M.E. comes up with anything suspicious, we'll look into things, but most of the time we don't have to bother. Can you imagine what would happen if we did a full-court press on bullshit like this?"

"Well—"

"Nothing personal now, but there's an obvious aspect."

"What 'obvious aspect'?"

"Now don't get defensive on me—" He looked up to thank Helen, who was carefully refilling his glass, tipping it sideways to keep the foam down.

". . . but the way I see it, deep down you'd like to see Paul Gruenfeld in the State Pen. That way, you see, your woman doesn't have a job in that New York company of his, and she comes back to your domicile, wagging her tail between her legs. Now that wouldn't be so bad, would it? Wagging tail?" He peered over the top of his glass, measuring Townsend's response. "Not that you ain't a Good Samaritan and all, but let's be honest here."

Townsend was pensive, cut to the quick. Mauro, not prone to deep psychological interpretations, had drawn blood.

"Point well taken," responded a self-restrained Townsend, "but that isn't my motivation here."

"Right," said Mauro skeptically.

"Besides," Townsend went on, "this guy is a V.I.P., and there's bound to be some interest over this whole thing. It might be advisable if your department had a leg up. You know a reporter named Rayburn?"

"Yeah. He's a squirrel."

"He seems fairly persistent. There's a big story in this." Townsend paused. Mauro gave a look of disgust, then reached into his back pocket and pulled out a small notepad. He removed a nubbin of a pencil that was tucked into the coil binding and opened the pad.

"I'll call Parker in on it. I'll nose around the room tonight—I assume that's why you chose this place instead of a *real* bar, right?—and we can seal it off until the morning. The lab boys can have a look-see and maybe take a few prints. In the morning, that is, it'll keep till morning. This ain't exactly a federal case."

"Great," said Townsend. "And I mentioned to you about the vomit on the carpet right? It's Philip's. But there might be some vomit also inside the toilet bowel. That's mine."

"You told me about all the vomit already," said Mauro. "I don't think I need to write it down, okay? Trust me, I'll remember the vomit. Let me just jot down some names here. How do you spell 'Grunefeld'?"

Townsend listed and spelled the pertinent names. "I don't remember Oscar's last name, unfortunately."

"Not a problem. I have to talk to him tonight anyway. Just to make sure he keeps the maids out."

"I really appreciate this, Tony."

"No prob."

"There's one little thing that caught my eye, nagging at me a bit."

"Oh?"

"It may be nothing, but when we pulled Gerard off the bed, I saw that the sheet corners weren't tucked in right."

Tony Mauro didn't know how to respond. His mind raced, trying to construct some reasonable connection. He tried to look intelligent. He said nothing, waiting it out, but was betrayed by his eyebrow merger into the elongated caterpillar.

"It wasn't that they weren't tucked in well," Townsend clarified, "they just weren't tucked in *correctly.*"

Mauro still didn't get it and was flustered. "What the fuck do you mean?"

"Okay," Townsend began calmly, hoping that if he articulated well, the discrepancy might elucidate itself. "Late yesterday afternoon I happened to be in Felicia Bradley's hotel room—"

"Wait! Wait!" Mauro's caterpillar levitated. "You're talking about the same Felicia Bradford—"

"Bradley . . . it's Bradley down on your pad, isn't it?"

". . . the same Felicia Bradley that's married to the OD person."

"Gerard. Correct. Except they aren't married in any real sense, as far as I can gather, more like a marriage of convenience. They live pretty much separately, like I said."

"Right, you mentioned that. But what were *you* doing in her hotel room?"

"From what I can tell, she wanted to seduce me, but I passed."

"Skip it," replied a disgruntled Mauro. "I'm not interested in your love life, I'm sorry I asked."

"Trust me," Townsend alleviated him, "it isn't germane to the story. My point is that the maid was making up her bed, and I noticed how tight and precise she was with her military corners."

"What the hell do you know about military anything?" Mauro asked, mental fatigue shortening his fuse.

"Be that way, call them hospital corners. Now *those* I know about. Anyway, the bed in Gerard's room was neatly enough made, but the corners weren't squared. I can show you how they do it."

"Never mind," Mauro interrupted. "Maybe it was a different maid, ever thought of that? Or maybe he made his own bed. What's your point?"

"Nothing, except I was wondering if maybe Gerard wasn't having a private party. Felicia made several references to him fooling around with some of the company girls. So maybe he was with someone when he overdosed. The person panics and runs out on him."

". . . being sure to make up the bed so Gerard can collapse on it? I don't buy it. The first thing someone's gonna do is clean up the drug tracks, not leave lines of the white stuff lying around on the table like you said it was. And how does that tie in with Grunefield and Devlin?"

"Gruenfeld and Devon," Townsend patiently corrected. "It doesn't, really, I just noticed it, that's all. Maybe someone's worried about having given Gerard some bad stuff."

"Or maybe Gerard provided himself with his own bad stuff," interjected Mauro, "and who the hell cares, that's what I'd like to know."

"The whole thing just strikes me as a bit odd, that's all."

"And I'll check it out, all right? Christ! What a guy has to go through to get a couple of brews these days!"

"I'll make it up to you, Tony. Maybe I can get Leslie to fix you up with one of her dancer friends, some nubile young thing whose taste runs toward the Neanderthal."

"Now you're talking."

"I'll get the tab. And while you're at it, would you mind retrieving my suit jacket for me? I think I left it on the bed in Gerard's room."

"Sure, why not?" said Tony, just acting miffed. "And you want me to have it cleaned and pressed for you?"

"Don't bother. It's enough for me to know that the coke on the table is 'the real thing,' if you catch my drift."

"The lab will check it out, okay?" Mauro stood up to leave. He tucked the pencil stub into the coils, and returned the whole pad to the back pocket of his jeans.

"Keep the wind at your back, guy," Townsend said with some affection.

"I'll count myself lucky," answered Mauro, "if I can just keep from stepping in all that fucking vomit."

10

Townsend was lounging on the couch, trying to concentrate on Tuesday morning's sports section and the travails of the boys of summer. The hapless Royals were having a lousy season, but Steve Rayburn's latest piece on Gerard Moreau was really what had distracted him from the box scores.

The three days since Friday's events had dragged by and Townsend felt overcome by ennui. He was observing the events in the dance community with increasing fascination, though, which unfortunately didn't obviate his obsession with Doris Humphrey and her insemination. He cursed himself for being duped by Lenny Oates, and fantasized about pressing his thumbs into the pulpiness of the tech's ebony throat. But mostly he focused on the birds and the bees, in detail not generally considered while occupied, hot and sweaty, pumping under the sheets.

Presuming one of the millions of Townsend's sperm had met its mark in the fallopian tube of Doris Humphrey, the zygote had cleaved and in a day perhaps, a ball of cells called a morula would pass from the tube into the uterus. Two or so days after that, a hollowed out ball of cells, the blastocyst, would begin its implantation in the uterine cavity. The little parasite would establish itself, manifesting a true work ethic; the evolutionary wheels would turn. And in less than ten days, a serum pregnancy test could confirm that all this business was happening. Townsend had circled the date on his Gary Larson "Far Side" desk calender. No annotations, just a circle around the date, June 30.

Townsend was joyful at hearing the phone ring. Perhaps it was the locum tenens service with a job offer. Better yet, maybe Rita needed him at the fertility clinic, and he could learn more about Doris. He wanted some excuse to get back there.

"Have you heard anything new, Town?" the voice asked without a preface.

It was Leslie. He concealed his disappointment.

"Not really," he drawled. He had been keeping her posted, relaying any information he got from his calls to Peter Weinberg, swearing her to confidence. He hadn't been completely forthcoming, though, neglecting to mention his meeting with Tony Mauro.

Townsend had not received follow-up from Tony and had resisted calling. Nagging the cop wouldn't play well, he knew. Townsend also assumed drug analysis took time, at least a week, depending on how backed up the state toxicologist's office was. And the Moreau OD wasn't high priority. On the surface it fell into the "crock of shit" category. Powder was powder was powder. Did Townsend seriously think otherwise? The circumstances of Gerard's discovery and subsequent downhill medical course continued to bother him. That unmetabolized cocaine was found in Gerard's blood didn't provide much solace, although it seemed to placate everyone else.

The stakes were higher now, since Gerard Moreau was officially brain dead, a flat liner on two consecutive electroencephalograms. Found down with an undiagnosed cause of death, he would by law require an autopsy, qualify as a medical examiner case. For the present, the dancer was being spared that final, humiliating ordeal, still in the St. Michael's ICU on a respirator, tubes in veins and orifices, a preserved specimen like Lenin in his tomb. Relatives in France had been contacted, Felicia had nodded her assent, the plug could be pulled at any time.

"Did you read Rayburn's article this morning?" Leslie asked.

"I skimmed it," Townsend understated.

"Anything new on his condition?"

"Brain dead is brain dead, Leslie. Finito. His condition will not change."

"But they knew that on Saturday," Leslie whined. "I just don't understand it . . . why don't they let him die?"

The reason for Gerard's present "stay of vivisection," as Peter Weinberg had speculated correctly, was the harvesting bonanza for transplantation. Gerard Moreau was equipped with a number of reusable parts, relatively young and quite healthy, notwithstanding the fact that they were currently housed in a dead man. Specifically, two corneas, a heart, two kidneys, and a liver. Especially a liver. As luck would have it, compatibility studies had shown that Gerard Moreau was a fine match for little Jesús Sanchez. Just in time, too, since the kid was tumbling downhill in irreversible liver failure. Townsend supposed that if the transplant team had their way, Gerard's autopsy report would be an abbreviated one. The pathologists would get the figurative and literal hind tit, vultures making due with whatever pickings were left to scavenge.

"I told you, Leslie, he's a perfect organ donor. Aside from his squash, he's in great shape."

"But what about the overdose? What about the drugs in his system? Won't they have to do an autopsy?"

"Any drugs in his system would be metabolized by now. They can arrange to get his organs, provided they have enough information to establish a reasonable cause of death, and unmetabolized cocaine in his blood seems to make their case. Leslie, you haven't told anyone else that he's brain dead, have you?"

"I swear, Town, not a soul."

The press had squeezed a good amount of ink over the tragedy, Steve Rayburn's byline dominating. The brain-dead angle, and especially the Sanchez transplant possibility, weren't public knowledge. The official word was that Gerard Moreau was in a deep coma, condition classified by the hospital spokesperson as "critical." Townsend assumed that Rosie and William Davidson knew what was going on but were keeping a lid on things. He wondered how Felicia was taking it—had the obvious animosity she felt for Gerard when alive turned into heavy-duty guilt now?

From what Rayburn's stories implied, Felicia was not too grief-stricken to be oblivious to the fate of the Van Buren funds earmarked for the Moreau Company. Apparently she contemplated grabbing the reins of the Moreau Company, assuming the choreographer's mantle. But she had never choreographed anything to speak of, and her capabilities in that regard were suspect. Dancing was a technique and a craft; choreography an art. Assuming a dancer could make dances was analogous to thinking that Townsend's abilities as a radiologist would qualify him as a neurosurgeon. But one couldn't blame Felicia for trying.

More qualified candidates hadn't wasted time in staking a claim, Nigel Devon heading the list and playing on the hometown connection. Why should Rosie Van Buren support a bunch of New Yorkers when there were needy artistes in her own backyard? Then there was Paul Gruenfeld, whose grounds were more firmly based in ability than in sentimentality. There was a Biblical sense of justice and fair play in his claim, blood money for enduring heartache and deprivation, just reward for walking through the fire.

A particular scenario given credence was a Gruenfeld–Bradley reunion, either the Gruenfeld Company merging with Moreau's, or Felicia simply deserting the latter and leaving her cohorts high and dry. Despite all the speculation about company reorganizations and the fate of the money, little, if any, centered on the circumstances of Gerard's death. The public was accustomed to celebrities and athletes self-destructing on drugs, and for a dance community, inundated with the ongoing tragedy of talented male dancers succumbing to AIDS, a cocaine-related demise was emotionally easier to take.

"What do you make of Felicia possibly getting back with Paul?" Townsend asked. "Heard any more rumors?"

"Anything's possible."

Townsend didn't get much out of Leslie. She had been guarded during their limited phone conversations, maybe anticipating an unsympathetic Townsend and wanting to avoid confrontation. Perhaps she wanted to deny any connection between Paul's presence in the balcony and the soon-thereafter tragedy of Gerard Moreau. She had shown an unswerving loyalty to her mentor and was increasingly defensive. Was it really about Paul? Or was it about her relationship with Townsend?

Townsend proceeded to walk on thin ice. "How's Paul doing, by the way?"

"Fine."

"You think he's going after the grant?"

"Of course he's going after the grant," snapped a peeved Leslie. "Everyone is. It's hard to tell the mourners from the lobbyists."

"You think Paul's discussed it with Rosie?"

"Paul, and Nigel, and Felicia, and I don't know who else. There isn't a company in the world that couldn't use Rosie Van Buren's support."

"Hold on, I'm just asking—"

"No you're not, you're baiting me! You still think that Paul had something to do with all of this, and you're full of shit!" She slammed down the receiver.

Townsend shook his head, got a dial tone, and immediately dialed her dorm phone number.

"What!" she hollered, answering the call before the completion of the first ring.

"I'm sorry," he said. "I didn't mean to upset you. Just trying to make conversation. Admit it, you're a bit edgy."

"Right," she replied glumly.

"I guess I won't see you until Friday night after the performance."

"That's a safe bet."

"We're still on, though?"

"I suppose."

Leslie had made herself scarce ostensibly because of rehearsals, the final push before a gala performance by five representative companies from the Dance Festival scheduled for Friday evening. The Moreau Company, originally slated as the major headliner, had been rescheduled, the Lar Lubovitch Company pulled in at the last minute as its replacement. Pilobolus, Nigel Devon's Kansas City Dance Theatre, and another company that Townsend couldn't recall rounded off the evening's entertainment.

Without the hype of *Desdemona,* and the thwarted confrontation of Gruenfeld's and Moreau's "dueling companies," the gala evening had lost its pizzazz. Tickets previously impossible to come by were available at the box office, and Townsend had picked up a single seat for Tony Mauro. Front row, not ideal from the standpoint of watching dance, but Mauro was probably more interested in seeing mounds of flesh pressed against the leotards anyway.

"I picked up a ticket for a friend," Townsend said slowly.

"Oh?" She sounded only mildly interested.

"I thought maybe one of the girls in the company might like a date, you know, we could sort of double, maybe take in a late dinner."

"That's fine, I could ask around. Karen, or maybe Janet."

"Janet would be great." Townsend vaguely knew both women, but voiced his preference with Tony in mind, opting for the one with larger breasts.

"Anyone I know? Somebody from the hospital?" Leslie asked.

"Not a medical type." He paused, took a deep breath, braced himself for her response. "Tony Mauro."

"He's the cop!"

"Detective."

"Damn you, Townsend—"

"Don't hang up, Leslie—"

"You got him involved in this, didn't you." Her voice was threatening. "You're doing this intentionally to punish me; it's all because you're angry."

"That isn't my motivation, dammit! He's hardly involved, nothing official, I just wanted him to check things out, just in case."

"I can't believe you!"

"The whole thing's fishy, Leslie. I'm not saying that it has anything to do with Paul. Be objective for a second. Listen to yourself, why don't you? Get the chip off your shoulder, for Chrissake!"

She was silent on the other end. He could hear her breathing. She didn't hang up.

"We're not exactly communicating if I hide things from you, right?" he asked, immediately cognizant of his hypocrisy. He hadn't dared tell her about Doris Humphrey, though it had been foremost on his mind for days. No doubt Leslie would take the situation well, possibly make light of it. What she would have real trouble with was how Townsend was reacting to the situation, how much he was aching. Leslie alone knew how badly Townsend wanted children, how a family had been sidelined because of her career. If Leslie could relate to his panic, then surely she would be threatened by it. So much for communicating.

"Right," she eventually responded.

"Trust me, will you?"

Leslie sighed heavily. "I've really got to get myself together for rehearsal, Town."

"Then we're still on for Friday?"

"I suppose so."

"And you'll see about Janet?"

"I'll ask," said Leslie. "And I know you chose her because she's got bigger boobs."

Townsend hung up the phone and felt a blanket of depression settle on him like a parachute collapsing upon its grounded cargo. He couldn't suppress his urge to learn about Doris Humphrey. If he could demystify her, he reasoned, maybe he could get the monkey off his back.

During the drive to the Lenexa Women's Specialty Clinic, he devised a variety of pretexts for the visit, but could come up with nothing more plausible than "being in the neighborhood." For what? Why would he willfully go to Lenexa? Real estate, that was it. He was thinking about buying some investment property, a little room to roam in the sticks, heaven forbid.

The waiting room was empty. Rita, thumbing through a magazine behind the counter, seemed so genuinely glad to see him, that Townsend decided to improvise.

"You were so nice to me last week," he said after her enthusiastic greeting, "that I thought you might let me buy you lunch." He added offhandedly, "I just happened to be in the neighborhood."

"What a sweetheart," crowed Rita, preening her hairsprayed coiffeur, "particularly since *I'm* the one that owes *you* the chicken and dumplings."

"How could I forget?" said Townsend. He was beginning to worry about what he was getting into. He hoped Rita Babcock was happily married.

"Howard back yet?"

"Sure enough, but he's in surgery all day, really behind the eight ball. I'm going out of my gourd just sitting 'round, but I gave the receptionist off and somebody has to mind the phone and appointment book."

"We could bring in something," Townsend offered.

They settled on sausage grinders and antipasto from a nearby Mario's. Townsend made the round trip in just over twenty minutes. They set up their lunch on the reception counter, cluttering it with paper bags and plastic containers, Townsend indulging Rita in idle chitchat for most of the repast. He learned about her nursing school years at the University of North Carolina, her cat, and, as feared, a failed marriage. Reflexively, he attempted to convey his unavailability by pointedly referring to Leslie a number of times, but Rita seemed oblivious to the references. Maybe she had heard otherwise—the actual state of their relationship—from Howard. Townsend craved information from Rita, but didn't want to lead her on, or worse, feel obliged to sleep with her to get it. He optimistically hoped she could be satisfied being pumped for information.

"If the VCR we've ordered were here," Rita was saying, "we

could idle away the time watching skin flicks. Course," she added smiling, "it might be kinda tight for both of us to squeeze into that back bathroom."

Townsend looked over his grinder questioningly and wiped off a moist spot from the corner of his mouth, presuming it to be tomato sauce. He automatically sucked the tip of his finger but couldn't taste much of anything. He was looking beyond Rita, at the shelves behind her. From floor to ceiling, the shelves were filled with blue ring binders. Each spine had a neatly typed name strip, one notebook for each patient. Townsend knew that one of the notebooks held the fertility story of Doris Humphrey, and a whole lot more. From where he sat, though, the names were a blur.

Since a distracted Townsend didn't respond, Rita volunteered the information that the office was installing a minitheater beside the commode Townsend knew so well, with a selection of blue movies to inspire arousal for fatigued, faltering husbands required to produce sperm on demand.

"Howard's giving me over two hundred dollars to choose the films," she beamed. "It's a tough job, but *somebody* has to do it!"

Townsend smiled noncommittally. "Leslie's not really into those kind of movies," he said.

"I feel terrible for some of those husbands, absolutely terrible!" Rita daintily picked out a Calamata olive pit from her mouth and set it on a spare napkin beside several others. "You can't imagine what a struggle it is for them sometimes!"

"Difficult, huh?"

"Difficult! Near impossible! Sometimes it takes them so dang long that they throw our whole schedule off! That's why we're going for the VCR. Better than me standing by the door asking 'em what's taking so long!" Her animation and obvious delight in the topic betrayed a perverse love of her work.

"We had this couple last year," she went on, lowering her voice to imply a breach of confidence, "and the hubbie just could not get anything to work in our bathroom. Now they were coming all the way from Joplin, ya see, and the only way he could do his business was to pull off the interstate on the way and have his wife help. Well, this one time, they're off the highway and he hears a police siren and misses the cup completely—gets it all over the steering wheel and dashboard of their Volvo. As you might imagine, that was it for the day. After they got here, he was in the bathroom for over an hour, with a break only to ask for some baby oil. I felt so bad for the poor dear!"

Townsend nodded, a practiced look of empathy on his face.

Unexpectedly, Rita snorted and started to laugh.

"Every time I think about it, it just cracks me up," she chortled. "You want this last olive?"

Townsend took the cue and exchanged his funereal look to one of gleeful camaraderie. "Go ahead, you take it," he said.

At least the conversation had turned to business, so Townsend seized the opportunity as Rita worked the olive in her mouth.

"I was curious about some things."

"Like what?" Rita removed the last pit and put it at the end of the line.

"Like how much certain things cost. I imagine the insurance companies won't pick up the tab."

"They'll cover initial visits," corrected Rita, "but then the patients are usually on their own."

"I suppose it's pricey."

"You bet, it really adds up."

Townsend took a leap, hoping Rita wouldn't perceive it as one. "How much for donor sperm?"

"Donor sperm? You mean from a bank?"

"As a 'for instance.'"

Rita twisted her lips to one side and pinched her eyes shut for an instant. "Just over two hundred dollars, as I recall," she said, "and nearly half that's in the shipping. But that's just the short of it. For us to wash and prepare the sperm, it's another eighty-five, then the insemination itself is another forty. And that doesn't include the cost of ultrasound exams and the initial consultation, but like I said, the insurance company will usually pick that one up."

"So, let's see," Townsend began, "for that lady we inseminated with donor sperm on Friday . . . what was her name?"

"You must be meaning Mrs. Humphrey."

"That was it, I think. Brunette, fairly young. . . ."

"Very attractive."

"Whatever her name was—anyway, her day's activities must have run around five hundred bucks."

"Near enough. But she's an exception. I can't imagine anyone getting by for any less than her, especially if she gets pregnant on the first go-round."

"That possible?" Townsend asked.

"It certainly happens, particularly in someone like her. She's functioning perfectly normally, as far as we know. She even went through the insemination without Clomid."

Townsend was attentive. "Why did you say you can't imagine anyone getting by for less?"

"Well," replied Rita, "as I said, she didn't require follicle stimulation, at least not yet. And her husband was worked up for his infertility elsewhere, so there wasn't any lab work or sperm analysis needed for him."

"So she's from out of town?"

"Apparently just moved here, can't recall from where." The office phone rang. Like a good hostess being drawn away from a guest, southern upbringing coming to the fore, Rita made sure Townsend would have something to occupy his time. Before answering the phone, she swiveled out of her chair, ran her fingers along the row of blue binders on the second row of shelves, and withdrew one.

"Have a look-see for yourself," she said, handing Townsend the office records on Doris Humphrey. "Lenexa Women's Specialty Clinic," she said into the phone.

Townsend's hands were shaking as he thumbed through the binder. The records were meticulously organized, with color-coded index tabs dividing the material into various sections: PROGRESS NOTES, CORRESPONDENCE, MONTHLY CYCLES, MALE, PATH/X-RAY REPORTS, LABS, PAST RECORDS. In the very back, under

ULTRASOUNDS, a pocketed plastic sheet contained several paper copy images from an earlier exam, presumably done to monitor follicle size. Townsend left them in their pocket, not bothering to look at what he knew best; instead he skipped back to the front of the binder.

The notebook was obviously the file of a new patient, with little substantive material. In fact, the organizing tab sheets made up most of what was present—all of the sections, with the exception of PROGRESS NOTES and ULTRASOUNDS, were void of information. Townsend strained to glean any meaning from Howard Gorell's crimped, upright script in the PROGRESS section.

Doris Humphrey was a thirty-one-year-old nullipara with an unremarkable past medical history; in particular, no prior pelvic infections or underlying gynecologic conditions. She had undergone menarche at thirteen and cycled normally, every twenty-eight days. Her prior form of contraception had been diaphragm in conjunction with condoms, although she had been on oral contraceptives ten years earlier for three years, opting to discontinue their usage because of bloating.

Townsend sighed. He had retreated into clinical calmness. Rita was still occupied with the phone caller. The information, albeit intimate, wasn't what he had in mind. He skimmed down to the SOCIAL HISTORY section, learning that she was a housewife (Howard had used the more politically correct "employed in the home"), married eight years to a self-employed financial consultant. They had been unsuccessful in their attempts to conceive, Doris not using any birth control for over six years. For the past three years they had been more serious about conceiving, consulting a specialist and shortly thereafter discovering the cause of the problem. Jason Humphrey had a markedly diminished sperm count, attributable to severe mumps orchitis in his early twenties. Copies of his workup by a urologist in Palo Alto were forthcoming.

Townsend double-checked behind the MALE divider, confirmed that the section was empty, and flipped back to the PROGRESS section. The treatment plan was straightforward. Artificial insemination with donor sperm, standard protocol, initial attempts without exogenous ovarian stimulation. After the first consultation, there had been one brief follow-up appointment. Doris underwent a routine ultrasound on day 10 of her next cycle to confirm a normally developing dominant follicle; she was instructed to monitor her luteinizing hormone level with a urine dipstick from day 13 onward, and to schedule an appointment for insemination as soon as her LH surge was documented. Townsend knew the rest too well. The cause of his current angst was given short shrift, summed up on less than half a line in Rita's flowery, looping, very legible script. She had jotted Friday's date in the margin, then simply, "AID performed (Dr. Townsend Reeves)."

". . . let me just get this down," Rita was saying. She leaned across the countertop toward Townsend, brushing aside the wrappings from their lunch, and grabbed a yellow Post-it pad.

Townsend glanced at her and smiled. Rita returned the smile, a silent apology for prioritizing business before pleasure.

He wanted the pad also, but didn't want to be seen copying any information from the chart. A black felt-tip marking pen was in easy reach. He picked it up in an absentminded manner—looking for something to fiddle with—and began tapping it quietly against the palm of his hand. He continued improvising a tattoo, watching Rita all the while. When she was looking down to scribble on the pad Townsend deftly slipped the marking pen into his pants pocket.

He turned his attention back to the face sheet of Doris Humphrey's chart. For INSURANCE COMPANY, none was listed. While a third party wouldn't pay for most of anything Howard billed for anyway, Townsend was still surprised that a carrier wasn't at least listed. No matter. The patient had signed the agreement that she would be responsible for the cost of services rendered. He scrutinized her signature, attempting to divine something about her character. He was no expert. It was a neat, standard script, the type drilled into students in parochial schools. Maybe she was Catholic, a right-handed Catholic.

He set about memorizing her address and phone number. Five-one-nine-four Charlotte placed her on the Missouri side in the neighborhood of the Art Institute, between Fifty-first and Fifty-second streets. The Humphreys also had a P.O. box for correspondence, probably a business address for Jason Humphrey's clients. Townsend recognized the Zip Code as belonging to the Brookside area, most likely the post office on Sixty-third Street, across from the Berbiglia liquor store. Townsend sequentially repeated all three numbers to himself. He covered each one on the sheet with his finger and tested himself, like a schoolchild drilling himself on spelling words. He had them down short term, but in his state of distractedness, they wouldn't remain in his memory banks for long.

Townsend caught Rita's eye and mouthed "bathroom," pointed back toward the lab, excusing himself. She acknowledged him with a nod, attention still focused on the medical concerns of her caller.

The lab was empty, Lenny Oates fortunately nowhere to be found. Townsend went inside the familiar bathroom, continually repeating the address and phone number of Doris Humphrey silently in his head. Door safely locked, he pulled the marking pen out of his pants pocket, intending to write them all down on some scrap of paper in his wallet. A Chevron receipt would do fine.

But his wallet wasn't in his back pocket. He remembered then that after paying for lunch, he had placed his billfold in the glove compartment of his car. His jeans had frayed and his left rear pocket was succumbing to a widening gap of white horizontal threads. He had worried that his wallet might slip out. Then he had thought to buy an iron-on denim patch. Simpler still to buy a new pair of jeans. At the moment he wondered why the hell he didn't just put the damn wallet in his other back pocket.

Townsend shook his head in frustration and reached for a paper towel from the dispenser. The dispenser was empty. He groaned.

In fear of losing his numerical mantra, he began chanting the numbers *sotto voce*. He turned on the exhaust fan to make him less conscious of his whisperings, like a woman prematurely flushing the toilet to prevent a new beau from hearing her tinkle. Men had no such hang-ups; rather, they didn't need to waste water, being blessed with the ability to quietly direct their urine stream along the side of the bowl instead.

He tore off two squares of toilet paper. Howard had scrimped here—the tissue was single ply. The paper absorbed the ink from the marking pen and smeared the numerals together. Townsend cursed, wadded up the toilet paper, and tossed it into the toilet bowl. He flushed with such finality that he was almost startled to watch the water rise yet again to its watermark on the porcelain.

His rummaging through the drawers and a check in the cabinet under the sink were fruitless. Finally, he unzipped his jeans and jerked them down over his hips. His white Jockey briefs were in good shape, but they had to be sacrificed. Meticulously, Townsend Reeves recorded Doris Humphrey's personal data along the front of his underpants.

Townsend had to gas up his Nova anyway, so after leaving the Women's Clinic he stopped at a filling station on Quivira Road and circumspectly eyed the pay phone at the far end of the lot. Townsend was a reluctant prophet, Ma Bell's equipment his personal burning bush.

When was the last time he had called a girl and hung up the receiver upon hearing her voice? Probably sophomore year in high school, before he had developed adequate nerve or sophisticated enough defenses for the universally vulnerable male ego. Sitting in his car, engine idling, Townsend felt very much like that sophomore in high school. Perhaps he was regressing even more, back to sixth grade when he chronically rode his Schwinn ten-speed back and forth past Edwina Conner's house in the hopes of catching the merest glimpse of her.

He decided to skip the gas—it was cheaper on the Missouri

side anyway—opting to drive his car directly past the pump and pulling up to park by the phone. He had a single quarter in his pocket, which he took for some kind of omen.

Not intending to actually speak to the woman, he wanted to hear her voice again. Nothing elaborate, no guise of pretending to want to speak with someone else, an obvious wrong number, none of the old adolescent standbys, like requesting that Prince Albert be let out of the can. And of course nothing threatening, no prolonged silence or heavy breathing. Just enough time to hear her say "hello," then he would click off. A good plan. Better yet, he might get an answering machine, and be able to listen to the recorded message of Doris Humphrey at his leisure, without anxiety. If need be, he could listen to it again and again.

Townsend didn't feel the need to consult his underwear; the number was fresh in his mind, lingering behind every thought like an annoying jingle. A continuously playing tape, a Möbius strip of numerical lyrics: phone number, address, P.O. box.

There was in fact a recorded message, but not the expected one. Prefacing the missive was a discordant tonal progression, an electronic version of a novice having at three bars of a glockenspiel.

"We're sorry. You have reached a number that is no longer in service. If you feel you have reached this recording in error, please dial again. Otherwise, please consult your directory or directory assistance for further information."

Townsend redialed twice more, with the same results. He considered it unlikely that he had transposed any numbers, but doubt nagged enough for him to confirm. He glanced around furtively, pulled his shirttail from his jeans, then grabbed the front elastic waistband of his briefs and pulled upward. The self-inflicted frontal wedgie was not without pain. He grimaced as he manhandled his testicles, stretching the fabric to the breaking point, his gonads trapped in an ever-tightening sling. The number etched in his Jockeys was as he remembered, his self-inflicted nausea for naught.

His next step was to consult the phone directory. No Jason Humphrey, J. Humphrey, Doris Humphrey, or D. Humphrey on Charlotte in the Kansas City listings. Then he remembered that theirs was a new listing, probably too recent for the current directory. So he consulted directory assistance, specifying "new listings." There was no such listing, the operator informed him in a nasal twang. He was baffled.

"Are you positive about that?" he asked.

"I'm sorry, sir, we have nothing."

"Wait. Maybe it's an unlisted number."

"I'm sorry, sir, I have no listing for an unlisted number."

It was nearing two in the afternoon, so Townsend didn't bother with the scenic route. He took I-35 north, exited onto the Shawnee Mission Parkway, and headed east to State Line. He followed Ward Parkway through the Country Club Plaza, then turned south on Main. Charlotte, he remembered vaguely, was somewhere off to the east. At Fifty-first Street he turned left, crossing three intersections before the road ended at Oak. Townsend went south to Fifty-second Street, then eastward again. To his relief, he soon spotted the street sign for Charlotte, and signaled for a left turn.

He slowed, then came to a standstill in the middle of the street. Charlotte didn't cut through to the north from Fifty-second Street. To the south, all of the addresses were greater than 5200. How the hell did he get to 5194?

Townsend drove around for ten more minutes, trying to find the 5100 block of Charlotte. From Troost to the east he was able to connect with westbound Fifty-first Street, but again Charlotte didn't cut through. The only habitation in the approximate vicinity was the R. A. Block Cancer Management Center, an unlikely residence for Doris and Jason Humphrey. The alternative candidate, on the corner of Fifty-second and Charlotte, was the Warkoczewski Observatory. Townsend flung a premonition from his mind.

Checking his glove compartment for a map, he found nothing other than old car registration forms, a crumpled first-aid auto emergency kit, a stained Chevrolet Nova owner's manual, and scattered debris. Aside from his wallet, of course, which he angrily snatched and crammed securely, almost punitively, into his right rear pocket. He made his way back to Troost and stopped at another gas station to spring for a street map.

"How the hell do I get to the fifty-one hundred block of Charlotte?" Townsend asked the attendant, taking the map and a quarter in change from the two bucks he had handed over.

"Ain't no fifty-one hundred block on Charlotte," replied the man, all skin and bones and grime. "Charlotte don't cut through. Not till bouts forty-ninth. Cancer observatory gits in the way."

"I see," said Townsend, looking at the map in his hands and rolling his tongue under the inside of his upper lip. He had gotten the picture. Doris Humphrey, whoever she was, had made off with his precious semen and disappeared without a trace.

11

YIELDING TO COMPULSIVE BEHAVIOR, BUT FULLY ANTICIPATING disappointment, Townsend stopped off at the Brookside Post Office en route home. He peeked through the small glass window of Box 169. The mail cubicle was empty. Surprise, no mail for Doris. Or was the box number another ruse?

He waited in line for a service window to become free.

"I'm interested in getting a P.O. box," he had told a diminutive, frosted-blond woman in her fifties. She cordially supplied him with a form.

"I was sort of hoping for the box that I had before," he went on. "It would make things a lot easier. I still have my old address inkstamp . . . and even some printed-up stationery." Lame sounding, but the worker probably heard equally lame requests all day. "Box 169. Is it available?"

The woman backstepped to a metal file cabinet and withdrew a card from one of the drawers.

"It's not available right at the moment," she said, "but unless it's extended, it will be free in just over a week."

"Damn," said Townsend. "Doris Humphrey still has it then. I'm sure she'll renew it."

The woman smiled. "Well," she replied, answering his question, "then again she might not, and we can put you on a wait list if you want to specifically request."

No need to squander his time on a stakeout. Townsend suspected Doris had procured the box as a backup, in case something were to be mailed from Howard's office. No doubt Doris was a cash customer, immediate payment for services rendered, explaining why no insurance carrier had been listed in her records. Townsend crumpled the form in a clenching fist as he walked back to his car.

His eyes burned as if he had been without sleep for days running and he felt a head pressure threatening to pop them from their sockets. The feeling had been a common one during his internship, sleepwalking through the stressful monotony of the hospital workdays, driven to the verge of a crying jag. In those days, exercise had been the only cure. Jogging, weight lifting, shooting hoops at the Indoor Athletic Building—anything to clear the head of its ensnaring cobwebs. Sex would do, too, on those rare instances when it was readily accessible. More often, though, what one had to go through to get it only exacerbated the problem.

Once home, after puttering aimlessly in the garden, spreading a couple of wheelbarrowsful of mulch around, Townsend overcame inertia and changed into his running clothes. It was nearing 5 p.m., and he had pondered the disappearance of Doris Humphrey since his failed tracking efforts of that afternoon. Anticipating that this might evolve into a run with a destination, he strapped on a fanny pack for his wallet and house keys. His route was uncharacteristic, along the main thoroughfare of Ward Parkway instead of cozy neighborhood side streets. He jogged unhurriedly toward the Country Club Plaza alongside rush hour traffic, then pointed himself beyond in the direction of the Mo State Performing Arts Center.

The excursion took just under half an hour, time well spent wallowing in self-pity. The Doris Humphrey affair, he concluded, was symbolic, a disruption serving to point out the purposelessness of his life. He was subsisting with little effort, sporadic moonlighting, no commitment. Medical career goals and professional drive had dissipated; only his personal life had been his ballast. That was a shambles now, and he was off balance, careening and teetering like a unicyclist with middle-ear problems. The harder he worked at getting back on track with Leslie, the worse things became. Given his circumstances, he couldn't give her the time and space she demanded, let alone support her efforts. His desire for kids—of late reaching a fevered pitch—was no more than an attempt to clip her wings. But Leslie Rosenthal had her own timetable and was not to be victimized. Doris Humphrey's uterus served only to mock him with bitter irony.

Townsend's self-image had taken it on the chin in another way. He had always viewed himself as a liberated male, taken great pride in his sensitivity and support of feminist issues. Leslie had nurtured him throughout his process of growth, throwing down gauntlets and refining her politically correct Pygmalion. As part of this personal evolution, he had come to ridicule those well-educated upper-middle-class men in the predictable relationship pickle: too demanding and intelligent to settle for bimbos, but not emotionally equipped to handle the alternative. The dilemma was terrible for the men, worse for the liberated women, and not altogether so hot for the bimbos, either. Townsend had considered himself immune. Now it appeared that he had never been tested.

He had jogged to the performing arts center on the off chance of catching Leslie at rehearsal. Maybe she wouldn't be too bone-tired to listen, to allow him some self-indulgent venting. More likely they would squabble at one another, but what was the alternative?

The lobby was deserted except for a munchkin of a woman in orthopedic shoes who was busily setting up photographs and other memorabilia in one of the display cases. Townsend brushed by her, catching the stenciled title of the exhibit: "Thirty Years of the Kansas City Dance Theatre." Underneath she had thumbtacked an eight-by-ten glossy of an artfully airbrushed and windblown Nigel Devon.

Townsend confidently opened the center doors into the theater and walked midway down the aisle before picking an end seat. Unlike his first sneak preview, this time he didn't feel the intruder. Didn't he belong, despite never having executed a *brisé* or a *battement?* After all, he shared a secret with Paul Gruenfeld, a choreographer of world renown. And he gave medical advice to Felicia Bradley, one of the hottest numbers in a leotard. Finally, he had come to the aid of that *enfant terrible* Gerard Moreau and nearly saved his life. Was it his fault that Gerard was vegetating in the ICU of St. Michael's?

The Gruenfeld rehearsal was in progress. Gruenfeld himself was seated in the front row, his demeanor a portrait of intensity. His company was running through *Outlaw,* the soon-to-premiere piece with a western theme. It was a semiabstract variation of the basic love triangle, with a misunderstood gunslinger Bret vying for the affection of Lilith, the classy broad from back east. The third corner was a law-abiding wimp named Willis, a dance version of the ineffectual Freddy from *My Fair Lady.* Leslie was one of a handful of townspeople, the local ensemble whose movements forboded what was to happen.

In truth, the dancers had not known exactly what they were forboding. Leslie had speculated about the ending with Townsend. Would Bret blow Freddy away, win Lilith back without using violence, or disappear into the sunset? It was Tuesday, and the premiere was on Friday, so Townsend sensed there would be an answer soon. The answer, in fact, was in the making.

Gruenfeld waved a hand and a male dancer manning the recorder stopped the tape.

"Okay, David," Gruenfeld rose from his seat and hopped onto the stage beside the gunslinger. "When you pull your gun out, extend your arm straight outward . . . not like that . . . exaggerate the motion, like drawing a sword from its scabbard. No economy of motion here, I want the full sweep. That's why I've got the holster on your left side. I want that sweep across your body. Forget realism here, just try it."

Gruenfeld guided the dancer through a series of steps, alternately counting, humming, clapping his hands for the rhythm.

"Better. Now, on that *ta-tum*—you know where I'm talking about?—that's where you do the *cabriole,* then you go into the turning combination that we worked on before, got it?"

The boy nodded his head in comprehension.

"But the key thing is," Gruenfeld continued to explain, "the key thing is to always keep that right arm extended and centered on Charles—Willis I mean—after each turn. Accent it! Ta-tum! You're grounded, home position, focused on his heart. Lunge out to the back *arabesque!* Really lunge! And again! And again! Arm extended, leg back!" He demonstrated the maneuver, punctuating his words with movement, David observing and nodding his head. Then the dancer looked perplexed.

"But what about during the turns? I don't get my right arm position—"

"Sweep it in, then extend it out again with each turn," Gruenfeld explained patiently. "But remember, always the drawing from the scabbard, that circular arm motion that pulls you around in the turn. Then you're grounded, focused on the heart, ta-tum!" Gruenfeld stamped his feet dramatically like a flamenco dancer, whipping his arm into extension. He took the gun from David and once again marked the steps. Not that long ago, Townsend realized, Bret would have been Paul's own role. From the way Paul Gruenfeld moved, no doubt he could still pull it off.

"Okay, let's mark it with the music," said Gruenfeld. As he was about to hand the prop to David, he reiterated. "At the heart!" He raised the gun straight upward, parallel to the floor, arm fully extended, pointing at Charles. There was a strange quiet among the dancers as they watched their mentor, transfixed. He seemed in an altered state, holding the gun perfectly still in the silence.

Townsend shivered in his seat. The image was as before: Paul Gruenfeld was in the balcony, hiding in the shadows, pointing the gun at Gerard Moreau.

Gruenfeld laughed abruptly, breaking the spell. "Except I did it wrong, didn't I? I forgot to pull it from the scabbard. Never straight up, always like a sword from the scabbard. Don't you forget." He handed David the gun, and jumped down from the stage back to his seat. "Okay, with the music."

Shortly thereafter, the ending was set. Bret rejects his past life of violence, dropping his gun to the ground and stoically heading into the sunset. Moved by his sacrifice, Lilith follows after him, leaving Willis behind in the dust, dumped but still alive. The nice-guy-finishes-last motif, always a crowd pleaser. The dancers applauded their leader after the final run-through and Paul Gruenfeld showed his appreciation with an understated, somber bow. Rehearsal ended on schedule.

Minutes before, Townsend recognized dancers from the Moreau Company milling around, helping themselves to the empty theater seats. When Gerard was alive, they would have kept their distance, waited out of sight to avoid crossing paths. But the battle had been between the directors, not the dancers themselves, and with Gerard out of the picture, there was no fight to be had. Besides, the situation in the Moreau Company was more than precarious; the working stiffs, deserters from the former enemy camp, might be begging Paul Gruenfeld for jobs in the near future.

Felicia casually made her entrance at the last minute, donning the long rehearsal skirt of a ballet matron. She carried a clipboard, clearly assuming the role of player-coach. Her blond hair was down and loose. She pointedly walked over to Paul, kissed him on the cheek, and had a few intimate words with him before his departure. Apparently the feud had ended for Felicia as well as her dancers. All seemed forgiven as mentor and protégée embraced. Gruenfeld left the hall in elevated spirits, spring in his step. He even acknowledged Townsend with a smile in passing.

Townsend stayed in his seat, hoping that Leslie would come to him. She had seen him there, all right, but was she going to make him jump through the hoops of trailing after her backstage? He saw her gather her things from the floor near the wings, and relieved, watched her make her way toward the aisle. Townsend, out of stubbornness, didn't budge.

"I was surprised to see you out here," she said.

"In the neighborhood. It's a great piece, by the way."

"Thanks, I think so, too."

Townsend licked his lower lip and took a good-sized breath.

"I was planning on some Chinese, and thought you might be hungry."

"I *am* hungry, but a group of us already made plans to go to Hoolihan's after rehearsal. It's Charles's birthday and we're going to have a little party."

"Oh." Townsend couldn't hide his disappointment.

"I don't think anyone would mind if you came along, though." Leslie wasn't overly encouraging. She didn't want him to rain on her parade and everyone else's.

He gauged the situation and his mental state. He was not up to the challenge, lousy company even for himself. He'd feel out of place and impatient, wanting to have Leslie to himself, wanting to monopolize her attention instead of bantering with a bunch of gypsies.

"Probably not a good idea," Townsend demurred, "but I'll see you on Friday. Did you arrange things with Janet?"

"All set."

"Great."

She smiled at him weakly, then turned around and headed backstage to join her cohorts. Back to her other friends, her other life, a life in which he shared no part. Townsend didn't know how to dance. He could identify with the music, the aesthetics, the athleticism of the movements, but he didn't know the lore or the history, didn't relate to the technique or the life-style. He couldn't conceive why dancers seemed so willing to victimize themselves. He didn't understand the inside jokes about the crazy Russian teachers that chain-smoked in their studios on the Upper West Side. But perhaps he was getting a firsthand glimmer of what it was like to live on the edge.

Townsend stayed in his seat, oppressed by fatigue. He wasn't hungry. He had nowhere to go, and nothing better to do than stay and watch the rehearsal of what was left of the Gerard Moreau Company and the newest piece in the repertory, *Desdemona*. How would they manage now that Hamlet had exited the stage before his cue?

The rehearsal was somber and businesslike. Gerard had been replaced by a handsome boy named Erik Crumm, a rising star plucked from the anonymity of the ranks of the corps. Felicia was gentle in her dealings with him, almost intimate, and Townsend wondered if they were lovers.

The postponement of their premiere to the following week had taken some of the heat off; Felicia spent most of the time running through portions already set by Gerard instead of breaking new ground. Erik lacked the passion and presence of Gerard, but did a credible job technically. Felicia was saving her energy, marking her part, never dancing full out. Townsend was amazed at seeing her so subdued and vulnerable, but imagined the fire was temporarily dampened, not extinguished.

The session ended with a whimper, even before their allotted time was up, an energy drain taking possession of each member of the company simultaneously. Intensity and commitment faded until they seemed at a standstill, despite the continued movement through space of body parts. Like leaves tossing in the wind, trapped in vortices, they were disoriented and unclear of their direction.

"We'll pick things up where we left off tomorrow," said a drained Felicia Bradley. She bore them no malice.

Felicia flashed a blank glance at Townsend as she stepped off the stage, then plopped down, rather unelegantly, into a front-row seat. No one came to comfort her, either lacking desire or out of fear. Erik hesitated on stage as if he were about to come forward, thought better of it, and proceeded backstage.

The two of them were alone in the house. Townsend pushed himself out of his seat, walked down the aisle, and sat down beside her.

"I'm terribly sorry about Gerard," he said.

"Thank you." She turned and looked at him intently, eyes welling with tears. At that moment, Townsend doubted that he had ever seen a more beautiful woman than Felicia Bradley.

"He's really gone, isn't he?" She was looking down at her bare, heavily calloused feet. The feet did not belong to a beautiful woman; they were like the coarse, roughened appendages of a physical laborer.

"Unfortunately, yes."

"I haven't told the company yet . . . I've been afraid to. I'm not really sure they have the confidence in me. But I suppose they haven't any choice." She took a deep breath. "The doctors are keeping him going artificially until Thursday; they're waiting to do a special transplant. I signed the release."

"I know."

Felicia seemed surprised. "How did you know that?"

"Friends at the hospital have been keeping me posted. It's a little Hispanic kid with bad liver failure. He can't hold out much longer. Gerard's liver will save his life."

She nodded, then rubbed her forehead with the palm of her hand.

"Is there anything I can do for you, Felicia? Business, shopping, errands of any kind?"

"That's sweet of you to ask, but you're doing fine. Sit here with me awhile, doctor."

They sat for a moment in silence.

"I can't do this," she finally said. "The dancers know it and I know it. It's like a joke with no punch line. You keep going on and on with the story, and there's no point to it. The entire exercise is a waste of time."

"*Desdemona* is almost finished, anyway, isn't it?" Townsend asked. He wanted to console her, but was also curious. He felt the pangs of guilt that accompany insincerity.

"It's not working. Gerard knew how to make it work. If I can't even finish this up, how could I ever tackle something like *Metamorphoses?*"

"You're just depressed. How can you expect to go on with this business after what's happened? Take it easy on yourself."

"I'm not sure you understand dance . . . what this is all about."

"I've heard that before. Maybe you and Paul could join forces again."

"It's a consideration," she replied. "I just can't believe Gerard's not in the picture anymore."

"What was your relationship with him like?"

The question was blunt. Felicia looked at him sharply and raised her eyebrows.

Townsend demurred. "I'm not meaning to pry . . . it's just I don't understand . . . you two . . . how it was."

"We used each other," she said, statement of fact.

Townsend tried to soften the blow with a mealymouthed "we all use each other in relationships, to one degree or another."

"No, no," Felicia corrected emphatically. "I mean really *use*. Exploit. Mutual exploitation, nothing more."

"You didn't love him at all?"

Felicia shook her head, an impatient, nonverbal "you're not getting it."

"I loved his talent," she said. "I loved him for what he could do for me, what he could transform me into with movement. I loved his pieces."

"And there wasn't anything physical?"

"He was gay, for Chrissake!"

Townsend let that one sink in. He was stunned, more so by his own naiveté than anything else.

"You mean you never slept with him?" He was baffled, uncomprehending. "I don't get it," he added, not waiting for her reply. "He must have been bisexual, right?"

"Did I sleep with him? Yes, I did once, long ago, before we were married. But only that one time. He could go through the motions, if there was a need, if there was something in it for him. It was a dirty job, but somebody had to do it, you know? That's hardly bisexual in my book. It certainly wasn't his preference."

"What was in it for him? With you, I mean."

"A green card, for starters."

"Oh, I see." Townsend tried to recoup, he didn't want to seem a complete imbecile. "I knew Paul Gruenfeld was gay."

"Of course, that's no secret."

"So," said Townsend, "both of these homosexual men were jousting over you. Don't get me wrong, I'm no homophobe or anything, I'm just trying to understand all this. Both of them fighting over you. It's a twist for me, that's all." He sounded stupid, even to himself. And he was shaken because this misjudgment forced him into a reevaluation of all his perceptions.

"I was the object of desire, all right, just not a sexual one," said Felicia, reflexively giving her blond hair the toss of a shampoo cover girl. "I was the instrument they needed to fulfill an artistic vision. Nothing against sex, believe me, but sex is of this world. It's irrelevant in the realm of the spiritual, as far as their art was concerned. We're talking a different level here."

"It's hard to fathom," Townsend responded, straining in his thoughts.

"Don't apologize for your heterosexual perspective. But even you had your chance with me and chose to pass. Still I'm flattered, Dr. Reeves—and nothing against your intelligence, but I imagine you'd make a pretty lousy choreographer."

The ambling dancers on stage were gradually coalescing into a troupe. Their mentor, an elderly woman who wore her completely gray long hair tied back in the ponytail of youth, had clapped her hands irritably to announce the beginning of rehearsal.

"I can't sit through this; I can't stomach Frieda Ekstein's stuff." Felicia stood up to leave, tucking her clipboard away under her arm.

Townsend bolted up alongside her.

"She's a museum piece." Felicia was talking in a normal tone, either oblivious to listening ears, or intentionally wanting the object of her scorn to be privy to their conversation. "She belongs back in Denishawn where she started. I'm depressed enough as it is."

Townsend glanced to the stage—if the old lady choreographer had heard anything, she wasn't letting on. Maybe, gratefully, she was partially deaf.

"My things are backstage," said Felicia.

Townsend felt awkward. He wasn't sure if he should stay with her, if he had overstayed his welcome.

"You had dinner?" he ventured cautiously.

"I'd love to," she replied, managing a smile. "I'll meet you in the lobby."

12

THE DISPLAY CASES PROMOTING THIRTY YEARS OF the Kansas City Dance Theatre were finished; the gnomelike balletomane had departed after locking the memorabilia behind sliding glass panels. Townsend killed time by browsing, looking at the progression of photos, pictures of faces and bodies that meant nothing to him.

"Ready?"

Startled, Townsend turned around. Felicia stood right behind him, having crossed the carpeted lobby soundlessly in her open-toed sandals. Her hair was still down. She had changed into loose-fitting beige linen trousers and an oversized lavender silk blouse, the two uppermost buttons unfastened. He marveled at how, despite the looseness of her clothes, the exquisite form managed to reveal itself beneath the folds. There was a profound irony in that, considering the millions of women who inconsiderately inflicted their unfit bodies upon the world through spandex.

"What are you looking at?" she asked.

"A pictorial history of the Kansas City Dance Theatre. Thirtieth anniversary."

"Believe me," she said, looking at some of the pictures, "they look much better in still photos than they do when moving."

"I'm no judge of dance," Townsend said diplomatically, not wanting to provoke a harangue.

"You know what you like, don't you?" Felicia was moving

along the length of the display case, continuing to peruse the photographs.

"I suppose."

"Then you're as much—," she stopped in mid-sentence, pressed her face nearly to the glass to examine a particular picture.

"—as much as an expert as anyone else," she finished absently. She was scanning the display purposefully now, a more directed search for something in particular. She squatted and scrutinized a photograph in the lowermost corner of the second case.

Townsend shrugged. "Food I do know something about, however. How does Chinese sound?"

Felicia didn't respond.

"Chinese sound okay to you?" he repeated.

"What? Oh . . . fine . . . anything's fine." She lingered in her crouch for a few seconds, then suddenly popped up. Townsend heard her knees crack.

"Shall we go then?" she said, snapped from her reverie.

Townsend's car being at his house presented a logistical problem. He proposed two options: taxi to a restaurant directly, then separate taxis home; or taxi to his house, where he could change clothes before driving them to a restaurant in his own car. Felicia proposed a third option: phone ahead order to the House of Toy, call a taxi and pick up the food on the way to his house. Casual home dining. Potential implications left unstated. Take out and eat in. Take in and eat out. House of Toying.

Townsend was a rock.

"Fine," he said, casting his vote for the third option and making it unanimous.

Townsend was heavy-handed with the order—moo shu pork, shrimp and scallops in brown sauce, almond chicken, fried rice, egg rolls, wonton soup—figuring he was in no frame of mind to cook for the next couple of days and the leftovers would tide him over. He had nearly forgotten about the pressure in his head. After picking up the takeout, he asked the cabbie to stop at a

Berbiglia's, where he purchased a fairly decent bottle of Pouilly-Fuissé. Maybe he could convert a stress headache to a hangover headache and feel less neurotic about his symptoms.

Felicia was duly impressed with Townsend's house. It was small but a gem, well kept and with fine interior detail work. He and Leslie had refinished all the wood floors themselves. They had also stripped and varnished the cherry wainscoting in the living and dining rooms, which had been painted over by previous owners. The entryway was marble, with an antique cut glass chandelier. Felicia nodded her approval silently upon entering, taking in the house and the man.

Don't make assumptions, Townsend warned her silently. The home reflected more of Leslie than it did of him. Her color schemes, her arrangements, her taste. Some of the furnishings had been purchased by them together at antique shops, yard sales, junk shops, estate sales. Still, Townsend always deferred to Leslie's judgment; her buying instincts were infallible. Leslie's imprint was on virtually everything, and each piece had its own history, a marker of their relationship and their life for seven years together.

The nesting tables were from Thailand, but were more significant as a memento of a trip to New Orleans. Leslie had discovered the small Victorian loveseat—all horsehair and straw pouring out from it—in the loft of a barn in Stanley, Kansas. The stained glass was salvaged by her from a demolition site. She had painstakingly removed the old varnish from the Queen Anne highboy in the corner with a toothbrush. Function was irrelevant; the pieces served as a chronicle in wood, fabric, and glass.

All that truly belonged to Townsend were the gilt-framed eighteenth- and early-nineteenth-century British medical caricatures that lined the living room walls. Leslie always thought them gross but had indulged him. He felt comfortable with depictions of the foibles of doctors; they made a statement about the presumptions of medicine, past and present. They also expressed the ambivalence about his occupation that would come and go with some unpredictable internal psychological rhythm.

147

"Lovely," said Felicia.

She self-assuredly walked from the vestibule directly into the living room without hesitation, leaving Townsend to fend for himself with the bags of food and wine. She was accustomed to being waited on. He went into the kitchen and set the packages down on the counter, already feeling remorse. Felicia Bradley, through no real fault of her own, was violating Leslie Rosenthal's space, intruding upon their intimate domain. He resolved that he couldn't sleep with her, not under that roof. It felt a sacrilege. Having decided that, for the moment, he would digest his food better.

The red light on the answering machine was blinking once, and out of habit, Townsend pressed the playback before going any further with dinner.

The voice was Tony Mauro's.

"It's me. Uh . . . sorry I haven't gotten back to you sooner. I checked the room out like you asked, since I'm such a nice guy. You owe me, doc. Uh . . . the report from the toxicologist showed mainly cocaine in Moreau's blood, and not the metabolite, Benzyl-lega something, I got it written down here [rustling of pages, pause]. *It don't matter.*

"What it means . . . uh . . . and I don't need to be explaining this to you—the cocaine wasn't broken down, which goes along with sudden death from the cocaine. There it is. So I didn't bother submitting the powder from the tabletop since it would have to go to the State Patrol Crime Lab for analysis and it would take at least two months, maybe more. And for what? So I'd use up a lot of favors with those guys and still end up looking like an asshole? Everything else looks clean, and there won't be any official investigation, in case you're still wondering. I do this for a living, remember.

So . . . uh . . . that's about it. You owe me one, like I said. I've been thinkin' 'bout those dancer friends of Leslie, and maybe . . . uh . . . I'd be up for that if you can work somethin' out. It's the least you can do. That's all. Good-bye."

The message didn't tell Townsend anything he didn't already know from Peter Weinberg, other than the fact that cocaine analysis was under the purview of the State Crime Lab, not the toxicologist's office. Tony had done his best. Doctored cocaine had been a long shot anyway. All his suspicions were farfetched, the more he thought about them.

Townsend rewound the answering machine tape. When he turned around, Felicia was standing rigidly in front of him. Her look was all business.

"What's this all about?"

Townsend could see the muscles of her jaw either working or quivering. His ploy was to play coy and casual. The usual.

"You heard the message? Just a friend of mine. Happens to be a cop. We go way back."

"What's this all about?" she repeated.

"I had some questions," he said flatly. "I wondered if maybe Gerard had been intentionally given some bad dope. It was just a notion, and I thought this friend of mine could just check it out."

"That's ridiculous! And what makes it any business of yours?"

Townsend shrugged like an idiot.

"Why would anyone want to hurt Gerard?"

Townsend shrugged like an idiot's dumber brother.

"Let's eat," he lamely suggested. He went back into the kitchen for two glasses, two plates and bowls, a corkscrew, and the fancy set of chopsticks.

For several uncomfortable moments, the silence was punctuated only by the soft crunching of water chestnuts. Townsend had set up shop on the dining room table. No tablecloth, just placemats. No classical music CD as background accompaniment. He didn't bother with candlelight either.

Already he had indigestion. And the headache was back. He hoped it was the initial rush of MSG.

Felicia swirled a small scallop around in the brown sauce with her chopsticks, as if she were trying to drown it. She set her chopsticks down. "Why did you get a policeman involved?" she asked.

"Hardly involved," Townsend said. "You're making too much of it." He had already gone through this rigmarole with Leslie, so he felt more rehearsed with his offhandedness. He coolly folded the pancake over the moo shu pork, making it into a tidy, tight package. It could only have been neater had he been able to use military corners.

"I don't mean that," Felicia clarified. "I mean *why?* Why were you suspicious in the first place?"

There was no reason not to confide in her, at least up to a point. He left out any mention of Paul Gruenfeld. He did explain that he thought he had resuscitated Gerard in time. He even mentioned the military corners, or, rather, the lack of them, on Gerard's bed. Felicia didn't bristle the way Mauro had upon hearing the latter observation.

"Gerard never made a bed in his life," she said.

"There you have it," said Townsend.

Felicia tapped her index finger rapidly against her lips.

"It didn't have to be intentional," Townsend went on. "Maybe Gerard was with somebody, they were doing the coke together, Gerard has a bad reaction, his companion panics and splits. Maybe someone was afraid they could be prosecuted for giving him the dope."

"Seems to me that the companion . . . or whoever . . . would clean up the powder before bothering to make the bed," said Felicia, echoing Mauro's previous line of reasoning.

Townsend had by now thought one step beyond.

"And turn a cut-and-dried overdose into a suspicious death?"

Felicia picked up her chopsticks. "In that case, if it were an accident, it really doesn't matter, does it?"

"You know where the powder came from?" Townsend asked casually, reinforcing the desired tone by picking up the wrapped pancake and bringing it to his mouth. The effect worked better than expected, since the bottom gave way and the entire filling spilled out onto his plate.

"You dropped your pork."

"Not to worry, I'm covered. Catastrophic moo shu insurance. You know where the powder came from?"

"I'm not my brother's keeper."

"When I was over at your place, you offered me a snort. Was Gerard using your stuff?"

"I don't think that's any of your business," Felicia said sharply. "And no, it wasn't my stuff. Gerard and I didn't share much of anything except dance."

"Where did you get yours?"

"I beg your pardon?"

"Your cocaine. Where did you get it?"

"I heard you, and I still don't think it's any of your business."

Townsend shrugged. "Don't get me wrong," he said, "I'm just thinking of your own well-being. If you got the stuff from the same supplier you might be careful, that's all."

"I appreciate your concern," she said coldly.

The conversation had roadblocked, but Townsend sensed that Felicia didn't object to the subject. She was as curious as he was, if not more so. He took a different route.

"Gerard do a lot of coke?" he asked.

"A reasonable amount."

"Addicted? That's not the right way to put it—was he more of a social user, or was he high a lot of the time? How about when he was choreographing?"

Felicia had calmed down enough to have some semblance of an appetite. She took her time in swallowing what was in her mouth.

"Heavy social. He was never high making dances. He never came to a rehearsal stoned. Lord knows he was tightly strung enough without any help. He'd bounce off the walls on coke. No one would be able to work with him. In that sense he could control his habit enough that I wouldn't call him addicted. No, he wasn't addicted. But he might do some coke alone, during the planning phases of a new piece, when he was trying to get inspired."

"You think it would be in character for him to get high right before a banquet that was more or less in his honor? I mean, a lot of people were going to be there, the press; they were going to announce this big grant and such . . . would he come to that high?"

"I wouldn't think so, normally," Felicia said slowly. She pushed a stray strand of blond hair behind her ear. "But this wasn't normal, was it? It wasn't every day that he'd be pulling in half a million to indulge his fancy. Maybe he was having an early celebration. The papers were signed, the grant—all the money— was a done deal. What did he care if the press or Rosie Van Buren saw him stoned?"

"So he'd celebrate by himself?"

"Philip and I had already left—we went to the coffee shop. In the hotel."

"So you—you and Philip—didn't celebrate with him before-hand? You'd think that the three of you would celebrate after the papers were signed." Townsend had rebuilt his moo shu pork pancake and gingerly took the first modest bite.

"That wouldn't have necessarily been politic. I'm not sure it would have been wise to offer Philip Van Buren a line. He might have disapproved, who knows?"

"You offered me some," countered Townsend, "and I dis-approved."

"I didn't want to sleep with Philip Van Buren," responded Felicia.

"You could have had some champagne," suggested Townsend, passing on her remark.

"No one thought of it," she replied.

"But everyone was in good spirits?"

"Philip was excited, Gerard and I were relieved. But even half a million doesn't change things. Gerard still had all the pressure over the piece, he'd been real tense, more driven than I'd ever seen him. And demons can't be bought off, no matter the price."

"Okay." Townsend was trying to keep things on track. He reiterated. "So you were there for the signing of the documents, you and Philip leave for coffee, and Gerard does cocaine all by himself."

"Maybe, like you said earlier, he was celebrating with someone else."

"Right. Any ideas who that might be?"

"Not offhand. If he'd hooked up with someone particular at the festival, I wasn't aware of it."

"But certainly not some corps girl, like you suggested the night we found him. You mentioned it twice, as I recall."

"For public consumption," she said, looking down at her plate, "Gerard chased skirts. It's just a little charade we had to play."

"Eggroll?" asked Townsend.

Felicia declined and he put it down on his own plate. He leaned over to top off her wineglass without asking. He felt obliged to refill his own. Otherwise, according to collegiate etiquette, it could be construed as plying some innocent young thing with drink.

"What's with the twenty questions?" she asked.

"You don't have to play," Townsend replied.

"I don't understand you. Why are you so interested?"

Townsend sipped his wine. "I'm not all that interested, it's just a puzzle."

"You mean you like puzzles, like some amateur detective?"

"Exactly the opposite. I hate puzzles. All of them—games, cards, crosswords, anything. They bother me. Ambiguity upsets my world order. I want puzzles solved only so I can go on with my life and not obsess about them. Purely self-defense. More almond chicken?"

"A little bit."

Townsend served her.

"I've actually got quite a headache," she said.

"Same here. Probably the MSG. Want an aspirin or Tylenol?"

"Maybe in a while." She poked around her plate with her chopsticks, then took a sampling of the recently procured helping.

"There's a ton of this stuff left over—"

"You can take some with you—"

Felicia shook her head, waving off the offer, then gave a slight grimace.

"What is it?"

"Nothing," she said, picking up her napkin. "A bad almond—rotten. Really bitter." She picked out the offending portion off her tongue with her fingers, set it in her napkin, then balled up the napkin. She gently dappled her lips with the rounded napkin.

Townsend felt light-headed, as if the alcohol in the wine had abruptly kicked in. Then he felt something more visceral, a total body rush, and not altogether a pleasant experience. He felt detached, his mind and heart suddenly racing.

"What did you say?" his voice was quavering. He had heard what she had said, had made the connection, and was already well beyond it. The question was more out of reflex than anything else.

"Just a rotten almond," she said, again dabbing her lips.

She had also said "bitter," which together with "almond" formed a medical catchphrase. It fell together in a torrent. He had offered her a Tylenol for her headache. Bitter almonds went with Tylenol like arsenic went with old lace. He flashed back to the CPR, that undesirable smell from Gerard's lips. He hadn't placed it then, only remembering that it was pungent. It hadn't been the odor of alcohol, nor was it the scent of ketones that he had been so familiar with from diabetic patients. It was, in fact, an odor that he had never actually smelled before. Which all explained why Townsend's efforts at resuscitation had failed. And the CT, of course the CT. The surprising finding of massive brain edema despite the brief passage of time. There was an article about that somewhere, and he was going to track it down.

"I . . . I'm not feeling well," said Townsend, rising from the table. Indeed he looked suddenly taken ill. "Maybe I can take you back to the Fairmont now."

"Don't bother, I can call a cab." Felicia scooted the chair back and stood up.

"No, I'd like to take you. I have to go out anyway. I have to stop by the hospital for a while. You're right on the way."

Felicia looked at him with interest, trying to comprehend the mood change.

"Well, I've certainly had less interesting evenings, doctor. Maybe we'll do it again sometime."

Townsend nodded, going through the social motions. His head pounded. He felt as if he might throw up. Was this the pure joy of finding a piece to a puzzle?

Gerard Moreau had been poisoned, that much Townsend knew. He also knew that for the time being he wouldn't say a damn thing about it.

13

TOWNSEND'S ALARM WENT OFF AT 6 A.M. on Wednesday. Without getting out of bed, he dialed the precinct from his nightstand phone. He couldn't recall if he had actually slept that night, since his dreams—were they real dreams or nighttime daydreams?—had been vivid, confused, and bizarre. He seemingly spent hours in the limbo between sleep and wakefulness, a fitful surreal night in the purgatory of consciousness.

"Is Lieutenant Mauro there yet?" he asked, knowing damn well that he wasn't. He'd have found it hard not to play straight with Tony on the other end.

"Oh." He tried to sound disappointed when the dispatcher responded that the lieutenant wasn't due in for nearly two hours. Could she take a message?

"Yes, please, if it isn't too much trouble," he began. "Tell him that Dr. Townsend Reeves called and that a ticket for the Friday night performance—seven o'clock at the Missouri State Performing Arts Center—is being held for him at the box office. And . . . uh . . . tell him that if I don't catch up with him beforehand, I'll meet him by the display cases in the lobby at the intermission. Got that?"

"And," he added, "I think he has a suit jacket of mine—I hope so, anyway—but tell him not to bother to bring it. I'll wear another suit."

"And one more thing . . . tell him to dress . . . uh . . . nicely. We've got plans afterward. He'll know what I mean."

The dispatcher read back the message nearly verbatim, then, after the last sentence, chuckled and added on her own:

"Does that mean he shouldn't wear his safari jacket?"

"No safari, no safari jacket," replied Townsend, cracking a smile. "Tell him to dress as if he were going to a wedding . . . or a funeral."

"I thought you said 'No safari jacket,' " she retorted. Her laugh was big and robust. Townsend had never met this dispatcher, to his knowledge, but by her voice he envisioned her as a husky black woman, a Leontyne Price in cop garb. Obviously she got away with irreverence toward her superiors. He made a mental note to ask Tony, just out of curiosity. That is, after Tony was through blowing his top.

He hung up the phone and rolled onto his back in bed and stared at the ceiling. Withholding information from Tony was tantamount to lying. But he couldn't be expected to drop such a bombshell with a dispatcher, could he? Was it Townsend's fault if Mauro wasn't at his desk first thing in the morning? Besides, he was procrastinating more than actually lying.

What would he do with himself for the next forty-eight hours, living alone with his secret? He'd get by. He'd mulch the garden, he'd jog, he'd wander about the Nelson Gallery. He'd drop by the post office on Brookside to check out Doris Humphrey's mailbox every now and again. And he might even call the job placement service to line up some relief work. He wouldn't be so choosy from now on. He'd go to Iowa if need be.

Townsend was acutely aware of how badly he needed a job. If he had one, though, he'd be too tired that morning to go into work anyway. His eyes still burned and he was hung over. A factitious hangover, certainly not from a measly glass or two of wine, but it felt as bad—even worse—than the real thing. His brain felt like a tangled mass of short-circuiting wires. His thoughts were ordered only to the extent that they were confined to the same heap.

After dropping Felicia off at the Fairmont—yet another awkward moment, a mirror-image of his most recent partings from

Leslie, as if all his relationships with women had fallen into some perverse, repetitive groove—Townsend had gone to St. Michael's. He again breezed past the security guards with a nod of recognition, but getting into the library late at night could have been another matter. First he tried to track down Peter Weinberg or any other resident he knew. No success. Fortunately, he didn't need a chaperon, as the access code on the library door had not been changed since he had taken his leave of absence. Three cups of watered-down hospital machine coffee and two hours later he had found everything he needed. One item in particular—a 1987 article in the journal *Radiology* from Harborview Medical Center in Seattle—he even Xeroxed for Tony.

Unless there was a change in schedule, he'd give the reprint to Tony on Friday. Until then, there was a stretch of ennui to endure, and he had to face it all by himself. The prospect was not a pleasant one.

Deluding himself, he rolled over on his side and forced his eyes shut. They burned as much closed as they did open. He lifted up his head and flipped the pillow to get to the cold side. He eyed the bedside clock: 6:06 A.M. He cursed and shifted to his other side. If only he could get back to sleep, he might be able to kill a couple of hours.

Immediately he felt as if an overheated alien had taken possession of his body, slipped beneath his skin. He felt a rush of heat, felt the opening of his pores. There followed a chill to the bone, and Townsend Reeves discovered himself drenched in sweat, sticking to the sheets.

"Nice suit, Tony," Townsend said.

Mauro smiled smugly. "I ain't no rube," he said. "You can take me places, you know?"

It was intermission. As planned, they had met each other in the lobby by the display cases commemorating Nigel Devon's Kansas City Dance Theatre.

"I looked for ya earlier, before the show started," said Mauro.

"Me too," lied Townsend. He had waited outside, lying low,

until nearly 7:30. He had spotted Mauro through the glass doors and ducked behind a large juniper. Then he had sneaked to his seat after the houselights had flickered and the lobby had cleared. Had he cut it any closer, the usher would have turned him away and forced him to wait out the Lubovitch piece in the lobby. His procrastination had delayed the inevitable only for the duration of the two pieces performed by the Lubovitch Company and the KC Dance Theatre.

"What do you think so far?" Townsend asked, unable to break his news. He yearned for a suitable transition point in the conversation, but what were the chances that small talk would turn to death?

"Not bad," Mauro said noncommittally. "Some great-looking babes, though. But skinny, you know."

"You want some coffee or wine? There's also some brownies and cookies over there." He indicated the concession area.

"Line's too long," said Mauro. "How about this fix-up you arranged?"

"Right. Well, her name's Janet Crosby, and she'll be dancing in the next piece. There's six corps girls—"

"Core?"

"Corps de ballet. Regular army, not the top brass."

"Gotcha."

"It's a piece called *Outlaw*. Both Leslie and Janet play townspeople. Janet's got light brown hair, and she's not as skinny as the rest of the gals in town. I think you'll be able to pick her out."

"Sounds great. Not as skinny, huh? But not fat, either?"

"Definitely not fat, Tony."

"Hey, that's great. You done good. You really like this suit?" He tugged at the lapels.

"Nice suit, Tony."

Townsend, starting to sweat, rubbed his mouth with the palm of his hand. Mauro was ebullient, and Townsend was reluctant to break the mood. But there was no way getting around it; intermission was almost half over. He tried to be as direct as possible, given the circumstances.

"You got a quarter on you?" he asked the cop.

"Dunno." He made to reach into his pocket. "Why?"

"I think you may need to make a phone call."

Mauro's face clouded. He had recognized that Reeves was acting a little strangely, but he wrote it off to problems on the home front, Leslie related. Instinctively he knew there was more to it. Reeves hadn't hounded him, had been content just to leave a message earlier that week instead of speaking with him directly. Mauro was a good enough cop to recognize a pattern.

"Spill," he said, totally deadpan.

"Maybe we should walk over this way a bit," Townsend said, nudging him away from other patrons hanging around the display case. It was difficult finding a pocket of relative privacy, so Townsend led him through the doors to outside, heading left down the sidewalk to the large juniper he had hidden behind earlier. It was just beginning to get dark, and the evening air was muggy. Townsend faced Mauro while nervously tugging at a prickly sprig of the bush.

"Tell me you're not going to ruin this evening for me," said Mauro.

"Well . . ."

"Shit," said Mauro.

"All you have to do . . . all you *can* do for now, really . . . is make a phone call," said Townsend.

"What phone call?" Mauro's voice was rising.

"You just have to call someone at the precinct and get the state toxicologist to run cyanide levels on some of the original serum drawn from Gerard Moreau."

Mauro closed his eyes for a three count.

"Any particular reason?" He was restraining himself, about to burst, like someone winded from a recent sprint trying to breathe at a normal rate.

"Just that it'll be positive. I suspect a concentration of somewhere in the neighborhood of two milligrams per liter. And if that white powder is still around, you might want that checked out for traces of cyanide as well. That might take longer, I realize now, given the State Crime Lab's turnaround."

"Cyanide," repeated Mauro.

Townsend was avoiding eye contact now. He squished the juniper sprig between his thumb and first two fingers, rubbed them together, then brought his fingers under his nose to smell them. Then he put his hand in his pocket.

"Right."

"And this is just some wild-assed hunch of yours?"

"I think you might want to take my advice on this one."

"I guess," the cop began, "I'd be asking too much if I just wanted to know how in the hell you came up with this cockamamie idea, right?"

"Not at all, Tony. I'm prepared to explain it all—I even have an article here for you—" He tapped his breast coat pocket. ". . . except it might take some time and intermission is almost over and you probably want to make that call first. There's a pay phone in the lobby."

"Son-of-a-bitch," Mauro muttered, whipping around in disgust and jogging back to the theater entry. He was opening the heavy plate-glass door with his left hand, his right was wriggling furiously about deep in his pocket. He stopped short, grimaced, and relaxed his grip on the door handle. The door slowly swung to. Mauro purposefully walked back to where Townsend waited, his muscles of mastication working in a grinding overtime.

"Gimme a fucking quarter, asshole."

By then, Townsend Reeves already had tossed the sprig and held the coin in the palm of his hand.

From an aisle seat near the middle of the house, Townsend saw Mauro returning to the front row just as the lights were dimming for the second half of the performance. Mauro was craning his neck as he walked, trying to spot Townsend in the crowd. Townsend caught his eye and wriggled his fingers in a coy wave. Mauro thrust his chin out with determined restraint and plopped down into his seat, crossing his arms tightly against his chest like a stubborn child. Townsend could see the stretch of

Mauro's jacket fabric, challenged by the bulging deltoids and *latissimus dorsi* underneath. If the public servant crossed his arms any tighter, the seams would bust apart. Townsend was counting on the mystique of Terpsichore to soothe the savage breast. And if that didn't work, maybe Janet Crosby could help.

Townsend couldn't maintain interest in the dance, a brooding abstract number performed by the Frieda Ekstein Company. He had never seen the company's work before, and sharing Felicia's opinion, wasn't all that impressed. He tried to remember the name of the piece, then attempted to read it from the program, but the lighting was too dim. Giving up, he set the program under his seat, closed his eyes, and leaned his head back, willing the music to take him somewhere else. The music was unmelodic, dissonant, and pretentious, and the recording was of such poor quality that the crackles and pops were freshly cut hairs under the collar, crumbs on fresh linens. Fortunately, the cultural torture would last only fifteen minutes or so; then Leslie would be on.

His mind wandered to the toiletries on the bathroom counter of Gerard's hotel room. If the cyanide turned out not to be in the cocaine, how had it been administered? Maybe the cocaine was a red herring after all. Who would be stupid enough to leave residual traces of poison in clear view? But on the other hand, if no one suspected foul play, who would even bother to analyze the adulterated drug? Was that a reasonable risk for a murderer to take?

Townsend strained, trying to re-create the mental picture. It was impossible. Somewhere among the electrical connections in his brain, the image of those few seconds was indelibly imprinted. But they had been chosen for burial because some other, more dominant connections in his cerebrum had deemed them inconsequential at the time.

Townsend casually flexed his neck forward to check on the progress on stage. A kneeling woman was spotlit center stage. Four other women were doing a swaying *arabesque* combination in a large circle around her. They alternated coming toward the center, interacting in a stylized manner, momentarily sharing the principal dancer's place in the sun. The process was boring, dragged out. Townsend had gotten the picture after the second girl had repeated the movements of the first. He watched with mounting annoyance as the third girl went through the same motions. It was filler, serving no purpose that he could discern. Choreographic laziness masquerading as artful repetition of a theme. *Dreck,* as Leslie might say.

But the fourth girl surprised him. Not that her movements were any different from those preceding, not that she executed them with a higher degree of proficiency. She surprised him, rather stunned him, by her very being.

Townsend's throat constricted and his entire body jerked involuntarily at the sight of her.

Doris Humphrey gracefully moved out of the spotlight.

Townsend jumped from his seat and fled up the dark aisle in a crouching run. Once back in the lobby, he crossed to the farthest entrance on the left aisle and reentered. He walked the entire length of the outermost aisle before coming to a blackout curtain; past that, a door a few feet away. He walked quickly up a short flight of uncarpeted, concrete stairs. The backstage door was open, and no one was there to stop him.

The enormousness of the wings and backstage area surprised him, reminding him of a darker, compressed version of the basketball arenas of his youth. Sets, props, and bodies, some busily occupied, most not or else in transit, milled about. No one paid him any mind. He couldn't escape the irritating musical score, but at least it was muffled. Through the tiers of black curtains he could glimpse a limited geometric portion of stage, the space intermittently violated by one of several moving bodies. For an instant he saw Doris flutter across his restricted vision.

It dawned on him that Leslie could turn up at any minute. He looked at his watch. Probably ten or twelve more minutes left in the piece. Was his ex still in her dressing room, or was she somewhere in the wings with him, concealed in the darkness?

He back-stepped into the nearest corner and tried to pull in the reins on his runaway thoughts. What in the hell was he doing? Would he confront Doris as soon as she made her exit? A bit obtrusive that, and subject to the risk that Leslie might see him there. He shuddered at the thought of that scene, explaining his presence to Leslie, his bizarre relationship with a Frieda Ekstein dancer. No doubt Doris would be as mortified as Leslie. No, the safest plan was to wait the piece out, allow time for the Gruenfeld Company to get on stage, then make his way to the dressing rooms. With any luck, he could catch Doris coming or going while Leslie was occupied under the lights.

But a community dressing room wasn't ideal for a confrontation with Doris. What would he say? Ask her why she lied about her address and phone number? What business was it of his anyway? Was he prepared to spill the fact that he had already spilled once for her? Definitely not, he couldn't do that any more than he could confess the business to Leslie.

His behavior was impulsive and ill-advised; he had focused so much on finding Doris that he hadn't really considered the next step. Clearly, the meeting would have to seem accidental, a fortuitous encounter.

What a coincidence! I just happened to be loitering backstage here, and who do you think I run into? Why, Mrs. Humphrey, the last time I saw you, you were in stirrups! Isn't life just a hoot!

Townsend did some serious reassessing. The sensible thing was to go back to his seat, watch the rest of the performance, then spend the evening as planned with Leslie, Tony, and Janet. He had the line on Doris Humphrey; undoubtedly she was in residence with the Ekstein Company, possibly even staying in the same dormitory as Leslie. He could easily track her down at his leisure, hang out at the dorm during Leslie's class or workshop periods, arrange a casual encounter. A cooler head needed to prevail, no need in being swept along by emotion and angst.

Townsend didn't budge.

And then he saw Leslie. She had been there all along, in the near wings, with Janet and other girls from the company. Their faces were highlighted by the glow from the stage lights. They wore sweats or knit warm-ups under their pioneer dresses, baggy cardigan sweaters on top, and were casually but methodically stretching, now and then checking on the progress of the Ekstein Company. Leslie sat in the splits, facing the stage, no more than thirty feet away.

Stupefied, Townsend watched her. With her arms in fifth position overhead, Leslie rolled her torso forward, arched her back, and gently rocked. Uprighting herself, she repeated the maneuver again and again, each time pushing a bit farther forward, chest closer to the floor, pushing out like a sprinter leaning into the tape at the finish line. Finishing that, she placed her hands palm down on the floor and shifted her body and leg position so that she was facing the left side, her legs split 180 degrees, the axis of her body occupying a perpendicular plane in space. Again she moved her torso, first back, then forward, pressing her face snugly against her knee before releasing. Then she twisted her torso from side to side. Like her cohorts, she was a superbly conditioned athlete, probably more so than he had ever been.

The left was her more limber side, Townsend knew. He also was well enough acquainted with her warm-up regimen to realize that she was about to turn toward him to repeat the same stretch over her right leg. When she twisted to his side, he'd be seen.

Townsend slithered along the side wall, keeping her in view the whole time. By the time she switched to her opposite side, he was well beyond her, undetected, deeper in the backstage bowels.

The area behind the stage was even more cavernous than the side wing space. Bare bulbs dangling from scattered ceiling cords defined almost palpable cones of light marginated by gradations of progressively deepening shadow. The quality was eerie, a haunted warehouse lacking only furniture draped in white sheets and gigantic cobwebs. One anticipated a musky smell that wasn't present; only a woodsy and vaguely medicinal odor, a mix of sawdust and solvents, like a construction site.

Townsend ventured away from the wall, walking past helter-skelter groupings of set pieces, props, ladders, electrical carts, and an occasional costume rack. Near the farthest wall, large set crates on wheels were parked like deserted railroad cars. Stenciled on the sides were the company names; some had specific piece titles as identifiers. Gruenfeld, Lubovitch, Ekstein, and all the other companies represented at the festival had their own boxcars in the graveyard; Townsend estimated thirty of them altogether. Given the festival performance schedule, with different companies performing each Friday, the shipping crates were more dynamic than static. Sets were packed in from New York, set up for rehearsal and performances, then efficiently struck and repacked for transport back to East Coast warehouses.

Townsend walked toward the boxes. An enormous loading dock was behind them at the rear; a square of outside Kansas City dusk cast a faint glow where an access door was open, and Townsend could make out the tail end of a transport truck backed into place, readied for loading. Staying put among the crates, he was hidden and out of the way, and if he had to make a quick exit for any reason, he could escape off the loading dock. Townsend paced around and between the wooden maze of transport crates. He leaned back on one that said EKSTEIN: PRIMITIVE PASSIONS and tried to harness his thoughts.

When he heard the hushed voices nearby, Townsend questioned the appropriateness of his hiding place. Not that it wasn't well suited for stealth; apparently its attributes were recognized by others. Townsend first imagined a romantic tryst, two unoccupied stage personnel pumping or sucking in the shadows. Little chance of discovery during the performance, more at risk for splinters in the backside. He quietly walked to one end of the storage crate and cautiously peered around the corner. Nothing to see, but he ascertained that the voices were coming from the far side of a different crate.

Tiptoeing across the hardwood floor, he placed his back flat against the side of the next nearest crate. The posture struck him as ludicrous. He was ten again, playing war, a G.I. Joe trapped in a German-occupied French village. The Germans were all over the place, lounging around with guns strapped over their soldiers, smoking cigarettes, while he was pressed against the wall of some picturesque stone building. But it had always worked for Vic Morrow in "Combat," and it was working for Townsend.

Except there were no Germans, and no pumpers or suckers. When Townsend stuck his head around the corner of the crate, leaving his back pressed against the side the way Vic would have done, he was disappointed. Two men in the shadows conversed in undertones, backlit by the outside dusk. Maybe discussing which crates to load. Truckers or stagehands.

Maybe not. One of the men was no stagehand. Townsend recognized the pretty-boy face and sculptured physique of Felicia's protege-cum-plaything, Erik Crumm.

And then Townsend saw Erik take the Ziploc bag.

Townsend groaned inwardly. Trying to hide from his ex-wife he lands himself smack in the middle of a drug transaction. Great move.

Townsend withdrew his head and resumed his Vic Morrow. The other guy . . . who was the other guy? He remembered Felicia bristling at the mention of the source of Gerard's cocaine. If Erik was involved in drug dealing, that could account for her response. Felicia was protecting Erik. Erik was linked to her cocaine and probably Gerard's as well. But was he connected in a more sinister way? Was Gerard's death tied in with drugs?

Townsend mustered his courage and peered once again around the corner. Erik's contact was portly, belly flopping over the belt of his jeans, balding with wispy light brown hair. He was a dissipated cherub, and Townsend had seen him before at the rehearsal of the Moreau Company. At that time he had paid him little mind, but assumed him to be the company stage manager.

Townsend strained to hear what they were saying. Then he

heard a creak. At first he cursed inwardly, attributing the noise to himself. When he realized it wasn't him, it was too late.

The blow came from the left side, whipping his face around and crashing his right cheek into the plywood. He fell to the side, and en route to the ground saw the startled look of Erik and his buddy. They gained their composure quickly, on top of him before he had done little more than hit the ground. He swung wildly, but it was no contest. Whoever had struck him initially was a sizable kind of guy, and Townsend felt the man's knee grinding into the small of his back.

And then the darkness came, not because he lost consciousness, but because one of them had thrown a packing blanket over him. With him covered and incapacitated, one of them took some cheap shots. The low blow fortunately missed its mark, landing on thigh bone rather than genitalia. The even lower blow, a sturdy kick to his shins, nearly compensated for the lucky miss.

Breathing was not easy. Feeling as if he would suffocate, he stopped struggling and let himself go limp. He was being man-handled by all three of them, but the purpose was more transport than infliction of physical harm. They shoved him, blanket enshrouded, into one of the packing crates. The door slammed on his ankle and he let out a yelp. His foot was kicked out of the way and the door was successfully slammed shut. He heard the crate being latched, then felt himself moving, being pushed backward.

He thrashed at the blanket and uncovered himself. The air was cool but stagnant. He filled his lungs with it, first deeply, then with panting breaths. He was in total darkness, rolling. He heard and felt the metal coaster against the floorboards, then sensed the vibrations as he was pushed up a ramp. He heard grunts, then laughter.

One of them kicked the door of his crate as a parting shot.

He and his shipping crate had been loaded into the truck. Townsend heard the corrugated rattle of the metal truck door as it was slammed closed. Then he heard the clanging of metal as the bolts were secured. At least he wasn't straightjacketed or in a pool of water, but extricating himself from his trap would be no mean feat. He waited in silence for a few minutes, then tested the strength of the crate with his shoulder. Some give, but not much. Eventually he could muscle out of his box and make himself more comfortable, but getting out of the truck on his own was another matter.

Townsend slipped off his suit jacket, folded it neatly, and placed it by feel on the floor of one end of the box. He loosened his tie and began systematically pounding his shoulder against the frame. There was little space to gather momentum; the physics of his confinement didn't lend itself to the generation of much force.

With each pounding, the entire case inched forward on its casters. Townsend doubted if the center of gravity were high enough for him to topple the damn thing, and even if he did, it probably wouldn't break apart. Then he felt more resistance, a clattering with each push.

He didn't feel at the top of his form. His face was swollen and bleeding, he had fallen fairly hard against the floor on the shoulder he was now using as his battering ram of choice. But there was more to his lack of success. The clattering. His efforts had propelled the storage box to the door end of the truck. Continuing to pound on that side was futile. He began ramming the opposite enclosing wall.

After a few more unsuccessful passes he changed tack, lowering himself as far down as he could squeeze by flexing his thighs, then pushing the opposing wall out with his legs. He strained and grunted, a Nautilus workout with actual purpose, then relaxed and regrouped for the next set. On the subsequent try he felt his groin give him a warning twinge. Townsend took heed. Enough that he was pathetic, no point in being stupid as well, like a bird persisting in trying to fly through a plate-glass window.

He stretched out as best he could, rolling up the blanket to prop up his head. His musings now took him down different passageways, through different doors. The silhouette of Paul Gruenfeld was replaced by a line of white powder and Erik

Crumm. Erik Crumm straddling one end of the line, Felicia Bradley—pudenda exposed—the other.

He lost track of time, and wondered if the performance was over. He wouldn't make his rendezvous with Leslie. The double date would not come off as planned, and Mauro would be furious with him for disappearing—it had become a pattern of sorts. Leslie wouldn't worry too much. Probably she had been dreading the evening anyway, and she had no reason to expect anything out of the ordinary. Leslie didn't know what Mauro knew, that a murder was involved. Had Townsend gotten himself tied up in the middle of it? Mauro had good reason to worry.

Townsend wondered what he was boxed up as: *Desdemona? Outlaw? Primitive Passions?* Then his thoughts took a different turn. Away from Erik and Paul and the cocaine and Felicia. Away from his evening plans and Tony and his deteriorating relationship with Leslie. Away from the mystery of Doris Humphrey, who had run off with his spilled seed only to be found again and lost again.

He became acutely aware of it, out of the blue. Like the headaches, or the burning eyes. But this was worse. Townsend changed his position but it did no good.

He really had to pee.

14

Townsend couldn't pull his car into his driveway the next morning because Tony Mauro's boat of a Buick was blocking the entrance. The car windows were open; Mauro slumped in the front seat, his shoulders uncomfortably propped against his folded suit jacket and the driver's side door, his feet sticking out of the passenger-side window. It was eight in the morning, another clear day promising sweltering heat, and both men looked as if they had slept in their clothes. Which, of course, they had.

Mauro jerked himself upright at the sound of Townsend's approaching Nova and ungracefully extricated himself from the car. Mauro had a strange look on his face. He took a deep breath, ready to explode into a verbal machine-gun burst, but his rounds were jammed.

Townsend pulled his car along the curb, cut the engine, and deliberately got out. He extended his arm, palm outstretched, a traffic cop gesture to stop oncoming traffic.

"Don't say anything you might regret, Tony," he said.

Mauro blew most of the air out through his nose. "I've fucking been here all night! Where the fuck you been?"

Townsend smiled through his exhaustion. "I'm touched, Tony, really touched. You waited here all night for me? I'm surprised the neighbors didn't call the cops."

"They *did* call the cops," said Mauro.

"Neighborhood watch," said Townsend. "Take a bite out of crime." He hopped up and sat on the hood of his Nova.

"You've got a real good explanation for this—," Mauro approached him menacingly.

"The best. I was locked in a shipping crate and loaded into a moving van."

"This have anything to do with the positive cyanide blood levels on Gerard Moreau?"

"I knew it. I knew the blood would come back positive."

"Like you said. Now we have a murder investigation on our hands, and you've got some explaining to do. Answer me now, did you get yourself mixed up in this bullshit?"

"Possible."

"Out with it." He pulled his notebook out of his pants pocket before shimmying himself onto the car hood beside Townsend.

"Relax with the notebook already. How about we go inside and make ourselves comfortable first? I'll put on a pot of coffee, and then I can take a shower before getting grilled."

"You don't need a shower any more than I do. I'll go for the coffee, but the shower can wait." He slid down off the car hood.

Townsend stayed put, weighed down with fatigue. "Tony, have a heart. I spent the night in a goddamn shipping crate!"

"And *I* spent the night in my fucking car, shithead!"

"Tony, I *peed* on myself!"

"Yeah?" Mauro sniffed the air and grinned with approval.

"To be truthful, I went in one corner of the crate, but it kinda rolled back over to where I was sitting."

"Yeah? Too bad. I'd say you chose the wrong corner."

"I'd say I didn't exactly have a level with me, all right?"

"Well," said Mauro, "I peed on your bushes. And I took a crap in one of your flower beds in back."

Townsend lifted his eyebrows. "Enough of this one-upmanship. Suffice it to say we both suffered plenty. We'll feel better after coffee." Townsend slid off the hood. Mauro grabbed a handful of Townsend's shirtfront in his fist.

"That ain't all. Because of you, you son-of-a-bitch, I didn't get to go out with that Janet chick, and I tell you she's some great-looking piece of ass," Mauro snarled, snapping his hand open, discarding Townsend and his shirt. His eyebrows were in a single channel, and his upper lip was curled into a fairly late stage Dorian Gray.

Townsend winced.

"That *is* bad," he said. "You win."

Mauro released him and they walked up the cracked cement pathway to the front door. Townsend fished for his keys. He found them in one pocket, then remembered that the folded journal article was in his other one. He pulled it out and handed it to Tony as he slipped the key into the lock.

"Reading material while I take a shower," he said, opening the door. He let Mauro walk in first.

"And I'm not so happy about you taking a dump in my flower bed, Tony."

Townsend poured out two steaming mugs of coffee and joined Mauro at the breakfast room table. He was shirtless, wearing only a clean pair of jogging shorts. He got himself situated, took a sip of his coffee, and rubbed his wet hair a few times with a hand towel. Townsend rarely combed his hair; instead, he fluffed up his curls with massaging fingers, and let them fall where they chose. While he was showering, Mauro had retrieved the morning's paper, riffled through it, and left it on the table. Townsend glanced at the front page and shoved it aside.

"So you smelled the stuff, that's how you knew," said Mauro.

"I didn't realize it at the time. I just thought Gerard had bad breath. Then it clicked. What triggered it was I was having almond chicken with Felicia—"

"Again with Felicia? What's with you and Felicia?"

"Nothing, I assure you, but we'll come back to her later. I'd never smelled cyanide before, but the odor is always described as that of bitter almonds. It was a bit more astringent, if you ask me."

"And nobody else noticed the smell."

"Apparently not. You read that article? Somewhere in the neighborhood of 30 percent of people are genetically unable to detect the scent of cyanide."

"I looked at it, but wasn't expecting a pop quiz, okay? Why don't you give me the *Reader's Digest* condensed version?"

"Okay." Townsend took a sip of coffee. Mauro was glaring at him over his own mug. "After the big Tylenol tampering case there was an Excedrin tampering case on the West Coast."

"I remember," said Mauro. "The Stella Nichols case. Lady poisons her husband for insurance dough, but also poisons a complete stranger to make it look like it was some crazy."

"Exactly. Cyanide in Exedrin. Two murders, and that journal article there reports the X ray findings. When both of the victims presented in the emergency room and had CT scans, there was massive brain edema, with what's called 'loss of gray-white matter differentiation.'" Seeing Mauro's face cloud with incomprehension, he added, "Don't worry about it, not important."

He went on. "The point is that there is very severe edema—brain swelling—early on with cyanide poisoning. With other causes of brain injury—let's say from a respiratory arrest—swelling of that magnitude doesn't happen for at least four to six hours. Gerard was scanned within an hour of his being found down. His edema was striking. Unfortunately, I just couldn't put things together at the time."

"Okay, I'm with you. But tell me this—" Mauro narrowed one eye in an accusatory stare. "Once you *did* put things together, why the hell did you hold out on me?"

Townsend reached for the paper and began leafing through it. For an instant, Mauro thought Townsend was avoiding the question. Then he realized that Townsend was looking for something in particular.

"Here's why," said Townsend. He folded the paper over twice into a manageable packet and thrust it in front of Mauro's face. Mauro's eyes tracked the section, like a smart missile trying to home in on a target. He floundered aimlessly, guidance system failure.

"Second column, very top," Townsend prompted.

The piece was a short one, a follow-up to the more extensive article that had appeared the previous day, front page. Both pieces carried Steve Rayburn's byline. Mauro read it silently. Townsend noticed that he moved his lips when he read.

LITTLE JESÚS DOING WELL AFTER
TRANSPLANT

Jesús Sanchez has spent the first twenty-four hours of his new life with his new liver. The nine-year-old is recovering from the liver transplant procedure performed late Thursday night by the St. Michael's Hospital transplant team. While his condition is still guarded, he has been upgraded from the critical to serious list, and hospital spokespersons state he is improving "faster than anyone could have foreseen." He is expected to remain in the Intensive Care Unit at St. Michael's for at least several more days.

"We just thank God for this miracle," said a tearful Juanita Sanchez, the boy's mother. While donations had been pouring in over the past weeks to help defray the expense of the costly procedure, members of the transplant team were doubtful an appropriate donor liver could be found in time. Sanchez was suffering from chronic liver failure, and his condition had been rapidly deteriorating over the last several days.

In the complicated seven-hour operation, only the right lobe of an adult liver was used, owing to the boy's relatively small size. Doctors were pleased with the initial results of the procedure, and were particularly encouraged by the excellent tissue compatibility of the organ donor.

"The kid's a real trooper," said Dr. John Santa Barbara, Chief Transplant Surgeon at St. Michael's. "With an eleventh-hour donor, he was lucky enough to get another shot at life, and we expect he'll make the most of it."

Mauro set down the paper and looked thoughtfully at Townsend.

"Gerard Moreau's liver," he finally said.

"You bet."

"You had wind of this beforehand."

"Hospital grapevine."

"And you figured that a murder victim's body parts might not be released for a transplant if the murder was under active investigation." Mauro paused, slurped at his coffee. Townsend bit down on his upper lip and nodded.

"Well, doc, you figured right," Mauro finished with a sigh.

"The kid was going to die otherwise," explained Townsend. "Once I found out about Gerard's tissue compatibility—that he was a near perfect match for Jesús—I couldn't set your hounds loose until it was a done deal." He got up from his chair and strode over to the coffee maker.

"What's a couple of days, right?"

Townsend grabbed the coffeepot from the coffee maker and hesitated, gazing out the window. He turned back toward the cop. His broad shoulders were hunched forward, both elbows on the table, fingers clasped together as if postured for prayer. This was just the beginning for Tony, he realized.

It was easy enough to apologize, now that it was too late, the deed done. Besides, he wasn't sorry, just showing Tony Mauro a little deference.

"You can work extra hard now and make up for lost time. I'll give you whatever help I can." He walked over to the investigator and topped off his cup.

Mauro sat silently. He pulled out a fresh pack of Camels from his shirt pocket. Townsend had noted the bulge and the logo through the material earlier, but declined to comment. Mauro had a hard time trying to quit when he was on a case.

"Mind if I smoke?"

Townsend shook his head.

"I'd just quit again, you know?"

Townsend shrugged passively. It was not the time or the place for an antismoking tirade.

"Bought it on the way over here. Rest of the carton's in the trunk of my car."

Mauro was daring him to say something, evening the score in a very small way. Townsend stifled himself, again out of deference.

"You done your good deed for the day," said Mauro, prolonging the ritual of unwrapping the cellophane from the packet. "A regular fucking fairy godfather."

Mauro tapped the pack, picked out the longest straw, and methodically lit up. He took in a first drag that sunk in his cheeks like a cadaver.

Townsend braced himself, an inward knowing smile, and reflexively held his breath. Mauro feinted, first making out to exhale from the side of his mouth, then propelling the smoke across the table to Townsend. Townsend took it stoically, the way the class wise guy might take a slap on the wrist from a ruler.

"So now maybe you can spread your good favors *my* way," said Mauro.

"Go ahead, get out that little book of yours," Townsend replied, feeling a lightness overcome his spirits. "There's got to be an ashtray somewhere around here."

Townsend was detailing his backstage encounter, the apparent drug transaction between Erik Crumm and the Moreau Company stage manager. He voiced his suspicions that Felicia might be involved, or at least knew enough about some type of cocaine shenanigans to be concerned about protecting Crumm.

"You see any money change hands?" asked Mauro.

"No."

"But you think this Crumb guy might have supplied Gerard with his coke."

"I'd say that's a good bet."

"Then maybe he wasn't buying from this other guy you saw, maybe just helping with the distribution."

"You know," Townsend said thoughtfully, "there'd sure be a lot of great hiding places back there to stash a lot of that stuff."

"Not to mention ease of transport," added Mauro. "Like in crates . . . in trucks. Like maybe there could be more in those boxes of sets than sets, know what I mean?"

"Wait a minute!" Townsend jumped up from his chair and ran into the living room. He returned shortly, holding the issue of *Dance Magazine* with Gerard and Felicia on the cover. He thumbed through it until finding the lead article, then quickly scanned the columns.

"Here it is, right here," he said, excitedly fingering a passage. "This past spring the Moreau Company was on a State Department Goodwill Tour of several South American countries. I wonder how close Customs checks out touring dance companies, especially when the State Department is sponsoring them?"

"You thinking a big-time smuggling operation?" Mauro grabbed the magazine.

"Why not?"

"And maybe Gerard Moreau was involved by being more than just a buyer," Mauro speculated. "I'll have to get Harris of narcotics to help on this one. I'll take this magazine, if you don't mind." He began furiously scrawling in his notebook.

"That's Crumb with a *b* at the end?" Mauro asked.

"Not Crumb, like bread crumb; Crumm as in *crummy*," Townsend replied, accepting such interruptions as a matter of course. He suspected that Mauro was not just bad at names, but weak at spelling.

"One *m* or two?" Mauro asked, flipping his pencil over in preparation to erase.

"Hell, Tony, I don't know. "And I don't know if it's Erik with a *c* or a *k* or both, so don't ask. Check with the Dance Festival office. They should have records on everybody."

Including Doris Humphrey, Townsend suddenly realized. But there was an easier and more discreet way to continue his search.

"By the way, Tony, would you happen to still have last night's program?"

In his haste to get backstage, Townsend had left his own under the theater seat, and had given the cast list for the Eckstein piece very little mind. Had Doris Humphrey been listed as one of the dancers? If the name was an alias, he could at least narrow down the possibilities. A minor problem, but an inconvenience all the same.

"In my car."

"Uh—," Townsend began, "do you mind if I get it? I mean, I'd like to have it if you don't mind . . . as a souvenir. Leslie might want it."

"Not now," Mauro dismissed, waving his hand as if to swat a fly.

"I'll get it," Townsend offered.

"Don't bother, not now. It ain't that important. One *m* or two, who the fuck cares?"

"You asked," said Townsend, wanting to get his hands on that program.

"Forget about it," Mauro snapped. He flipped back one or two pages in his small loose-leaf pad.

"Let's go over this again. Some guy named Tommy lets you out this morning. Opens the truck door, you hear him and start banging. He was real surprised."

"Extremely surprised."

"And you had never seen him before."

"Never. Some stagehand. He was planning to load the set pieces from the Frieda Eckstein Company. They had struck the set last night after the performance and crated things up, apparently. If I had been fortunate enough to have been packed in an empty Eckstein crate instead of a Lar Lubovitch one, I might have been rescued twelve hours earlier."

"These company names aren't important, are they?"

"I don't think so."

"Good." Mauro thumbed through his pad and made a motorboat sound with his mouth. "That just about does it. Unless

181

you're leaving out something. Are you leaving out something?" He looked at Townsend suspiciously.

"Not that I know of," Townsend replied, consciously working to maintain eye contact. "I'm sorry I fouled up your evening with Janet."

"Couldn't be helped, could it? At least I got her phone number. Maybe we'll take a rain check."

"Was Leslie worried that I didn't show up?"

"More irritated, I'd say. She had no reason to worry. But I figured you might be putting your nose in places where it shouldn't go. She doesn't know about the cyanide, does she?"

Townsend shook his head. "I need to call her now, though, so she doesn't worry—or get more irritated."

"Keep a lid on the cyanide," said Mauro. "We don't want any word out until we get a chance to interview the principals involved; that's the job for Parker and me, starting now." He looked at his watch, then consulted his notebook. "Erik Crumm is new to the list. And the stage manager, whatever his name is. And Tommy the stagehand, regardless of what you think. We also got Felicia Bradley—I'm doing that one personally—the Van Burens, mom and son; Paul Gruenfeld; Nigel Devon, William Davidson; Oscar Brewer; and both medics. Full day."

"Nobody knows Gerard was poisoned? Not even Felicia?"

"No point in letting the suspects know how much we know. Just you and me, the state toxicologist, some friends and brass at the precinct. And the murderer, of course. But we can keep a secret, right? We'd put out the word if we figured this to be some random tampering case, but it ain't. When the time comes, we'll tell Felicia and everybody else in the world. I'll even call that squirrel Steve Rayburn personally."

"You sure it's not random tampering?" Townsend tried to conjure up all the toiletries on Gerard's counter.

"Sure enough to keep it quiet for a day or two. I checked the room out, remember? And I kept all the bottles and medicines in an evidence bag, just in case. Aspirin, some Sudafed tablets, vitamins, nothing that could easily be tampered with. Didn't bother with the mouthwash, since you used more of it than he did. A week's gone by and nobody else has dropped dead from over-the-counter drugs. That's good enough for me."

Townsend smiled, gratified that Mauro had taken the initial request seriously. "I guess sometimes it pays to take a doctor's advice."

"Maybe this time."

"Then you think the cocaine was laced?"

Mauro shook his head vigorously. "Checked that out too."

"But I thought it took two months—"

"Under normal circumstances, yes. When the serum came back positive at about 11 P.M. last night," Mauro explained, "we got the lab boys to come in special just to run a specific assay for cyanide on the coke. I did some heavy leaning, ruffled some feathers. But they came in and did it. See, I did more last night than just buy cigarettes and wait in your driveway. The M.E.'s eating crow right now. He's reviewing his autopsy findings, stomach contents in particular."

"You're smarter than you look."

"Just one thing—" Mauro seemed distracted.

"What?"

Mauro didn't respond for a moment. He looked down into his coffee cup, but there wasn't enough left to justify the effort of picking it up.

"So why were you backstage?"

The question came out of the blue, but was inevitable. Townsend never had any illusions of slipping that one by him, although he had tried. A large part of Mauro's strength was his affect. He acted like a dolt, maybe, but little got past him. Townsend always assumed Columbo was Mauro's favorite TV cop, but had never bothered to ask.

"You like Peter Falk?" Townsend asked.

"Who's Peter Falk?" answered Mauro, so deadpan that Townsend didn't know if he was serious or not. He wasn't going to find out, either, since Mauro immediately pressed again. "Why were you backstage?"

"Not germane."

"C'mon, cut the horseshit."

"I can't tell you. But it's not important."

"Let Officer Friendly be the judge of that."

"Sorry, Tony, I really can't. Trust me, it has nothing to do with this."

Mauro pounded his fist on the table, rattling the empty coffee cups.

"Damn you to hell! You always pull this shit!" He rubbed his eyes, then his mouth and chin. Townsend knew better than to lie to Mauro, but Mauro knew that intimidation would do little to budge the stonewalling doctor. Mauro pointed a finger at him, squinting one eye nearly closed. The expression set his eyebrows in an unusual serpentine shape.

"I'm warning you—"

"Duly noted."

"You win for now." Mauro relented, not pretending to be a good sport. "Thanks for the coffee."

Their parting at Townsend's front door was awkward, rather like a couple on the first date jockeying about a goodnight kiss. They stared each other down on the threshold. Townsend hadn't wanted their visit to end on a sour note, but it couldn't be helped. Maybe he should have confided in Tony; perhaps even solicited help in tracking down Doris Humphrey. At the moment, though, he didn't need any help. All he needed was a copy of last night's program. But he didn't ask again for the one in Mauro's car.

"Later," Mauro finally said.

"Keep me posted," said Townsend.

They held their stares longer than they might have otherwise, until Townsend shut the door.

15

Townsend phoned Leslie at the dorm as soon as Mauro left. He wanted to assuage any worries she might have about his whereabouts, dampen her irritation with him if need be, and most important, determine when he would have free rein in searching out Doris Humphrey.

He wasted no time in setting an apologetic tone.

"It's me. Sorry I didn't show last night, and hope you didn't worry, but let me tell you what happened—"

"I *was* worried about you," Leslie interrupted, not sounding especially worried, or particularly irritated, either. "To tell you the truth, I was exhausted anyway, so I wasn't all that upset about being stood up. I figured there'd be some reasonable explanation—you always seem to have one—but your cop friend really seemed bent out of shape. I think because you fouled up his date with Janet."

"They could have gone out by themselves," said Townsend.

"That was an option, but your friend didn't seem comfortable, for some reason. Maybe they'll do it some other time, though; Janet thought he was pretty cute. Anyway, so what happened? And how did you like the performance?"

"Great, really great. I was really proud of you." Yet another lie. Before Doris Humphrey, Townsend had never lied to Leslie, not during their courtship, not during their marriage, not during their breakup. Now their trust had been violated, the lies multiplying like some unleashed virus, threatening the underpinnings of their relationship.

"It's a nothing part," she said in a deprecating manner. "So what happened?"

Townsend related the episode with one modification. He altered the timetable, claiming that he rushed backstage after, not before, her performance and was roaming around, waiting to meet up with Tony, when he witnessed the drug transaction and was trundled into the set crate.

"My God! You're lucky you didn't get yourself beat up worse, or even killed!"

"Naw . . . they just wanted me out of the way so they could go about their business. You hear any scuttlebutt about drugs going around at the festival?"

"They're available, if that's what you mean, but nothing out of the ordinary," Leslie replied. "I don't exactly run around in those circles," she added defensively.

"I wasn't implying that." Then, offhandedly, "So what's up for this afternoon?"

"Tied up all day."

"Too bad. Where you going to be?"

"Regular festival classes start in an hour, and I'm slated for beginning and intermediate modern. Then I have to give a master class over at Westport Ballet School. I won't be back until dinnertime, then Paul's holding an extra rehearsal to change some of the things he didn't like last night about *Outlaw*."

"I see." The day was free and clear for him to nose around the dormitory. He assessed the situation, then suddenly felt brazen.

"You know a dancer named Doris Humphrey?"

Leslie laughed. "Of *course* I do, Town. Not personally, of course."

"You do?" He was dumbfounded. Was that so surprising? The modern-dance community was relatively small and close-knit, and the companies at the festival were working in tight quarters. Didn't Townsend at least know of most of the physicians practicing in Kansas City?

He stammered, not knowing what to say next, finally coming out with, "the Doris Humphrey in the Eckstein Company?"

"Other way 'round, you mean," said Leslie. "Frieda was one of Doris's dancers way back when. Doris Humphrey died in 1958 . . . Townsend?"

"Right," said Townsend, his voice sinking somewhere in his throat.

"You knew that, right? I can't believe you didn't know who Doris Humphrey was!" she harangued. "Started out with Denishawn? Contemporary and rival of Martha Graham? 'The Art of Making Dances'? Charles Weidman? None of this rings a bell?"

He was silent on the other end.

"My God, Town, you're a cultural illiterate!"

"I can name all the bones in the wrist," he said.

"Unbelievable! So what's with your asking about Doris Humphrey?"

"Just my meager attempt at becoming culturally literate," he replied peevishly. He didn't bother to mention that someone posing as Martha Graham's rival had run off with his jism.

Townsend changed into clean jeans and a polo shirt and drove to the Performing Arts Center. A company was already on stage rehearsing. Townsend paid it no mind—merely confirmed that it was not the Frieda Eckstein troupe—and lingered only long enough to scrounge a previous night's program from under a seat in the back row.

Program in hand, he narrowed Doris's true identity to five names. Four, by throwing out Wendi Chu. Was she a Suzanne, Kate, Amanda, or Lauren? He repeated each name to himself, trying to imagine the best fit. He remembered her in the stirrups that morning in the Women's Specialty Clinic—now the calluses on her feet and the bruises on her legs made sense. Leslie had them too, from dancing half the day barefoot and rolling on the floor like a wrestler with no opponent besides weight and gravity.

It was just after ten—despite the lengthy interrogation by Tony—so Townsend still had a chance of finding her in her room, sleeping in after the big performance. Otherwise, he'd have to stake out the dormitory lobby.

Gibson Hall was one of two L-shaped dormitories, mirror images, fused at their apices like Siamese twins joined at the hip. The entrails Gibson shared with its counterpart Grayson included the entranceway, parking lot, cafeteria, and recreation room. In the early days, Gibson had been a female house, Grayson designated for males, but now they were both coed, segregated sexually only by floors.

The major expenditure University Housing incurred thanks to the sexually liberated sixties generation had been the cost of moving urinals from every other floor of Grayson and transferring them to Gibson. There had been a big flap during the transition, taxpayers grumbling, the papers having a heyday. The longhairs may have not changed the world, but at least they moved the latrines. Other than that relative extravagance, the taxpayers had no cause to complain. Both structures were plain-Jane, primarily slabs of concrete with interspersed gray brick to disrupt the architectural tedium. Built to last, like prisons, and equally uninspiring from a design standpoint.

Townsend parked in the nearly empty front lot and walked through the front entrance. The reception area was deserted. The floor was a fake marble linoleum that always reminded him of the bowling ball he had wanted as a kid. The dorm was sparsely populated, Townsend knew, dedicated exclusively to the visiting summer dancers. Grayson was closed entirely; other dorms on campus were designated for the regular summer-school students. An appropriate arrangement, logistically and morally, since university officials didn't want to subject their innocent collegians to the bad influences of a community of professional dancers. The dancers were not officially allowed to cohabit, their room assignments adhering to the odd-even floor arrangement by gender.

The coed manning the Gibson reception desk was a brunet, perky-looking thing. She looked up from her paperback and gave Townsend a sweet smile. Security was lax; adult dancers could take care of themselves.

"May I help you?"

"You remember me," he said, never having seen her before. "I'm here to pick up Leslie Rosenthal, one of the Gruenfeld dancers. I know the room number."

"Oh, all right," she replied, as he breezed past her.

He took the stairs instead of the elevator. Leslie and the rest of the Gruenfeld females were on the second floor. Maybe Eckstein's troupe was too, but Townsend skipped it—no point in exposing himself to Janet or any of the other company members who might recognize him if he didn't have to—and proceeded up to the fourth.

Townsend stepped into the institutional hallway, struck by the spartan accommodations of the rank and file relative to the luxury enjoyed by the V.I.P.'s at the Fairmont. Then again, maybe Gerard Moreau would have been better off had he been assigned an odd-numbered floor at Gibson Hall.

The hallway was empty, all the doors closed as far as he could see. He hesitated, unsure of how to proceed. No names were posted on the doors, just numbers. He thought about asking the desk clerk more directly. She looked like the trusting type, and not a mental giant.

"Hello again. My friend Leslie isn't in her room. She said she might be with one of her friends: Suzanne, Kate, Amanda, or Lauren. Could I have their room numbers please?"

No need to consult the clerk, as a woman emerged from the bathroom, bath towel wrapped around her sinewy body, a second towel wrapped around her hair. She carried a container of hand soap and a bottle of shampoo.

"Excuse me," Townsend said, as she unselfconsciously made to walk past him, "I'm looking for Suzanne Ryan's room."

She unceremoniously pointed at a closed door two rooms down, and proceeded down the hall several doors beyond to her own room.

Townsend approached the indicated room, inhaled fully, and knocked on the door.

"Come in, it's open," came a woman's voice from inside.

She was sitting cross-legged on one of two beds in the room, mending something with needle and thread. She looked up from her handiwork expectantly when he entered, then her face dropped.

"Hello, Suzanne. It's Suzanne, isn't it?"

"Actually, no—" She became rigid, a posture of defiance. She instinctively pulled the end of her nightshirt over her knees, but didn't demur by assuming a more feminine posture. Her body language was unsubmissive.

"Well, it certainly isn't Doris."

"It's Kate. Suzanne is my roommate." She put aside her material. Effortlessly, like a dancer, she got up from her sitting position in one fluid motion and reached over for a terrycloth robe that was slung across a side chair. She slipped it on over her nightshirt as Townsend watched silently. Her modesty seemed becoming, given the circumstances.

"Well, I must admit this certainly is a surprise, Doctor—"

"Reeves, Townsend."

"Doctor Reeves, that's right, I remember."

It struck him unfair that she was struggling to place his name, while he had been obsessed with hers for well over a week, albeit an incorrect one.

"Kate Jordan," said Townsend, placing the full name from the program with the face. It was a lovely face, and at the moment a quite determined one.

"There's nothing you can do now. Why are you here?"

"I just wanted an explanation."

"How did you find me?"

Townsend paused. "Coincidence, really. I just happened to be at your dance performance last night."

"And you're a curious sort of guy."

"You might say that."

"It's not as if you can call the Fertility Patrol or anything. I paid my bills."

"It's not that. I just wondered about you, that's all . . . why you lied."

She walked to the battered veneer dormitory-issue dresser and picked up a bristle brush. She ran it through her hair casually, almost hypnotically, watching herself in the mirror on the wall.

"I'm not a criminal or anything. I just made the choice that I wanted to be a single mother, and I didn't think I could find many fertility clinics that would be willing to go along with that. I'm an out-of-towner, the opportunity was here, and I took it. So I lied. Simple enough, not that I owe you any explanation. I paid my bills." She gave her hair a final once-over, then set the brush down and turned around to confront him directly.

"Are you satisfied with that?"

Townsend sighed.

"Yes," he said sheepishly. He continued to stand there, looking down at the ground. He couldn't bring himself to leave. He had been expecting more, and was nagged by an overwhelming sense of incompleteness, one of life's near circles needing completion, inches away from closure. He wasn't sure how to connect it, but he couldn't just leave the ends hanging there, so close.

"Any other questions?" she snapped.

Townsend shrugged, then looked up to make eye contact. Her eyes were a piercing blue, and behind them, yet another strong-willed beautiful woman.

"Would you like to go for a cup of coffee?" he asked.

"You give all your patients such individual attention?" Kate Jordan had opted for more than coffee, Townsend springing for a complete brunch. While he waited in the dormitory lobby, she had quickly changed into jeans, a Dance Festival T-shirt, and *huarache* sandals. Now they occupied a corner booth at a Plaza breakfast haunt. She hungrily took the first bite of her Denver omelette.

"Not usually." He sipped his coffee, which was bitter. He had passed on solid food, not sure his stomach could handle it. Now he wasn't sure his stomach could handle the coffee.

"You're not really my patient. I was just a hired hand, covering for Howard. In fact," he paused, "I'd never done an insemination before. Not that it was tricky or anything, just not in my usual job description. I was filling in, and I winged it."

"Winged it?" Kate's eyes widened. "Well, it was excellent service anyway. And now brunch included." She smiled, revealing perfect rows of white teeth. "A great idea. Original, too." She paused. "Maybe not all that original. I've heard of hospitals serving free steak and lobster dinners after you have a baby."

"Don't spoil your appetite. Look what you have to look forward to."

"I wonder if they'll give me both dinners, and I can take one home in a doggie bag. . . ." Her expression clouded.

"What you're doing . . . it won't be easy."

"Being a professional dancer isn't easy. But being married wasn't so easy, either."

"You'll have to quit the company, or at least take time off."

"This is my last season, my eighth." she said. "It's quite enough, thank you very much. I made a choice. I'll do the fall New York season with Frieda, then go back home."

Townsend thought about Leslie, the choice she wasn't ready to make. It was all timing. Kate Jordan had done her thing, achieved some degree of stature in dance, thrown the career monkey off her back.

"Where's home?"

"Small town outside Seattle."

"Does it have a name?"

"Fall City. Heard of it?"

"No," replied Townsend.

"Didn't think so."

"The name suggests something autumnal, or else a bunch of clumsy townspeople. I see red leaves in October and old folks slipping on ice. Am I close?"

She shook her head. "Red leaves, sure, but mostly Douglas fir. And some snow and ice, but not like ten miles away in the mountains. It's named after a big waterfall, Snoqualmie Falls. The town's on the Snoqualmie River, downstream from the falls. But you being a midwesterner, I wouldn't expect waterfalls to come immediately to mind." She spread fruit jam from a foil packet on half of her English muffin.

"This is odd, isn't it?" she went on chattily. "Here we are on sort of a date after what you've done to me. The doctor's office bit. I mean, it's weird. You walked into my room this morning and the first thing I did was pull down my nightgown to cover my knees. I feel at a disadvantage. Like here you've seen me intimately in this very unflattering light, and I haven't poked or prodded the untanned part of your body with instruments of torture. Is that fair? Specially when you're sitting there so quietly just looking at me." She chomped on her muffin. "You know, back in my real dating days many years ago I really used to hate being with men who I felt were undressing me with their eyes. It drove me crazy. And here you've already undressed me, and this is much worse. Are you always this quiet?"

"How about pensive? And this isn't really a date . . . it's brunch. And I don't feel weird about having seen you professionally."

"Good. Because if you wanted to see me socially, you'd have to start at ground zero, like everyone else. Besides that, I'm leaving town forever in a week. Besides that, I'm definitely not in the market. Are you still going to pay for all of this food, now that you know the scoop on me?"

Townsend smiled. "It's tax-deductible, all part of services rendered. I don't collect on the brunch, I write it off."

"You're writing it off," she laughed. "But let's talk about this weirdness some more. You can completely divorce seeing me on that examining table from seeing me now?"

"Pretty much."

"You're making me feel better. And it's always like that? Let's say you have this really beautiful woman—"

"Like you?"

"Don't get personal, now. I'm talking dishier . . . younger . . . blonder. You stay absolutely detached?"

"It's not a sexual issue, it's a question of aesthetics. Most physicians—male or female—would prefer examining a young, thin patient to a big ugly fat one. But it's nothing personal and it's only a question of aesthetics. It's the difference between looking at a painting and looking at a billboard. The whole situation is too clinical to be provocative. So relax. You're just another pretty face."

"Whew, what a relief! I feel much better. You want half of this muffin?"

Townsend was feeling comfortable enough for a muffin. She tossed him a butter pat, a second foil packet of jelly, and handed him her dirty knife.

"If you're not dancing—and even if you are—," he asked, neatly applying the jelly and wiping the knife clean off an edge of muffin, "how are you going to support a child, that is, assuming you get pregnant?"

She responded with the confidence of one who always planned things well ahead. "I've scrimped and saved for eight years, plus my ex-husband bought me out of our townhouse. And my daddy's quite supportive. Besides, he has plenty of money, if it comes to that."

"What's his business?"

"Lumber."

"He owns a lumberyard?"

"You're still thinking like a midwesterner, Townsend—I can call you Townsend, can't I? You don't see real trees around here, only planks in some building supply company lot. My father owns a logging company and mills. Several mills, in fact." She told him the specific company name, which Townsend thought he had heard of. He made a mental effort to memorize the name of the company, somewhere in the environs of Fall City, Washington.

"So you're well heeled, you won't end up on state assistance."

"Nope. You think any less of me?" She waited for his "who am

I to judge" look before continuing. "I'll go back home, buy a little place on some acreage, maybe teach dance or even open up a school, you know, 'Kate's School of Ballet, Tap, Jazz, Tumbling, and Hula.' I'll do fine."

"I'm sure you will."

"So tell me about the doctor business."

Townsend listened to himself speak as if he were an outsider. Where he was, and where he had been for the past year, seemed hard to explain. Credentials were simple enough to present—he had a fifteen-page curriculum vitae for that—what he was doing with his life was another matter. Unlike the self-assured and -directed Kate Jordan, Townsend was meandering, out of step. He had strayed from his medical script. He was almost embarrassed to talk about his life after taking leave of St. Michael's. He stammered his way through a condensed version, glossing over the marriage-breakup part. Kate Jordan watched him reflectively. She didn't raise her eyebrows at any of his disclosures.

"Pretty gutsy," she said.

"What?"

"Walking away from your job like that."

"Not really. I'm marketable. There will always be work for me out there. I can moonlight for as long as I want, and I can always get back into a long-term private practice or academic job. Finding one with some appeal is the problem."

"Not that," said Kate. "What I mean is, it took guts to change your game plan, look at your life and career from a different perspective."

"That's a nice way of looking at it. At least it's preferable to being viewed as unstable, flaking out, or heaven forbid, trying to find oneself."

"You're not lost, Townsend."

"I've strayed from the script."

"You've made the conscious decision to ad-lib. You'll get used to that in time, and the process will have been worth it. I'm a dancer, remember? Almost everyone I know flies by the seat of their pants. And even though we try to control our bodies—and to some extent we succeed over the short haul—we can't control much of anything else about our lives. Big risks, big gains."

"I'd have to say that most of my medical colleagues wouldn't see things that way. I appear on the edge."

"Maybe you do, to a bunch of doctors trapped by a style of life. You're a free man. You can smell the roses. Welcome to the real world."

Townsend sat quietly. If he were to be convinced to feel heroic, he would have to be the guy who gets the medal for being lucky enough not to get blown to smithereens. Heroism as a passive action, a quirk of fate, the Angel of Death skipping past because of a cosmic clerical error.

"I'll have to say," admitted Townsend, a bit uncomfortable with himself as fodder for public dissection, "that dancer types don't seem so alien to me anymore. We're not exactly kindred spirits or anything—"

"Who does your ex-wife dance with?" she asked.

Townsend hesitated, squirmed.

"All right—don't tell me, I don't want to know. I'd probably know who she is, anyway, and that might make you uncomfortable."

"Yes," said Townsend. "But you could find out easy enough."

"I won't try," she said. "And I'm sorry about the relationship limbo. I know all about that."

Townsend found his opening to gently pump her about her own ex. He was an investment banker in New York; they had been married three years before things had begun to irreparably unravel.

"He didn't want a wife, he wanted a maid," she said. "And now that he has one, things are working out better all 'round. Certainly the townhouse isn't messy."

"He couldn't deal with your dancing?"

"Deeper than that. He couldn't deal with my doing anything. Dancing was just taxing him to the max. Bryan's a nice man, really, just unable to free himself of certain traditional values. Modern man is a disguise he doesn't wear well."

"Relationships these days are tough on men. They're not prepared. They weren't brought up that way. Not that I'm defending anybody . . . but I can empathize."

"The difference is," said Kate, "that at least you make an effort."

"I'm hardly an exemplary model," he said.

"Men are graded on a curve," she said with a smile. "Maybe all this with wife number one has just been a rehearsal period so you'll get it right next time. A crash course in preparedness."

Townsend had thought of his relationship with Leslie as a never-ending struggle. The idea of its being finite had never occurred to him. He looked up at her. She was watching him carefully.

"Such a sad face," Kate said. "Maybe if I had met someone like you a while back, I wouldn't be in this fix." There was the slightest beginning of a smile from the corners of her mouth. His eyes met hers and they looked at each other in silence. He didn't want the meal to end, not yet. He was just beginning to feel comfortable, he was close to shedding his guard. How long had it been since he had felt that way with anyone?

A busboy appeared from behind him and cleared off the empty plates.

When he had left, Kate broke the mood. "Let me ask you a professional question before I forget, Townsend. Since I don't intend to go back to Dr. Gorell's clinic, how soon can I tell if I'm pregnant if I use a home pregnancy test?"

"Check, please," Townsend said to the waitress passing by.

Neither Kate nor Townsend seemed particularly interested in parting company after brunch. After leaving the coffee shop, they ambled around the Country Club Plaza window shopping. Townsend was surprised to learn that Kate had seen little of the city, so he offered to drive her around and show her the high spots. She accepted.

"I've heard a lot about Kansas City barbeque," she said in the car, "but I haven't had any since I've been here."

"You hungry enough for barbeque?" Townsend asked incredulously.

"Not now, I'm stuffed!"

"Maybe some other time," said Townsend, first thinking of Lamar Oates, the barbeque king, then nephew Lenny, the bumbler who had invoked chaos theory and brought them together. Their being together had gradually assumed the quality of a date. Paradoxically, the more comfortable he felt with her, the more discomfiture he began to experience.

Keeping the secret was what was really eating him. He had wanted to know more about Kate Jordan; now the more he knew, the more he wanted to tell her the truth. He couldn't confide in Kate any more than he could confide in Leslie. If he needed to vent, Lenny Oates was currently his only option, a depressing thought indeed.

"In college I played basketball with the king of K.C. barbeque, Lamar Oates," said Townsend sullenly. "Heard of him?"

Kate shook her head. "The king? Sounds impressive. He give you a good deal?"

Townsend recalled he had a free dinner coming, but that, certainly, was the exception.

"Maybe he'd go a little heavy-handed on the sauce if he knew the rib plate were for me," said Townsend.

"I'm impressed, I just love powerful men," she quipped.

Townsend glanced over at her; his appraisal one of admiration. Would he want the mother of his child to be any different?

"You been to the Nelson Gallery yet?" he asked.

Townsend returned home, physically agitated, emotionally exhausted, shortly after 4 P.M. He had spent a delightful but stressful afternoon with Kate Jordan. He had dropped her off at the dorm; they parted with a handshake. Such was the extent of their physical contact, aside from their inadvertently brushing against one another during the tour of the gallery. Neither mentioned a repeat engagement, or referred to her leaving in a week. No

198

addresses were exchanged, no expectations were verbalized. His sperm remained anonymous.

There was a single blinking red light on his answering machine.

"Townsend, dear, this is Rosie. I've just had the most disturbing visit from two policemen. They're asking many odd questions about Gerard and the night of the banquet. They're not being very specific, they're very closed-mouthed about the whole thing, but my impression is that they suspect foul play might be involved. If they haven't already contacted you, they probably will, because I mentioned your name. The Lieutenant—Mauro is his name—made a point of writing it down, so I think he'll be contacting you. This whole thing has been quite upsetting, so please let me know if you have any idea about what's happening. I never got a chance to thank you for all your help and support that night. Without you I don't know if I could have pulled through it in one piece. And Philip is grateful too and sends his best. And by the way, I think your friend Leslie is an absolute peach! Please call if you feel like it. Bye-bye now."

Yes, Townsend felt like calling. Anything to keep from brooding. He was becoming a candidate for intensive occupational therapy. He had no modeling clay, though, no Styrofoam craft balls or construction paper handy. A phone call would have to do; he could milk it for a few minutes. Then he could pace in earnest.

Townsend reached under the counter for the White Pages. He thumbed through to her listing, under the first initial *R*. He hesitated before dialing. It might be rude to show up unannounced, but then again, he could really drag things out if he went there in person.

He could gas up the car on the way back. Maybe stop for a burger, rent a movie. Or even better, head down to a Westport watering hole for a drink, chase it at home with a 50-milligram Benadryl to put him to sleep. Good plan. Acclimating to a life of quiet desperation wasn't all that tough, he thought.

16

IN DEFERENCE TO HIS MOTHER'S TRAINING, which he had rebelled against and spurned for many years, Townsend changed clothes. Nothing extravagant, but he abandoned his jeans and polo shirt for a pair of pleated slacks and a short-sleeved striped dress shirt.

Proud of me, Mom? He fished for a compliment by telepathy to his mother in New Mexico, like someone devout anticipating an answer to a prayer. A time zone earlier there, he imagined her to be just off the links, chatting with friends under the shade of an awning, drinking some syrupy, barely alcoholic hybrid of a Shirley Temple and a real drink.

"High-class people dress up," his mother told him *ad nauseam* as a youth. "It's all right for you to wear those jeans and basketball shoes around the house, but don't expect me to be seen in public with you looking like that."

Such subtle tirades at an impressionable age had left Townsend contemptuous of fashion. Overcompensating, in fact, he tended to judge anyone well coiffed—male or female—as hopelessly shallow until proven otherwise. In more recent years he had eschewed attractive women who were too dolled up. He was presentable and always clean himself (he had habituated to at least two showers a day during his athlete days), but that was as far as it went. He ordered his shirts, pants (one variety of chino or another), and shoes from the L.L. Bean catalogue; underwear and socks he procured from Penney's. Straightforward, hardly stylish, but all in good, traditional taste. Which set him apart from

Tony Mauro, another non–clothes hound, who sought out double knits the way the fashionable esteemed designer labels. But in common, neither he nor Mauro owned anything that required ironing.

The black and brown saddle Oxfords demanded something other than gym socks. Townsend rummaged around in his dresser drawer and found the thin ribbed pair that his mother had bought for him years earlier. They extended to his upper calf (knee-highs on someone of average height), and had a tendency to slip down around his ankles if he walked for any great distance. Thus, they were only acceptable for the occasional evening out; otherwise he would have trashed them long before.

Townsend sniffed his usurped white socks before tossing them into the wicker dirty-clothes hamper in the corner of the bedroom. They had served just half a day and were approaching the edge, like orange juice after five days in the fridge. But Townsend was accustomed to drinking bitter orange juice, and likewise accustomed to slicing surface mold from a hunk of cheese. Habits tending to reflect more general outlooks and life philosophies, Townsend tied the socks together in a knot and placed them back in his drawer. He'd wear them jogging tomorrow.

The trip took less than five minutes by car. The Van Buren residence had been referred to as a "mansion" when he was growing up, one of many older stately homes lining Ward Parkway Boulevard south of the Reeves's more modest neck of the woods. As he pulled his Nova into the circular driveway, Townsend had a peculiar sense of déjà vu. Yes, he had been there before, the place was the same, but his perspective was different. He recalled a similar feeling when he returned to his elementary school to visit an ailing teacher during college. The once-spacious corridors had been transformed by some wizard into a claustrophobic tunnel. Belinder School was just a box, the Van Buren mansion was just a house.

On his first, and only other, visit to the place, his father had been driving, pulling the '66 red T-bird into this same circular drive, and Townsend had been crammed into the backseat, trying to accommodate his spiderlike legs into the narrow confines of a luxury car that was only luxurious in the front half. He had argued with his mother before the trip, wanting to sit in front with his father. He had been thirteen then, and not at all anxious about having dinner with the Van Burens.

He's an old dear friend of your father's, Townsend, so please try to make a good impression. And don't you feel much better now that I made you change out of those awful jeans?

If only a house, it remained an elegant and solidly constructed one, built by craftsman with materials that were now exorbitantly priced and out of reach for all but the obnoxiously well-heeled. By square feet, though, it was no larger than many of the newer presumptuous homes in outlying suburban developments, hastily planned, poorly constructed, overpriced. Such was the distinction between "stately" and "making a statement."

The entry was much as Townsend remembered it, although he was greeted at the door by a younger and thinner maid than Luella, who was probably long since dead. Townsend waited in the vestibule somewhat nervously while she went off to announce him, having second thoughts about his brashness in dropping in. Middle-class casualness seemed inappropriate here—these types didn't go next door to borrow a cup of sugar from a neighbor; they sent out to a specialty shop for a delivery.

Any reservations were immediately dispelled by the outgoing Rosie, who greeted him as if he were a long-lost relative of comparable social standing.

"Oh, you needn't have dropped by like this," she effused, leading him into a living room that looked like a setup for an *Architectural Digest* cover. No visible personal effects, no family portraits on the wall or framed snapshots on the mantel. Nothing to betray the fact that a family actually inhabited the premises.

Townsend reconnoitered the room for a chair that looked as if it had been sat upon before, and finding none, selected a wingback that was closest. Rosie sat kitty-corner to him on the matching sofa. She wore a belted lightweight floral summer dress; and against the differently hued pattern of the divan, resembled a stray patch of annuals in an otherwise ordered garden of perennials.

"I didn't mean to intrude," Townsend apologized.

"You're not, silly boy. It's always a pleasure to see you. Would you like Teresa to get you some coffee?"

Townsend declined, but Rosie forced hospitality upon him with "Well, *I'm* having some."

"In that case—"

"Teresa!" Rosie shouted for her woman servant, who obsequiously appeared in the doorway, took the request for coffee, and exited in military fashion, all but saluting.

Rosie crossed her legs tightly and jimmied herself to the edge of the sofa. Townsend caught a good whiff of her perfume, identity unknown, but clearly expensive and applied with characteristic abandon. She interlocked her hands, palm to dorsum, and rested them on her uppermost knee. Her arms and legs formed a V, apex pointing directly at Townsend, attention likewise. She leaned toward him, expectantly, as if he were an oracle. The pose was deferential, implying absolute interest, even seductiveness—the rapt attention of a much younger woman placing herself before the altar of a suitor.

"I got your message—," he began.

"I didn't mean to bother you."

"You sounded upset. I mean, you were trying not to show it."

Rosie Van Buren inhaled deeply, allowing a layer of veneer to pull itself away. The transformation from hostessing to confessing was striking.

"This whole thing is so horrible, Townsend. I don't know if I can really explain to you what Gerard's death has meant to me." She nibbled on her lower lip as if to keep it from quivering.

"I didn't know him all that well, really," she went on, "but he and his company had become the focus of my life. Overwhelming and suddenly, like a love affair. It sounds all so stupid, telling it like this."

Townsend adopted a Freudian pose of attentiveness, leaning forward to rest his elbow on his knee, resting his chin in the cup of his right fist. His silence and demeanor conveyed that it didn't sound stupid at all and she should proceed with her venting.

"You're a young man and may not relate well to this, Townsend, but I'm well past middle age, despite the efforts of Mort Feingold and the miracles of cosmetic surgery." A restrained grin, wrinkle-free, attested to Mort's competence. The admission was not overly candid, though, thought Townsend, since she refrained from volunteering information about more substantial body work. Revealing the latter would have truly amounted to baring her soul, a dip into disarming honesty.

"And despite what many people thought years ago when I married Alex—that I was a golddigger or some such thing—I loved the man with all my heart, and no one's been able to take his place. Even after all these years."

Townsend hoped that Rosie wasn't pointedly referring to his own mother vis-à-vis the golddigger remark, although undoubtedly Margaret Reeves was included among that number. He kept his mouth shut.

"I'm just trying to justify how I was absolutely taken by Gerard and his work when I saw the company perform in New York last spring. I used all the influence I could muster to get him invited to the festival this season. And no matter what I could do for him and his company financially, he'd be giving me much, much more in return. Do you understand that?"

Townsend didn't quite get it, but couldn't bring himself to finesse his denseness with a lie.

"I didn't before," he replied.

"Gerard had tremendous talent," she proceeded to clarify. "I'd never been moved by dance like that before. I just knew from the first time I saw him that he could become one of the great choreographers of all time. And I wanted to play a part in all that. Accomplish something of real worth through Gerard's genius . . . channeling that genius."

"You're involved in a lot of worthy projects," he interjected, a haphazard and clumsy compliment.

"Nothing of this magnitude," she countered. "Nothing where I could really make a difference."

Teresa entered with a coffee service and set the tray down on the coffee table between them. She left without being acknowledged.

"Cream and sugar?" Rosie asked, pouring for Townsend from an ornate silver coffeepot into a Limoges china cup.

"Black," answered Townsend. "Thank you."

Rosie poured a cup for herself, adding cream and sugar from an antique serving set. The sugar bowl and creamer looked like refurbished Victorian era to Townsend. They had scalloped rims and rested on three rather simple feet, like a windup novelty item that could walk across a breakfront.

"*Metamorphoses* was meant to be a tribute to Alex's memory. And what a tribute that would have been!" she added wistfully. "The project had consumed my life. Everything fit together so perfectly, like fate leading me by the hand. The farm, for instance." She barely moistened her lips with the coffee. Townsend figured she had feigned interest in coffee only to encourage him to acquiesce to her hospitality.

She carefully set down the cup and went on. "Three hundred acres outside Stanley. There's a caretaker's house, of course, but no one's living in the main house—it was always a weekend retreat for us, but we haven't used it in years. Other than the herd of Black Angus—which all started as more or less a hobby for Alex—it really isn't a working farm anymore. So much unused space and a beautiful, pastoral environment. The entire Moreau Company could have taken up residence in the house and the outbuildings—with some minor remodeling, of course—and one of the barns was going to be converted into a studio. All to Gerard's specifications."

Townsend listened with interest. He hadn't heard before about the artist community that Rosie intended to create, always assuming that her patronage would be in the form of a cash gift. She obviously had her heart set on a considerable investment, both financial and personal.

"Not only would the arrangement have helped Gerard realize his potential," Rosie continued, "but it could have had a tremendous impact on the culture of this city. Can you imagine? Kansas City as the world's center of the contemporary dance movement?"

Townsend couldn't; to him the project sounded like the pipe dream of some out-of-touch chamber of commerce type.

"Perhaps Gerard wouldn't have thrived in such a nurturing environment," Townsend offered, playing the devil's advocate with great delicacy.

Rosie looked at him questioningly.

"Not that I'm any expert on the artistic temperament or anything," he backtracked. "But what little I knew of Gerard, he was a fairly tempestuous sort of guy. Sometimes those kinds of individuals—from what I've heard, anyway—need to overcome adversity to . . . uh . . . maximize their—"

"Oh, I don't buy any of that hogwash," Rosie cut him off. "And you don't either, do you Townsend?"

"Not really," he agreed too quickly. Unsettled, he took an overly large gulp of coffee and burned his throat. He converted his grimace into a "great coffee" expression.

"Anyway," Rosie sighed. "So much for *those* grandiose plans."

Townsend allowed a train of thought to settle upon him. The project sounded overblown, but admittedly he was no visionary. Money worked wonders. And what if the project didn't pan out? No real loss for the company, getting a free ride, and a big tax write-off for Rosie. His thoughts congealed on Leslie, and how convenient it would be for her to be based in Stanley, Kansas. Rosie's patronage could perhaps save their marriage. Now that was something to lobby for.

"You can still do it, can't you? Obviously not with Gerard, and maybe not even with his company—"

"There *isn't* any Gerard Moreau Company without Gerard," she interjected morosely.

"But there are other companies. Good companies. Established companies. They'd jump at the opportunity to get out of New York. Like, for instance, Paul Gruenfeld."

"Paul's already been here. Today in fact."

Townsend raised his eyebrows.

"And so has Nigel Devon and Frieda Ekstein. And I've had calls from virtually every company at the festival, and several other inquiries from New York, Philadelphia, L.A. Sharks smelling blood in the water."

"Times are tough in the dance world. You can't blame them for trying, even if it does seem indecorous. I'm sure they all feel bad about Gerard, but life goes on."

"Oh, I don't blame them for trying," replied Rosie. "After all, I set the bait. But I can't just behave like some jilted lover on the rebound. This was all about Gerard, from the very beginning. I need time to regroup."

"Understood. But if and when the time comes, don't forget Paul," Townsend pressed.

Rosie gave him a curious look.

"You must be a big fan of his."

Townsend shrugged. "Only indirectly."

The cloudiness cleared over Rosie's face. "Of course! Your lovely Leslie! I can understand why you'd want the Gruenfeld Company to hang around."

"I didn't intend to be leader of the sharks," he apologized.

"Don't be ridiculous, dear boy! I perfectly understand. And it's an argument that holds a lot more weight with me than most of the pandering garbage I've been hearing lately. If it comes down to that, I certainly won't forget your recommendation." She smiled sweetly and took another pseudosip of coffee.

Townsend was torn between flattery and embarrassment. He didn't expect Rosie Van Buren to dole out hundreds of thousands of dollars on his behalf, just to give him a shot at working out some relationship problems. He rather preferred to assume her insincere. Lifting his coffee cup to his chin, he gave the murky surface a precautionary cooling blow before taking another drink. Uncomfortable with his extraordinary lobbying efforts, he felt an overwhelming urge to drop the subject.

"So what's this business about the police asking questions?" he asked.

"They didn't contact you yet?"

Townsend shook his head, afraid his voice might crack if he lied outright.

"You don't think Gerard was involved with drugs, do you?" she asked, nudging her cup and saucer away from the edge of the table.

"I really don't know what to think. Obviously he indulged—after all, there was cocaine in his room on the table when we were there. You saw it."

"I don't mean that," Rosie jumped in. "I've accepted the fact that he may have been a dabbler—it disappoints me, of course, but I'm sure he's not the only one in the dance world. . . ." She trailed off, then recollected her thoughts. "What I meant was, do you think he could have been heavily involved in drugs, so much so that—I don't know—some deal could have gone sour or something and somebody was out to get him? Maybe bad debts or something? You know what I mean, don't you?"

"Yes, I do," he answered, "but I really have no idea. Felicia would be the one to talk to about that."

"It's a rather delicate subject, isn't it?"

"You bet. But from what you say, people are asking questions, and since it's their business to find out, well, I'm sure they will."

"Well, the policeman didn't actually come out and say it, he just referred to 'suspicious' circumstances and asked the kinds of questions that made me think—it just sounded like he was investigating a murder."

"Maybe routine stuff," Townsend offered, having decided that the tack was to keep all his cards tight against his chest.

Rosie shook her head vigorously. "No, no, I don't think so at all."

"Maybe they're trying to nail someone from the drug angle. Go after the person who sold Gerard the cocaine, even if it wasn't an intentional homicide. I've heard of that before."

"Maybe." Rosie didn't seem particularly convinced. "But you don't think someone could do such a thing because of the grant, do you? If they were jealous about the endowment and thought they might be able to get the money themselves if Gerard were out of the picture? I know it's a silly thought, but the way all these companies have descended upon me, like vultures, I just can't keep it from crossing my mind. I'm just being silly to feel that way, aren't I?"

"Did you mention that to the police?" Townsend asked, skirting her question.

"Not in so many words, but maybe I should have."

Townsend shrugged as if it made no difference either way, and it didn't, thanks to his own duplicity.

"Do you think I should call the policeman back specifically to let him know?"

Townsend shrugged again.

"Maybe you could mention it when he calls you," she suggested, not seeming very anxious to handle the detail herself.

"Sure," Townsend agreed. Keeping in character as an ignoramus, he asked the name of the policeman.

"Mauro," said Rosie. "Detective Anthony Mauro."

Townsend couldn't resist. "How does he spell that?"

Rosie spelled it correctly, then chuckled. "Funny . . . he wanted to know how you spell your name also," she said.

Both felt a sudden awkwardness. Townsend didn't want to press his luck by pushing matters any further; Rosie seemed at a loss for social banter. She became aware of her coffee, as if it were a great insight, and took a sip that was hardly worth the effort of bringing the cup to her lips. She took an extra sip, again mainly air, for good measure.

"I really should be going." Townsend pushed himself out of the wingchair.

"Are you sure you can't stay and chat some more?" Rosie had also stood up on cue, her action negating her words.

"Positive." He took a couple of hesitant steps toward the entry and paused, waiting for her to take the lead. In the interim his eyes inadvertently settled on the wall adjacent to the French doors. Gilt frame and sky blue velvet matting enclosed a book-sized space with no picture, only a brownish central blot. Beneath it hung a similar, but smaller and less ornate display. Taken by curiosity, he smiled at Rosie, then permitted himself a side step to the objets d'art. Townsend hunched before the fancier frame and peered, his nose about a foot from the glass.

"This must be one of Philip's moths," he said. The desiccated creature, crucified on the backing board with a pin through its thorax, spanned less than two inches. It was basically a medium chocolate brown, but with further scrutiny, Townsend could make out a pattern of spots, black circles with a white dot in the middle. A subtle orangish flush radiated outward from each spot. Townsend never recalled paying quite so much attention to a moth before, his previous contact limited to either swatting them away under a porch light or tossing their carcasses out of light fixtures.

"It's a butterfly," corrected Rosie.

"Really? It's so drab, I thought it was a moth."

"Look at the nameplate," replied Rosie.

Townsend read aloud from the engraved brass plate affixed to the lower margin of the frame. *"E-re-bia van bureni.* Ah, one of the doctor's, then."

He looked over at Rosie for confirmation. She was smiling broadly, fairly bursting with pride.

We should have brought up the subject of butterflies a long time ago, thought Townsend. *A real icebreaker in this house.*

"That one has sentimental value. A special summer in the Riding Mountains of Manitoba, twenty-five years ago. Of course," she sighed, "at the time I probably didn't realize how special that summer was. I thought all those expeditions were a bit tedious, you know, me being more suited for the city life. Understand, I pop up with moguls every time I get bit by a mosquito. I literally went through *cases* of Off back then. And for one who loves perfume so much—no perfume, just insect repellent! But the boys—how they loved those summers!"

"Summers in Manitoba were a tradition?"

"Not just Manitoba . . . Alaska, the Yukon, all over the place. Any fairly hot spot for *Erebia* species. Particularly in bogs or openings in deep forests, where forest meets prairie."

"Interesting," said Townsend, not completely lying. "Is this the only butterfly named after your husband?"

"Oh, no," replied Rosie. There's an *Erebia gloriosa* Van Buren, an *Erebia fabulosa* Van Buren, and a host of subspecies."

Rosie was acquainted with laypeople not understanding zoological nomenclature; she usually dropped the subject. Townsend's face, as she perceived it, though, betrayed more than the usual curiosity. She was prepared to expound on things a bit, step up to the next explanatory level, as he didn't appear the type to politely nod his head and feign comprehension. Townsend, of course, who had always hated nomenclature as a student, thought that he *had* attempted to feign comprehension.

"It's very simple, really," Rosie went on. "You can't exactly discover a species and name it after yourself—well, I suppose you can, but it's fairly gauche. The expert who describes a butterfly in the literature need not be the person who discovered it. The discoverer will be credited, but not necessarily bear the species' name. Now this little guy," she pointed at the case, "was named by a gentleman named Wolfgang Kruger, who chose to pay particular homage to my husband Alex."

Townsend wrinkled his face. "That name is really familiar to me," he said. "I must be thinking of someone else, because I don't exactly travel in butterfly circles, but somehow the name seems—"

"You *have* probably heard of him," said Rosie. "He's the biological museum curator at Mizzou State. Has been for years.

Internationally renowned, but makes his home here, off Harrison, in fact. Family friend for years, delightful man."

Townsend made two immediate associations. One was the street name Harrison, which he recalled having crossed several times in his search for Doris Humphrey's imaginary abode near campus. The second was a deadly guest lecturer during his freshman year basic biology course. An hour on insects and lepidoptera, an inordinate amount of time devoted to nomenclature, the subject matter as dry as the man's specimens. The man mumbled, to boot, which made him very hard to hear over the snoring.

"Funny little guy, bald, hunched over?"

"That's him."

"He actually lectured for my freshman biology course, that's how I know the name."

"Must have been a memorable lecture."

"Yes, yes it was," said Townsend. "But I guess I didn't pay enough attention, because I could have sworn this here *Erebia* was a moth."

"Just a drab butterfly."

"Right." Townsend stooped lower, diverting his attention to the neighboring display. The framing was simple—a thin oak border with neutral matting—but the encased specimen was striking in its colors. Hind wings were a bright yellow, forewings bore a golden metallic comma-shape. "And this butterfly here?"

"Moth," laughed Rosie. "A colorful moth. A species of *Syngrapha*. One of Philip's. And while it isn't yet official, that beauty will go by the name *exotica rosa*. A moth of my very own."

Townsend nodded appreciatively. "Just when I thought I had it. A drab butterfly and a colorful moth. So much for my liberal education."

"A common mistake," said Rosie. "Typically the arctic and alpine butterflies are drab, brown or gray monotones. Most moths fly at night; the colorful ones often are diurnal, like that one, flying during the day."

"Okay. It's all coming back." Townsend closed his eyes and

concentrated like a struggling clairvoyant. "The difference between butterflies and moths?"

" 'Rhopalocera' is the old name for butterfly, from the Greek *rhopalin* meaning 'club,' and *ceros,* 'horn.' Moths, on the other hand, used to be called 'Heterocera'—"

"Hetero meaning 'different.' "

"Exactly. Moths don't have clubbed horns like butterflies; they can be threadlike, brushlike, or comblike. *Exotica rosa* has threadlike horns."

Townsend nodded, then again nearly pressed his nose to the display.

"You might need a magnifying glass to really tell," she added.

Townsend scanned the specimen, as if he were looking for a hairline fracture on an X ray.

"And you sure can't tell where they squished this little gal's thorax to do her in," he said slowly.

"No, no you can't," said Rosie.

When he turned back to face her, Townsend tried to manage a smile. He worried that it looked forced.

That fossil Kruger hadn't been such a bad teacher, after all. Townsend hadn't forgotten everything.

17

MAURO'S BUICK WAS AGAIN PARKED IN THE DRIVEWAY when Townsend arrived back at his house. He once more pulled the Nova alongside the curb, unhurriedly got out, and sauntered over to the policeman's vehicle. Mauro tilted his head and watched him approach in the rearview mirror, but otherwise remained motionless, sitting erect, both hands gripping the steering wheel of the stationary car.

"You better not have crapped in my flower bed again, Tony," Townsend opened jovially.

"Felicia's dead," Mauro answered.

Townsend felt light-headed. He leaned forward and rested both his forearms on the roof of the Buick, ignoring the pain of the hot metal.

"I need to sit down."

"Better inside than suffocating out here." Mauro gingerly pushed the car door ajar slightly, giving Townsend time to move out of the way. "You're not going to hit the deck on me, are you?"

"I'm fine."

They walked to the front door, Mauro clinging to Townsend's elbow, as if he were a wedding usher.

"Where ya been, today, big fella?" Mauro asked while Townsend fumbled for the door key.

"On a date. Brunch on the Plaza, then the Nelson Gallery." He slid the key into the lock, twisted, then pushed the door inward. "Then I went and had a brief chat with Rosie."

"Ahhh," said Mauro, crossing the threshold and penetrating an invisible billows of cooled air.

"Maid found her in her room a little after noon. Came in and there she was, slumped over the table. Apparently reading the newspaper at the time. Probably dead for an hour or two."

Neither man was exploiting the limited comfort of Townsend's Victorian living room sofa. Both hunched on the edge, poised to rise in an instant, as if the tufting were a carpet of nails. Neither wanted to bother with making coffee.

"Naked?" Townsend asked.

"Fully clothed. This was a rush job, nothing fancy. No pulling the wool over anybody's eyes this time. Somebody spiked her Tiger's Milk—some kinda breakfast vitamin drink. From the smell of what was left of the stuff, the cyanide probably improved the taste."

"The murderer didn't even have the presence of mind to put the DO NOT DISTURB sign on the doorknob," Townsend said.

"Pretty rattled, I'd say."

"Any dope around?"

"None visible, but we dug around and found a small stash of coke tucked in a bureau drawer with her dainties."

"Was it the same maid who found her, the little Hispanic lady with the mustache?"

"Yep. The name's Esmeralda Martinez."

"Anybody but her been cleaning those rooms?"

"Not for two weeks, anyways," Mauro answered. "The little lady's working overtime. Got two daughters in college and a third in medical school. You still hung up on a lousy bed that wasn't tucked in up to standards? Cause you're sidetracking me here—"

"Hold on," Townsend interrupted. "Did you find out who from the Dance Festival was staying in the hotel? And where their rooms were?"

"Sure I did, but—"

"Run it down for me."

Mauro wrinkled his brow, looking peeved. "It's in my notebook here, I covered everything. Just to make you happy." He pulled out the notepad from his back pocket, flipped over a few pages, and handed it over. Then he reached into his shirt pocket for his pack of Camels. "Mind if I smoke in here?"

"Go ahead. But I'll have to get an ashtray," Townsend replied absently, perusing Mauro's list of festival room occupants.

Mauro eyed him. "Never mind."

Townsend recognized many of the ten or so names. All the room numbers indicated the ninth floor, in close proximity to Gerard and Felicia's rooms. Each of the major companies at the festival seemed to be represented. William Davidson had a suite, so did Paul Gruenfeld, Frieda Eckstein, even Nigel Devon.

Townsend looked up at Mauro. "Why does Nigel Devon need a room at the Fairmont? He's got to live somewhere close."

"He does. And if you ask me where, I've even got it written down. All the trivia you want. But the reason is that the festival provided one complimentary hotel room for each dance company. For whoever wanted to use it, which translates to the biggest cheese. Sort of a perk."

"Except the Moreau Company got two rooms, one for Felicia and one for Gerard."

"Special treatment. Even more special treatment for your friend Rosie. Except she got use of the Presidential Suite in the penthouse . . . biggest and best in the house."

"Some expenditure. The festival sprung for that?"

"Didn't have to," Mauro replied, reveling in the fact that he had the answers to even the most inane of Townsend's questions. "That one was courtesy of the Fairmont. Included with rental of the ballroom."

"Seems like William Davidson would have taken it."

"Nope," beamed Mauro, "since he needed accommodations for the whole festival, and they just had use of the Presidential Suite for a couple of nights."

"I see," said Townsend. "And what's this 'Hospitality Suite' all about?"

Mauro sighed impatiently, but complied. "All-purpose room.

Information center, T-shirts for sale, lounge for the festival volunteers to hang out, lost and found, you name it."

"Who had access to it?"

"Who *didn't* have access to it?" Mauro snapped.

"Room 922. That must be the one right next to Gerard's room, right? Adjoining, in fact. There was a door in Gerard's room, next to the closet."

"Locked from both sides on the night of the murder. The first thing I checked. Hey, I do this for a living, remember?"

Townsend, for the moment, was silenced.

"Now let's get back on the track, not that I have anything against pointless conversation to kill time," Mauro continued, "but what I've been trying to tell you—"

"Just one more thing, Tony."

"What for Chrissake?"

"Do you happen to know if Esmeralda's been making the beds in the hospitality suite?"

"You know, that's a great question. A really brilliant question. We've got a double cyanide murder here, and the guy with degrees out his wazoo wants to know how many beds the maid is making. Well, you want the answer to that question? I'll tell you right now." Mauro jerked himself off the couch and started to pace. "The answer is, 'I don't give a rat's ass!' Is that a good answer?"

"It's an answer," said Townsend contritely.

"And why do you want to know, anyway?"

"Just wondering."

"Just wondering," Mauro repeated. He pulled out a cigarette and stuck it in his mouth, but didn't reach for his lighter, placated for the time being just to suck anything, even if only air.

"You want an ashtray, Tony?"

"I don't need a fucking ashtray," he said. "Will you let *me* talk now?"

"I didn't mean to upset you, Tony, honest. I'm just thrashing things around is all." He gave Mauro's notebook back.

Mauro seemed satisfied. He tucked the pad into his back pocket, then took a drag on his unlit cigarette and whistled the air out. "Don't mind me if I take the liberty of bringing this discussion back to earth, from science fiction to hard facts. Like the fact that the stage manager of the Moreau Company, one Chip Larsen, is nowhere to be found. His assistant, a big dude named Carl Sander, must have went with him. I figure Carl to be the guard dog that grabbed you from behind. Thought you'd be interested to know that."

Townsend nodded politely.

"And thought you might also be interested to know that Erik with a 'k' Crumm 'double m' is also nowhere to be found."

Townsend nodded again.

"Except"—Mauro clipped himself off like a prosecuting attorney dramatically preparing to reveal a damning piece of evidence—"except, before he disappeared from the face of the earth, he was in the lobby of the Fairmont Plaza, carrying a travel bag. He even asked the desk clerk for Felicia Bradley's room number so he could call her on the house phone. Three witnesses place him there at ten-thirty this morning, and two saw him leaving the hotel a few minutes later. In a real hurry, too." Mauro puffed some more air. "So what do you say to that, huh?"

"You guys will find him . . . you'll find the three of them."

"You bet your ass we will."

"But I don't exactly follow." said Townsend. "The big picture, I mean. Like motive. Why would Erik want to kill Felicia? That's what you're getting at, right? I mean, here she's given him the lead in this new ballet, the career chance of a lifetime. And I bet she was shacking up with him as well. The last time I saw them, at the rehearsal on Tuesday, they seemed to be getting along well enough."

"There are still a few loose ends," Mauro said, not exuding complete confidence, "but the way I see it, Felicia figured out about the foul play with Gerard—"

"And the reason for that?"

"That's a loose end," said Mauro defensively, "but Harris is working on the drug angle. Smart money says Gerard was up to no good with Larsen and Crumm."

"With all due respect," said Townsend, "I think it's more a dead end than a loose end. I mean, is this guy Erik trying to win some kind of stupid award? He goes to the Fairmont to kill Felicia, but he gets seen by practically everybody in the lobby, and just in case he doesn't, he goes to the desk clerk and asks for her room number. Not to mention her room's right next to the fire escape. Wouldn't it make more sense to sneak up unseen, or at least escape that way afterward?"

"These guys don't always think straight," Mauro lectured, "especially when things start to unravel. Besides, maybe he didn't originally intend to do her harm, just meant to make a deal with her, keep her quiet. She doesn't buy what he's selling, and he loses it."

"And he happens to have cyanide with him, sparing himself the trouble of strangling her?"

"So he's a criminal Boy Scout, always prepared."

"And what's with the travel bag?"

"You think he's gonna stick around after a murder?"

"Now you're talking premeditation. You can't have it both ways, Tony."

Townsend was not being tactful. Things would go more smoothly if he could nudge Mauro in a different direction, but the cop had intellectually dug in his heels. Townsend had no choice but to drag him by the nose, even if he didn't himself know where he was leading. Mauro was chewing on his lip, cigarette dangling and wriggling precariously.

"Erik's not going to stick around when the cops are nosing in on his illicit drug dealings," Townsend went on. "Neither are Chip Larsen and this goon Carl. And Erik must have been tipped off by Felicia. She got wind of your investigation on Tuesday, when she overheard your message on my voice machine. And I'm assuming Felicia was the first on your list to interview this morning, right? She calls Erik to warn him that things are heating up, that police are suspecting a drug connection with Gerard's death, and he's packing his bags."

"So why does he go to Felicia?" the cop asked, starting to climb out of his mental foxhole.

Townsend rubbed his chin. "Maybe to borrow money for his trip, I don't know. But I guarantee you he either left her alive, or found her there already dead."

"Okay, smart ass, so you got any better ideas?"

Townsend finally had the opening he had been waiting for.

"Not without my own loose ends. But there's another angle on this."

"All right," said Mauro, "but keep it simple."

"Right," agreed Townsend. "You know anything about butter-fly collecting?"

Mauro crinkled his brow, unfurrowed, then furrowed again, his eyebrows an undulating sine wave. For an instant his face went blank, then approximated a bemused smile. Blank once again, then another cycle of brow furrowing. Mauro's furry fore-head caterpillar was doing the hootchie-cootchie.

Finally he withdrew his lighter from his pocket. "You got thirty seconds to get me an ashtray, or I'm gonna burn a hole in your Persian carpet here—"

"Antique Chinese," said Townsend. Within seconds he had returned with a soap dish from the guest bathroom. Mauro was already puffing away like a 1940s expectant father.

"You told me to keep it simple," said Townsend with an impish grin.

Mauro grabbed the soap dish, tipped his ash, and sucked so hard on his Camel that the paper crackled.

"Simpler." Exhaled smoke gave the word a tangible, swirling form.

Townsend resumed his position on the edge of the sofa; Mauro remained standing.

"It's like this," Townsend began. "Van Buren senior collected butterflies, but Philip specializes in moths. Butterfly collectors usually kill a specimen by gently pinching its thorax. But that's not how it's done with moths; they're too delicate."

Mauro's face revealed a glimmer of comprehension.

"So they use killing jars," Townsend went on, "mini gas chambers, if you will."

"Cyanide gas," anticipated Mauro.

"Exactly. Potassium cyanide mixed with sawdust. The water vapor released from the breathing of the moths flying around in the closed jar converts the potassium cyanide to hydrogen cyanide, a gas."

"How you know all this?"

"A college biology course that I'd forgotten all about until this afternoon. This old professor I had—named Kruger—made a point in a lecture of how he had a pound of cyanide in his lab. That part stuck with me; not much else did."

"Philip Van Buren has access to cyanide," said Mauro.

"At least that's something solid."

Mauro nodded, then closed his eyes, straining in thought. When he opened his eyes, he looked troubled. He pulled the notepad from his back pocket and began leafing through the pages. He found the page and started moving his lips.

"We have a time problem here," he finally said. "Felicia and Philip left Gerard alive at approximately six-thirty. Shortly after that they both show up at the hotel coffee house, corroborated by a waitress and a cashier. William Davidson joins them in the restaurant at about seven."

"What for?"

"Final preparations, grant business, from what all three of them said. It wasn't a done deal until Gerard had signed the legal papers, so Philip let Davidson in on the details, gave the go-ahead for the announcement at the dinner."

"Then what?"

"Davidson and Felicia stay until seven-thirty; Davidson leaves to meet up with Rosie at the reception. Felicia goes back to her room to finish dolling herself up. Philip stays in the coffee shop, has a couple of beers until ten of eight. Then he meets Felicia at her room and they go to the party together. Somewheres around eight o'clock. That doesn't leave much time for Philip to take care of Gerard."

"Maybe the time frame's off."

Mauro shrugged.

"Did he ever leave the coffee shop, even for a few minutes? Go to the john?"

"He went to make a couple of phone calls, but used the cashier's house phone. First Mother Rosie to tell her about the signing of the contract; then Davidson to arrange his coming to join them in the coffee shop. The cashier overheard both calls; short and to the point. Philip was in a good mood and very excited, says the cashier. She even remembered the conversation." Mauro consulted his pad and read " 'Mother,' he says, 'Gerard signed the papers and it's a done deal. Congratulations.' "

Townsend frowned, thinking of killing jars. "There's got to be a way. Did the medical examiner come up with anything?"

Mauro ground his jaw. "Nothing in the stomach, no burns in the esophagus. No real evidence to help us figure out how it was administered. But the M.E. said sometimes it's like that."

"Poisoning with gas doesn't show anything internally or externally," said Townsend. "Just nonspecific signs of asphyxiation, which Gerard would manifest anyway because of the respiratory failure. But they usually go really quick from the gas." He shook his head, puzzled. "Still, there's got to be a way."

"Don't forget a reason," added Mauro. "Phil doesn't strike me as the type to get his ass involved in drug smuggling."

"Agreed," said Townsend, "but look at it this way. Let's say your mom has all this money—"

"She didn't get paid that much for spending her time trying to keep my old man sober."

"Hang on. Let's say she's got all this money, and instead of leaving it to you, she decides she's going to give all—or much of it, anyway—to some pretentious French asshole dancer. What would *you* do?"

Mauro crushed out the smoldering butt. "You made your point. I'd kill the sucker," he said.

Mauro left with renewed energy. Philip Van Buren was in for some heavy grilling, but nailing him for the murder might be another matter altogether. Wolfgang Kruger was a new lead, though, possibly the source of Philip's cyanide. The search for Chip Larsen, Carl Sander, and Erik Crumm would continue. Still, things didn't sit right with Townsend.

Now alone in his house, finally sinking back into the sofa, he pondered killing jars, cyanide gas released by crystal potassium cyanide reacting with water. Could Philip have rigged a killing jar in Gerard's shower? Cyanide crystals sequestered in the drain trap, the deadly gas released when Gerard turned on the water? That explained a naked Gerard, all right, but unfortunately, not a dry one. And Gerard was quite dry when Townsend had found him. Had he been lying there long enough to air dry, the bedclothes would have been still damp.

Townsend jerked himself up from the couch and began to pace the room. Gerard would have been wet *unless someone had dried him off.* The troubling loose ends of the poorly executed bed remake and the adjoining hospitality suite began to intertwine, and a scenario tumbled into place.

Townsend played it out in his head. Philip rigs a water-activated gas chamber in Gerard's shower. The gas released is less than an immediately lethal amount, or perhaps the ventilation fan reduces the concentration enough to make a difference. Gerard either collapses in the shower, or makes his way back into the room and the bed. No matter. Philip has enough time between leaving the coffee shop and meeting Felicia to dry Gerard off and change the damp bedsheets. Dry bedding and extra towels come from the adjoining hospitality suite.

Townsend focused on the door to the adjoining suite, locked from both sides according to Mauro. Logistically it didn't present a problem. Before Philip leaves Gerard's room after the document signing, he makes sure the connecting door is unlocked. For the cleanup, Philip enters and leaves Gerard's lodging through the adjacent room, making sure to lock the connector from the hospitality suite side on the way out. And from Gerard's room? Philip manages to be first on the scene, along with Oscar Brewer. Amidst the initial confusion, Philip locks it without Oscar noticing. Maybe his vomiting on the rug was a diversionary tactic. A nice touch in any case. At least Townsend had thrown up for real, not crocodile barf.

But if Philip eliminated the major obstacle between him and a hefty inheritance, why was Felicia murdered? Was cocaine trafficking the link? Or was Philip making sure that Rosie couldn't still divert the money to a Moreau Company under her direction?

Townsend needed to run his theory by Mauro. He dialed the precinct and got the female dispatcher with the husky voice.

"I know Tony isn't there yet," he told her, "but ask him to call me as soon as he checks in. And give him a message in the meantime. Tell him to count the towels in the hospitality suite." He paused for a second. "And the bed corners—tell him not to forget to check the bed corners. Got that?"

"Sure do, doctor. Towels and bed corners." Nonjudgmental, nothing but the facts. Her voice betrayed no sentiment that she might be considering him a crazy man. Townsend thought that Mauro should see to it that the woman got a raise.

He phoned Leslie's room, but no one answered. He needed very much to see her, to affirm their relationship. He was feeling guilty, troubled by how much he had enjoyed the afternoon with Kate Jordan. Why hadn't he left well enough alone and kept himself in the dark?

He called Leslie's dorm again, letting it ring over a dozen times. Then he remembered the extra rehearsal for *Outlaw* that evening; he looked at his watch and calculated that it was in progress. Much too jittery to stay at home waiting for Tony's call, he locked up the house and jogged out to his car. He'd try Tony again from a pay phone at the Arts Center.

* * *

225

Once at the Performing Arts Center, Townsend was too antsy to even sit through what was left of the rehearsal. He tried, though, able to contain himself in his seat for almost five minutes, at least managing to catch Leslie's eye. Hopefully she had no plans, or wasn't too exhausted to have dinner with him.

He unobtrusively returned to the lobby, where he could at least pace while he waited for rehearsal to end. He called the precinct again, but Mauro hadn't returned. Townsend didn't want Mauro to think he was skipping out or flaking out on him again, so he told the dispatcher that he had left home but would keep calling back. In the meantime, he left her the number of the lobby pay phone.

The empty lobby offered little in the way of diversion. Aside from the display cases, there were no newspapers or magazines, only a small table with stacks of brochures advertising upcoming cultural events. The pictorial history of the Kansas City Dance Theatre held little interest for him, but Townsend haphazardly glanced at some group photos. He skimmed the faces, thinking he might come across an old shot of Leslie from her earlier days in the company. Nothing caught his eye.

But something had caught Felicia's eye, he recalled, the evening they had Chinese together. She had been kneeling, scrutinizing one of the group photos in the lower-right-hand corner of the first display case. Townsend's knees creaked as he squatted; it was a position he couldn't hold for long. The color glossy was a performance shot from five years earlier, the piece entitled *Concerto in Blue*. Five dancers in blue unitards were darting past each other in a circle, simultaneously airborne. The dancer in front looked vaguely familiar, but it wasn't Leslie. All the dancers in the photograph were male.

His knees were aching. Townsend settled down onto his rear end and sidled up to the display case to read the rest of the caption. *Concerto in Blue,* choreography by Nigel Devon, was first performed at the Lyric Theatre in 1985 and had become a perennial favorite in the company repertoire. Townsend never finished reading the cast list; a chill and an involuntary convulsing of his head caused him to lose his place. Besides, he had no particular interest in the other four dancers in blue. Just the dancer in the foreground, the vaguely familiar one. The dancer listed in the credits as Brian Van Buren.

Townsend grunted when he lumbered to his feet, as if the wind had been knocked out of him. He bumped a knee against the display case in the process; the glass rattled threateningly but didn't break. By the time Leslie came looking for him after the *Outlaw* rehearsal, Townsend was long gone.

Before leaving for the precinct, though, he took the time to make a single call from the lobby pay phone.

He called collect. Prompted by the long-distance operator, the party at the other end gladly accepted the charges.

How could Margaret Reeves refuse a collect call from her son?

18

Townsend had nervously straightened up the house. The antique Chinese rug was vacuumed, the knickknacks on the lacquered coffee table were neatly arranged, the kitchen counter-tops were wiped down. There was a full pot of freshly made coffee; a couple of clean mugs had been brought out of the cupboard. And he had even gotten in forty-five minutes of jogging. Not bad for a Sunday morning, and not yet ten o'clock.

He forced himself to sit down on the living room sofa, like a patient trapped in a doctor's waiting room. He was personally laying off the java, running unaided on nervous energy. There was a limit to what could be compressed in twenty-four hours. Only the night before he had been imprisoned in a truck. Since then, he had met with Tony Mauro twice, visited Rosie Van Buren at her home, and spent an afternoon with Kate Jordan. Aside from the activity, he had squeezed in at least a week's worth of cerebration. Just over an hour earlier he had made his call, extended the invitation.

At least he could see out the window from the sofa. Spotting the white Mercedes 480 SL slowing down in front, he hurriedly retucked his lime green cotton shirt into his chino shorts and fluffed up his hair with an abbreviated scalp massage. Not wanting to appear overanxious, he waited a full ten seconds before answering the door, during which time he again checked the back door to see if it was locked.

"I got over here as fast as I could," said Rosie Van Buren,

stepping across the threshold. She was wearing a different cotton floral dress, belted and sleeveless, with a scooped neck. She carried a summery peach-colored shoulder bag.

Townsend inhaled her fragrance. It was strong, as he knew it would be. He escorted her into the living room and led her to the Victorian lady's chair; he faced her on the near edge of the sofa. He didn't offer her any coffee.

"I think the police are going to arrest Philip," he said.

"What?" Rosie's voice rose in a shrill crescendo. "Why, that's absurd!"

"Felicia was murdered yesterday."

"I know that. I read the papers. The whole business is sordid, that's what it is. And it's the drugs, I tell you." Rosie was running on at an uncharacteristic fast clip. "Gerard must have been in it way over his head. Did you read where Erik Crumm and two others are being sought by the police? Why would they arrest Philip? Besides, Philip left for the weekend yesterday morning—he couldn't possibly have—"

"You're a good mother, Rosie, protecting your son, making sure he has an alibi."

"He didn't do it, I tell you. And he'll have the best lawyer, you can bet on that. I've already contacted Schiffman."

Townsend shook his head and held up his hand to stop her.

"I know Philip didn't do it, Rosie. *You* did." He paused, watching her face closely. Social graces could go only so far.

Rosie Van Buren was silent. She stared blankly at the butterfly and bird design on Townsend's lacquer table. Her eyes revealed nothing. Then she brought a hand to cover her lower face and chin, as if she were warding off a bad smell. She stroked her face when she pulled the hand away, smearing her lipstick.

"What in the world would possess me to do something like that?" she asked in a low, measured monotone, just over a whisper.

"Brian," Townsend answered.

"I'd like a drink now, if you don't mind."

"I don't think that would be wise just now," said Townsend.

He tilted his head like a parrot, struck by the grotesqueness inflicted on her by a simple smudge of lip gloss.

She gave him a piercing look, relented, and sank back into her chair. "What does Brian have to do with anything?" Her voice was weak now, defeated, but she was going through the motions, moving her pawns pointlessly until the inevitable checkmate.

"Felicia recognized him in the photograph in the display at the Performing Arts Center; that's when things really began to unravel. Of course, she knew him as Brian Vance when he was an apprentice with the Paul Gruenfeld Company a couple of years ago."

"Felicia told you he danced in New York as Brian Vance?"

"No. You saw to it that she didn't get the chance. What the papers didn't mention this morning was that the police caught up with Erik Crumm late last night. He's the one who identified the photo of your Brian as Brian Vance."

Rosie nodded wearily.

"Erik and Brian got into Gruenfeld's Company at the same time, and both took similar paths," Townsend continued. "Erik hitched his star to Felicia, and Brian got involved with Gerard. I'd lost track of Brian; I only found out yesterday from my mother that Brian had committed suicide over a year ago. She'd heard rumors that Brian was gay, but didn't know much else about the circumstances. But Felicia knew the circumstances, and so did Erik—"

"Brian was young and impressionable," Rosie interrupted, "and he wanted so much to make it as a dancer, more than anything. He lived for dance. But he was an innocent, not calculating enough to sleep his way to the top. You have to believe that. I have the letters from him to prove it. He idolized Gerard, he thought that Gerard was his mentor, taking him under his wing. I'll show you the letters from him, Townsend, I will."

Townsend tensed when she reached into her purse, but she only pulled out a handkerchief. She carelessly dabbed at her eyes, managing to smear her mascara.

"Gerard was scum," Rosie went on. "He used my Brian, led

him on. When he and Felicia broke from Paul's company, Gerard convinced Brian to desert Paul and come with him. Then he found another plaything, reneged on his offer to have a place for my Brian. Brian took pills the night he found out. But he wrote me a letter first, Townsend. I have that letter."

Rosie neatly folded her handkerchief over twice and replaced it in her bag. "I don't have to cry anymore. Justice has been done."

Townsend inhaled deeply. "The grant business . . . the whole thing was a hoax, bait for the trap. You had a hand in all the preparations. With your sponsorship, it wasn't hard to lead William Davidson in whatever direction you wanted. Like the hotel room assignments. Setting Gerard up adjoining the hospitality suite, in an out-of-the-way corner, an emergency exit close by."

Rosie wasn't ready to be taken off track. "Gerard Moreau was a whore; he'd do anything for money," she said.

"And that included sleeping with you, even though it wasn't his particular bent."

"I never let the scum inside of me, Townsend, I can promise you that. I couldn't bring myself to that, even for my Brian."

"But you came to Gerard's room to seduce him. When Philip called you from the coffee shop, that was your cue, wasn't it? You were staying in the penthouse. Philip's call let you know the coast was clear. He had left Gerard alone, and to make sure Felicia didn't stumble upon the encounter he brought her with him on the pretense of business—"

"Felicia was to have certain responsibilities in the dance colony in Stanley, for which she would be handsomely compensated," Rosie volunteered. "Felicia was a whore as well, it appears."

Townsend didn't bother to defend Felicia's honor. "You walked down the back staircase to Gerard's floor," he said instead. "Gerard had signed the papers, but you hadn't. And you needed one small sexual favor from him before you signed, right?"

"Most men wouldn't need any convincing to sleep with me, Townsend." She smiled coyly, extended her long neck back, and ran the spread fingers of one hand through her red hair provocatively. She heaved her bosom out as far as possible without slipping a disc. The seductiveness of the maneuver was dampened, unfortunately, by a mussed makeup job and the fact that, great lay notwithstanding, Rosie Van Buren had killed two people.

"You knew that Gerard had a penchant for cocaine, and you suggested that he might indulge beforehand." Townsend was putting out feelers, hoping to elicit a denial if he was too far off base. Rosie was looking at him passively, dry-eyed, so he went on. "The cocaine was critical. It provided a plausible cause of death, while still ensuring that Gerard would be a medical examiner's case. Any suspicious or drug-related death is an M.E. case, and that worked in your favor. Being a pathologist's wife, you knew that the routine hospital autopsy includes examination of the entire alimentary tract. But the M.E. only checks the esophagus, stomach, and the proximal small intestine to the ligament of Treitz.

"There were no signs of cyanide poisoning in the esophagus or stomach, and using gas would have been too dangerous, too unpredictable. That doesn't leave much in the way of entry portals except the rectum, right, Rosie? Which posed some logistical problems, but nothing you couldn't handle."

"I never let the scum inside me, Townsend, I promise you there was no penetration."

"I believe you, Rosie. But you took him to bed, didn't you, and all his clothes were off, and maybe yours were too. And amidst the fondling, you managed to insert the suppository. A glycerin one, possibly, hollowed out for the powder, or maybe just a standard gelatine capsule. Either way, once the casing dissolved, the poison would be absorbed by the rectal mucosa."

"He found out, Townsend, I made sure to tell him. It was important for him to know that justice had been done."

Townsend had expected an admission, knew it inevitable, but was nevertheless stunned by it.

"It was so simple, really," Rosie filled in the silence. "He couldn't tell, even, not the way I did it. He didn't exactly have rectal hang-ups, as you would imagine, thought I was just tickling his fancy, I suppose. And then I saw it in his eyes, all of a sudden." She leaned forward, bringing in her audience, a teller of tall tales and ghost stories.

"He was astride me, with that disgusting hairy body of his, gripping his own disgusting member. His eyes glazed, then they jerked all around, like they were looking for something. He let go of his penis as if it were a hot potato. It was comical really, because it didn't drop; it just stayed there, erect, as if it were suspended by magician's wires. And then his eyes rolled back in their sockets, and he fell with all his weight on top of me. That's when I could smell it on his breath. And that's when I told him, that's when I whispered, 'You killed my son Brian, and you are dying for it.' "

She finished, and didn't seem inclined to say any more.

"You made it to the ballroom by seven-thirty," said Townsend professionally, as if the grisly description were a mundane history conveyed by a patient, and he was moving on to the next organ system. "I imagine you went directly from Gerard's room, right? When we were in the elevator together I couldn't smell your perfume. You intentionally weren't wearing any when you saw Gerard, but you didn't have time, or else forgot, to put some on afterward. I could always smell your perfume, Rosie. I even remember how you smelled from twenty years ago."

She eyed him curiously. " 'Joy,' " she said absently.

Townsend continued. "Philip stopped by to clean up on his way to accompany Felicia to the gala. He entered through the adjoining room, since you had made sure the access door was unlocked from Gerard's side when you left. Everything had gone according to plan, except Gerard was still breathing, which must have been a nasty surprise. Philip switched the linens from one of the beds in the hospitality suite. That was less risky than pilfering new sheets from a housekeeping cart. Except he wasn't as skilled at making beds as the housekeeping staff. No military corners. That was the first thing that bothered me."

"We always had maids when Philip was growing up," Rosie

reminisced. "Still do, you know that." She crossed her legs and clenched her knee with prayer-clasped hands. "Not enough cyanide, that was the problem. And I was counting on you, Townsend, but you overplayed your part."

"Knowing that a doctor was at the gala, you were hard-pressed not to get me involved," said Townsend. "And your performance was convincing. Unfortunately at the time, you had no idea that Gerard was still alive, since Philip didn't have the opportunity to alert you. The plan had been for Philip to send Oscar to break the news, giving Philip more time to confirm all the tracks had been covered. When I gave the CPR, I smelled the cyanide on his breath, though I wasn't really aware of it at the time."

"You knew more than you let on when you came to visit me yesterday."

Townsend nodded.

"So it was you who told the police about the cyanide."

Townsend's second nod was barely perceptible. "I had figured out the cyanide part, Rosie, but I didn't know it was you. Not that it would have made any difference. And then I saw the moth."

"*Syngrapha*," Rosie enunciated.

"*Syngrapha*. You tried to lead me to believe that moths were killed by pinching their thoraces—like butterflies—but I remembered differently. In retrospect, I thought that perhaps you were distracted, weren't paying attention to my question. How could you not know something that basic? Then I thought that you were protecting Philip. Problem is, you protected Philip too well."

Rosie lifted her eyebrows in slow motion.

"You sent Philip to discover the body, for starters," Townsend answered. "But what was striking, really, was how well Philip's time could be accounted for. Always an alibi. In the hotel restaurant, while the murder was taking place, he was with Felicia. Then with William Davidson. Philip even stayed in clear view to make his phone call to you. The cashier overheard him tell you that the papers had been signed. The call was your cue that he and Felicia had left Gerard, that the way was clear to make your move. Odd, wasn't it, that he called from the cashier's desk rather than using one of the house phones in the corridor? He was drinking coffee and beer for an hour, for heaven's sake, and he didn't even disappear for five minutes to empty his bladder."

Rosie showed no emotion. Townsend nervously looked out the window.

"When Felicia put things together—," he continued.

"That stupid bitch didn't put anything together," Rosie erupted from her tranquillity. "She was legs and feet and no brain. When she recognized my Brian in the picture, she called to feel me out. I wish I had a tape of that conversation. I played dumber than she was, if you can fathom that. I expected her to at least have the sense to try to blackmail me, but she thought the whole thing was a big coincidence. She actually believed I didn't know a thing about Brian's relationship with Gerard and what that bastard did to my boy." She shook her head in renewed disbelief, looking earnestly at Townsend. "I have to show you the letter sometime, Townsend," she trailed off.

"I'd like to see it, Rosie." He was not feigning compassion. He swallowed, let some time pass in the quiet. "So Felicia wasn't trying to cut a deal."

Rosie laughed. "Now, I wouldn't say that. As soon as she concluded I didn't know anything, she started a pitch on her own for the grant. I said her proposal sounded reasonable, and agreed to meet her in her hotel room. And you might say that her Tiger's Milk had more than its usual bite." She started to laugh again, and then sensed she was violating decorum, even for a murderer. Her look became funereal.

"She might never have figured it out, Townsend, but someone else might have. Like you. I couldn't take the chance. You understand that, don't you?"

Townsend held his head motionless.

"I have to get the police involved, Rosie."

"Dear Townsend," she replied. "I never had any illusions of buying *you* off."

She stopped as Tony Mauro sauntered in from the direction

of the kitchen, hands in his pockets. He seemed dressed for church, with gray slacks and a navy blazer. Even his paisley tie was straight, knot neatly tightened. Townsend could make out the bulge near his armpit; Tony was packing one.

Rosie raised her eyebrows, then her facial muscles relaxed with comprehension.

"I'm sorry, Rosie," said Townsend, averting his eyes.

"Franklin and Margaret Reeves always did have a smart boy," she said. "Good morning, Lieutenant. I hope I didn't take you away from services."

Mauro pursed his lips, wondering why he couldn't get away with being dressed up once in a while. He had spent an inordinate amount of time that morning debating what he would wear for this collar. He had dismissed jeans or khaki out of deference to the broad. He needn't have bothered.

"I don't go to church."

"Well, then, I certainly hope you didn't go to all this trouble for my sake."

"Naw, no trouble," said Mauro. "I'm all duded up for the celebration afterwards." He reveled in not letting her spoil his moment, but never took his eyes off her as he continued walking her way. "Let me take this from you, Mrs. Van Buren," he said, gently picking up her purse. She didn't resist.

Townsend gazed out the window and saw that three squad cars had pulled up behind the Mercedes.

Epilogue

TOWNSEND SAT AT THE BREAKFAST ROOM TABLE and double-knotted his high-tops with a flair. He was dressed for hoops in a faded pair of twelve-year-old Missouri Wildcat workout shorts and a misshapen rust-colored tank top. Just like workouts in the old days, except he hadn't shaved. Coach Woijak had always insisted that his boys be clean-shaven, even for practice.

He gulped the remaining orange juice in the glass and stared at the thick Sunday paper. He shoved it further away, unopened. A week had passed since the arrests of Rosie and Philip Van Buren, and he had reached media satiety. Felicia and Gerard's stage tragedy of Othello and Desdemona had been warped into a true-life pas de death. Kansas City was stricken by a civic ambivalence—thrilled with the attention but embarrassed by the notoriety. It had sought to become a cultural center and had instead ended up as the modern dance murder capital of the world.

Steve Rayburn was clinging to the story like an adolescent girl on the back of a motorcycle squeezing a hulky biker. He was the undisputed local maven, a self-styled investigative Carl Bernstein with the psychological insight of Carl Jung. But he was fighting a losing battle in keeping the claim he had staked. The story was too big to be contained. The news blitz was on an international scale, with the tabloids leading the pack. There was even talk of a television docudrama. Madonna had expressed interest in playing Felicia Bradley. Townsend found the obsession prurient and sickening, but did occasionally indulge in speculation over who could do his own portrayal justice.

His phone machine was on continuously so he could screen all calls. He had made it a policy to refuse all interviews, but was still constantly being hounded. An enterprising female newscaster from Nebraska had even tried to gain admittance to his home under the guise of being a Jehovah's Witness. As for Mauro, he had given news briefings in an official capacity but was maintaining a relatively low profile. To his credit, he had not downplayed Townsend's role in the unraveling of the mystery.

Paul Gruenfeld was reaping the most benefit from the turn of events and the publicity barrage. His quasi confession, "The Last Time I Saw Gerard," had made the front page of *The Enquirer*. With angst and sensitivity he disclosed the precise moment of a personal and artistic catharsis as he spied on a rehearsal of *Desdemona*. In the balcony of the Missouri State Performing Arts Center, he had aimed a prop gun at his true-life rival and determined that in the denouement of *Outlaw*, the gunslinging Bret would walk away without pulling the trigger on Willis. Paul Gruenfeld confessed: in the darkness that summer afternoon he had reached a separate peace with Gerard Moreau, rest his soul.

The same article detailed Gruenfeld's plans for a major new piece, a full-length modern ballet about the New England witchcraft trials. Leslie Rosenthal had been promised one of the solo roles in *Salem*, and would soon be heading back to New York with the company to begin rehearsals. Gruenfeld was optimistic enough about his company's future that he had signed three additional dancers from the now-defunct Moreau Company. Returning to the Gruenfeld fold was his prize pick, Erik Crumm. Not mentioned was the minor detail that Crumm had recently beaten a drug rap due to a weak case and lack of interest by the prosecutor's office. There had been no big-time smuggling from South America after all, only backstage shenanigans, nickel-and-dime stuff.

Townsend gave his laces a final tug, rinsed out his juice glass in the sink, and was digging out his basketball from the winter boots and scattered outer garments that had fallen off their hangers onto the closet floor when the doorbell rang. On his way to answer the door, he grabbed the shoelace tied end to end with his extra house key from the side table and slipped it over his head.

Tony Mauro stood on the threshold, similarly attired, holding a basketball of his own. Rather than a tank top, though, he sported a navy blue National Dance Festival T-shirt.

"Well, well," said Townsend, stepping outside and pulling the door shut behind him, "if it isn't celebrity cop, undercover as the world's shortest basketball player."

"This ain't gonna be a cakewalk for you, Mister Doctor. I've got a wicked outside shot."

"Right. Right. You're talking to a former All-American here, Lieutenant. The real thing. You know what they called me in those days?" He didn't wait for the answer that wouldn't come. " 'Down Town.' You know why?"

"Sure," said Mauro. "Your mommy took you downtown to buy you your knickers and Buster Brown shoes."

Townsend grinned. "You're asking for it, no mercy. But since I'm such a humanitarian, I'll spot you twenty points before I wipe your ass."

"In your dreams, man. Just don't call me for any pussy fouls."

"No tackling, Tony. Remember—this is basketball." He twirled the ball on his index finger.

"Where's this showdown comin' down?" asked Mauro. "You want me to drive?"

"Roundball funeral services for Tony Mauro will be held at the Pembroke Hill School. We can walk. If any of those prepster daisies are hogging our court, you can wave your badge, maybe even pull out your gun."

They sauntered down the cracked cement path toward the sidewalk, each with his own ball held in the crook of an arm.

"Not to change the subject," said Mauro, "the prosecutor has Rosie by the short hairs, as if he needed anything more to make the case."

"Yeah?"

"Short red ones, in fact. Esmeralda was cutting corners. She never did get around to changing those dirty sheets that Philip put on the bed in Room 922. So what do you think of my new shirt, huh?" He faced Townsend, outstretching his arms in a no-frills model's pose.

Townsend didn't answer, distracted by the Yellow Cab that had slowed down, then pulled curbside in front of Mauro's Buick. Kate Jordan emerged from the backseat. In a beige linen power suit, she looked a businesswoman. Or more accurately, a beautiful actress playing the part of a businesswoman.

"I'm glad I caught you, Townsend," she said, seeming short of breath. "I'm on my way to the airport."

Mauro gave her a good once-over approvingly, then looked at Townsend. Townsend was forced to introduce them. He referred to her as "a friend."

"I've seen you being interviewed on TV," she said to Mauro, shaking his hand. He beamed.

She addressed Townsend. "The company's through performing at the festival, and I couldn't handle teaching any more master classes. With this whole Moreau Company thing, everything's a real zoo. Frieda can't say much about it, since I've already resigned from the company anyway."

"Kate was with the Frieda Ekstein Company," Townsend explained to Mauro, playing host. "You saw her dance the other night in *Primitive Passions.*"

"Yeah, right, I remember. The five girls. Nice moves."

Kate graced the compliment with a smile. "Thank you, Lieutenant." Her eyes quickly turned to Townsend. "Could we speak privately for a moment?"

Mauro didn't seem to feel slighted by the brush-off; after all, a beautiful classy woman had seen him on TV and treated him with a modicum of respect. He was used to Townsend getting the prize. And no real loss anyway, since this one was leaving town. He told her how pleased he was to make her acquaintance, and took a stroll a few paces down the sidewalk, bouncing his basketball to an unobtrusive cadence.

Kate Jordan waited until Mauro was out of earshot.

"I need to tell you a couple of things," she said softly. "First, I wanted to thank you for last week, it was a wonderful afternoon for me. Just what the doctor ordered, in fact."

She reached into her purse and pulled out a card.

"Here's my address," she said. "I thought, if you ever get out to the Northwest—"

"You never know," Townsend picked up the cue. "Maybe I'll be out there moonlighting one of these days, who knows?" He looked at the card, realizing he didn't have a pocket for safekeeping. He didn't want to lose the card. "Let me put it in the house, real quick," he said, leading her to the front door. He bent down and unlocked the door without lifting the shoelace key ring from his neck.

He invited her in, but she declined the invitation, so he stayed in the house only long enough to place the card on the entryway side table.

"My pregnancy test was positive this morning," she said as soon as he was back outside.

Townsend swallowed a wad of saliva that had materialized in the back of his throat. "Congratulations."

"I know, Townsend." Her eyes were piercing his own. "I said I *know.*"

"You know *what?*" Townsend wasn't very convincing at playing dumb.

"The whole business, the sperm. I was suspicious about your interest in me. Above and beyond the call of duty. So I went back to the clinic. I talked to the technician Lenny. I wrung it out of him."

"I see."

"And I'm grateful to you."

Townsend cleared his throat. He seemed to be having an acute saliva problem. "You're welcome," he managed to say softly.

"I wanted you to know that I knew. It's important to me. It doesn't change anything, really."

"No, it doesn't."

"I have to go now, or I'll miss my flight." She reached up and clenched the front of his tank top. She guided him down to her, then kissed him on the forehead.

Townsend's eyes were closed, and when he opened them, straightening up, he could only see her back as she took long, rushed strides to the taxi. She got in the car hurriedly, and settled back into the seat. He couldn't see her face, and she didn't look out the window as the taxi pulled away with a screech. Townsend knew then that Kate Jordan shared the pain of knowing with him.

Mauro, near the curb, watched the taxi disappear from view. "I thought you have reached the legal limit in the woman department," he said loudly, increasing the tempo of his dribbling.

"Just a friend."

Mauro moved to where Townsend's walkway intersected the sidewalk. "Okay. So what are you waiting for?"

"I'm ready, let's go." Townsend slowly walked to meet him, still cradling the basketball under his arm. Mauro could sense something was amiss.

"We're still on for tonight, right? I've been waiting all week for this date with Janet and you're not gonna mess things up again for me, are you?"

"We're on."

"Everything's okay with Leslie?"

"Okay."

"Great. So before we take in the flick, I thought we could go to one of Oates's places for barbecue. How does that sound?"

Townsend thought for a moment.

"I'm feeling more like fried chicken," he said. "Let's make it Stroud's."

"No prob. So you ready to wipe my ass or what?"

"You're a dead man, Tony."

They walked down the sidewalk, side by side, each dribbling his own basketball, a small forward and a small guard.

"Hey, wait," said Mauro, stopping in his tracks. "You never told me how you like this shirt. The official Kansas City Dance

Festival shirt. Janet got it for me. Nice shirt, huh? What do ya think?"

"Nice shirt, Tony," said Townsend. He reached over and affectionately squeezed Mauro's thick neck, as if he were palming a basketball.